J. Weck

Crimson Ice

A NOVEL OF MYSTERY AND SUSPENSE

J. WECK

Originally published by
DigitalPulp Publishing
611 S Palm Canyon Drive
Palm Springs, CA 92264

www.DigitalPulpPublishing.com

ISBN:978-0-578-02695-4

joanneweck.com

CRIMSONICE@me.com

Cover Design by Margaret Carson

Back Cover Photo by Elisa Chalem

For my sister Jeannie.

Her sun is gone down while it was yet day
(Jeremiah XV, IX)

CHAPTER 1

Frankie was groping for a blanket when the bedside telephone broke into her dream. She snatched it up and mumbled a sleepy hello.

"Is Rocky there?"

"What? Here? No."

"Have you heard from her?"

"Tonight? No. What's happened?"

"She's disappeared." A thick muffled voice. Gordon, she realized, Rocky's husband, sounding desperate. Frankie freed herself from the tangled sheets and swung her feet onto the cold floor. "Disappeared? What do you mean?"

"She left! She's gone!"

Her brain felt sluggish. It was Rocky who sometimes called in the early-morning hours, concerned that Gordon had not come home.

"When did she leave?"

"About four."

She peered at the clock on the bedside table: 2:45 AM. "It's . . .not even three."

"Yesterday afternoon. About four. I know she usually runs to you after we have a . . . spat." His voice was choked, the words slurred. Jeffrey, her three-year-old son, who slept in a crib near her bed, stirred, popped a thumb into his mouth, fingering the silk edge of his blanket.

Frankie felt for her slippers and, by the dim glow of an Elmo nightlight, found her way to the living room. She sank down on the worn leather sofa. Miniature lights were twinkling on a tiny Christmas tree in a corner of the room.

An image of her sister's bruised and swollen face flashed unbidden. A spat? Shit! More likely another battle, she thought. She was shaking with anger by then but drew in a breath deep and held it, keeping her voice steady. "Gordon, please--was she okay when she left?"

"I didn't mean to hurt her!" His voice broke. "I'm sorry!"

Frankie covered the receiver with her hand and swore softly. "Son of a bitch. Bastard! Yes, you're always sorry!" Speaking into the receiver again, she asked, "You think she was coming here?"

"I don't know. She just drove off." She heard his raspy intake of breath. "If she's not with you. . . ." And then, after another breath, "I don't know what to tell the kids."

A shock as electric as the touch of an exposed wire flashed through her. "She left the kids?" No matter how angry Rocky had been or how injured, she would have bundled Gordie and Autumn into the car. Gordon in a rage was not a person with whom you would trust a child.

Frankie had been beyond anger after her sister's last visit, when she found her packing. "What are you doing?" she'd demanded.

Rocky'd had the grace to look embarrassed. "Going home."

"Are you crazy? You should be getting a restraining order! You should be filing for divorce."

"I'm not divorcing him." She had continued to stuff children's clothing into her large Vuitton valise, thick reddish-gold hair pulled back into a ponytail, face young and hopeful. When upset or unsure, Rocky rubbed at the bridge of her nose, a strong nose that balanced her wide Polish cheekbones and made her face interesting as well as lovely. Below her left eye the shadow of a bruise had still been visible.

"It's my fault, too." She'd slammed the valise shut. "You know I instigate. And I can't back down."

Frankie knew exactly when this role reversal had begun--the first time Rocky had gone back to Gordon after he'd hit her. She stared at her older sister. Both had inherited their mother's looks, but Rocky had a creamy ivory complexion minus Frankie's splash of freckles. They had the same green eyes flecked with gold, the same wide smiles, but Rocky's figure was rounded with curves, while Frankie was tall and lean, with muscled arms, long, coltish legs, and hair a fiery red.

"Christ, Rocky! I wish I'd taken a picture of you!"

"You should have seen him!" She'd raised an ironic, perfectly arched eyebrow, but Frankie detected a flicker--anger, indecision--shadowing her eyes.

"The bastard's going to kill you if you don't get out!"

"I love him." Rocky had tucked Wilby, Autumn's stuffed bunny, into Gordie's diaper bag. Frankie had wanted to grab her, hold onto her, lock the door. Rocky'd gone on with a hint of mischief, "Besides, he really knows how to make up after he's been a bad boy."

"Bad boy?" Frankie, horrified, had searched for a gleam in her sister's eyes. "Nothing could make up for the way you looked last week! I don't care how terrific the sex is--"

"You can't imagine how terrific the sex is--"

"What are you teaching your kids?"

"It doesn't affect them. And I told you--he's going to change. It's not your business anyway." Rocky had zipped up the diaper bag, picked up the valise, and shouldered her Givenchy handbag. "Maybe you're jealous."

"Jealous? Of what?"

"Maybe you need to get laid."

"Maybe you need to get your head examined!"

"He's not like Angelo!" Rocky had spat out. "Angelo was a loser! You should have run out on that thug, but that doesn't mean I should leave Gordon!"

Frankie'd winced. One thing their father, Teddy "Tornado" Witokowitz, had taught them, was to fight fair.

"Because Gordon has more money? Because he'll buy you another diamond bracelet when you go back? He *is* like Angelo, but you can't face it!" Why, she wondered, were the daughters of violent men invariably drawn to similar men? Had they been infected with some sort of virus?

Rocky had backed off, already sorry and flashed her most conciliatory grin. "Stop it, Frankie! Don't fight with me. Who do we have but each other?"

"Well, don't come here next time--when he breaks your jaw!"

"I won't!" Rocky'd snapped. Their farewell had been cool, each feeling misunderstood.

Was that why she hadn't heard from Rocky this time? Frankie heard only Gordon's intake of breath.

"Gordon--" she managed the soothing tone that would keep him on the line-- "she left the kids?"

"I was taking them to visit my parents," he stammered. "So they could watch them open presents." His parents? But hadn't there been an estrangement?

"Did you hit her?"

"I pushed her a little," he admitted. "I didn't mean to. I, I just lost it."

"How bad was she hurt? Would she have gone to the hospital?"

"No. I--well, maybe. Her head was bleeding a little." His voice became defensive. "She tripped on the rug and fell against the fireplace."

"Did you check the hospitals?"

"Yeah. I called the emergency rooms, Stroudsburg and Geisinger."

It was two days before Christmas. Frankie had planned to spend the holidays at the home Gordon had designed, perched on a ledge above the glassy expanse of Lake Nakomis, that looked as though it had grown out of the rocks. But the way the couple could lately turn a quiet evening into a melee had made her visits less frequent.

Yet she was also aware of the passion between them-- when Gordon was late, Frankie would see her sister's nervous, darting eyes and her relief when he walked in, their kisses so intense that Frankie, embarrassed, had to look away.

Heart thumping, blood pounding in her ears, Frankie tried to focus. "Have you told the kids anything?"

"No. Maybe I said she was at the theater." His words were thick. "I got them into bed without too much trouble. But I thought she'd be home by now. She's always here when they wake up."

"She had a show last night?"

"She never made it. The director left a message on her voice mail." Frankie felt another adrenaline surge. Rocky had been known to perform with a sprained ankle and a 102-degree fever. "Have you reported her missing?" Frankie asked.

"I was hoping she'd be with you," he groaned.

"Why don't you call the police and see if they'll take a report? Meanwhile, I'll drive up." Intuition, or growing distrust, told her she was not getting the whole story.

"Should you?" he asked. "What if she's on her way there?"

"I was planning to come up Tuesday anyway, for the holidays. I'll leave her a note," Frankie assured him. "And if she does come here, she has a key."

In a few moments, she was tossing a single battered suitcase into the trunk of her green '96 Honda, strapping her sleepy son, still in pajamas, into his car seat, and heading out through the quiet streets of Springfield toward Route 78. The early storm had abated, and Christmas lights were visible on neighboring houses. Huge mounds of snow had been plowed from the streets, but the surface still felt icy. Fat snowflakes blew against her windshield and disappeared. The northeast was enduring its worst winter in seven years, and she knew driving would be even more hazardous in the mountains.

Jeffrey's sleepy voice broke into her thoughts. "It's dark out, Mommy. Where are we going?" She glanced at him in the rear view mirror. His eyelids were already drooping over huge dark eyes, his thumb seeking his mouth of its own accord.

"We're going to see Autumn and Gordie. You can play with them when they wake up." The motion of the car soon lulled him back to sleep and allowed her mind to race.

Gordon was lying.

She fought down panic and her most horrible fears. No, no--Rocky had left in a rage, driven further than she had intended, decided to sleep off her anger at a friend's. Or she had been injured and gone to an emergency room and been kept there. The blow had dazed her--she had amnesia. No, that happened only in movies. Maybe she'd had an accident. Maybe the car had slipped off the edge of an embankment somewhere and was hidden from view. She'd read of such an incident, a car hidden by underbrush for days before it was found.

Frankie sped over familiar highways through the winter night, foot heavy on the gas pedal. She cranked up the music while she drove, musical scores from shows she and Rocky had worked on together, Rocky starring, she as stage manager. Stage manager. In control. Not a puppet like the actors. Only her first independent gig, at the Playwrights' Theater in Madison, New Jersey, had prevented her from working on Rocky's current show.

She was headed northwest, climbing steadily into mountainous country where the snow was deeper and there was more wind. Finally, the outline of dark mountains indicating the Delaware Water Gap appeared dimly ahead. She slowed for the E-ZPASS at the bridge and crossed into Pennsylvania. Her Honda, one of the few cars on the highway, ate up the empty miles. She was unaware of the state trooper behind her until the lights flashed and a siren sounded.

"Oh, shit! Damn it to hell!" she moaned as she edged over to the side of the highway.

"You said bad words, Mommy!" Jeffrey had chosen that moment to wake and point out her moral lapse. Then, noticing the trooper approaching, excited, "Look, Mommy, a police!"

The officer leaned down into her window. "Let me have your license and registration, please." About forty, with a chiseled face, he looked stern. She'd been doing at least twenty-five over the limit.

"Was I speeding?" she asked. "I'm sorry. It's an emergency." Surprising herself, she blurted, "My sister's disappeared! Her husband--he's violent, and now. . ." The cop stood there for a moment while she put her head down on the steering wheel.

"Ma'am," he said, "I need your license and registration." She reached for her handbag. Jeffery, in the back seat, was trying to get the trooper's attention, waving, then cocking his head shyly when the man glanced at him. She fumbled in her bag and found the required items. He took them wordlessly and went back to his cruiser.

In a few moments he returned. The flash of oncoming headlights illuminating his face and then plunging it back into darkness made him look like a gargoyle. He tapped at her window, and she rolled it down.

"You've had two speeding tickets this year. I should write you up." He paused while she waited. "I'm only going to give you a warning this time," he said. "But you keep driving like that, and you're likely to hurt that little boy back there." He hesitated. "About your sister, was that story supposed to keep me from writing a ticket?"

"Christ, no!" Frankie searched his face for a trace of concern. "Her husband beats her. Now he says she's disappeared. His temper--"

He cut her off. "Now, Mrs. Frances Witokowitz Lupino--" he articulated each syllable, reading her license carefully-- "I want you to catch your breath. Most likely you'll get there and find the two of them in the sack. If that's the case you can throw this away. But if it turns out she's really missing and you need help finding her, you call this guy." Along with her documents, he handed her a card that read: *Roman Sarvonsky, Private Investigator* and a number. She tucked it into the glove compartment and was soon on her way.

CHAPTER 2

It was almost dawn when she reached the estate at Lake Nakomis. The sky had grown lighter as night retreated. The wind on the mountain was fierce, hurling the snow into drifts, with clouds that promised still more. Behind wrought iron gates, the house rose like a ship against a background of towering pines.

She pressed the intercom button, waved toward the security camera, and after a moment the gates slid open. Snow was piled high on either side of the circular driveway; the branches of the spruce and white pine were heavy with blue-white clouds, and the lake shimmered in the early light, but Frankie was oblivious.

A single light was burning in a downstairs window. The approaching car triggered automatic sensors, spilling light over the driveway. Gordon opened the door just as she was lifting Jeffrey out of the car seat. He lumbered down the driveway and locked his arms tightly around both of them until the little boy squirmed and yelped in protest. Frankie pulled away, conscious of aftershave and whiskey.

They stumbled in. Gordon made no offer to help with the child or suitcase, so Jeffrey toddled across the flagstone breezeway into the large kitchen. Still sleep-dazed, he asked, "Where's Autumn? Where's Gordie?" He found a yellow dump truck and sat down to play on the white-tiled floor. Frankie realized, even as she unwound her scarf and took off her parka, that her eyes were sweeping the kitchen and the room beyond.

"You haven't heard from her?" She dumped her handbag and suitcase on the work island, and pulled out a chair. Gordon slouched onto another one, looking confused and disheveled, a drink in front of him, a Dewar's bottle behind him on a counter.

"No, nothing." His hands muffled his voice. Frankie wanted to see his eyes, to read what might be hidden there. The fragrance of coffee filled the room. She realized she was cold. Separate bits of information entered her brain in disjointed sequence. This house felt so empty without Rocky, she thought, and then, Gordon's face had several deep scratches.

"And the police?"

"They took a report, but they probably won't do anything for twenty-four hours. Sergeant Benton seemed to think I was jumping the gun." Gordon glanced up. "Want some coffee?"

She nodded, scrutinizing the fresh-looking claw marks going up into his hairline. He poured her a mug. Rocky loved her coffee, taking pains with choice of coffee maker, grinding fresh beans for each pot. Frankie's hands, cradling the mug, were shaking as she took a sip. Everything had her sister's imprint--the copper pots hanging above the work island, the warm-colored prints above the green marble counters, the bouquet of poinsettias and berries in a white vase.

"What happened to your face?" she asked, trying to keep it from sounding like an accusation.

He fingered the scratches almost absently. "I guess Rocky did it." His voice was a little blurred. A look of amusement flickered across his face. "You know your sister's temper."

Then she must be all right, Frankie thought. If he'd done something terrible, he wouldn't be smiling at the thought of her temper. "You fought about what?"

"Nothing. Something stupid. I don't remember." His eyes evaded hers. At fifteen she had first looked into those eyes——a clear wolfish blue, like those of a Siberian husky--and been as fascinated as Rocky. The memory of her childish crush now brought only a shiver of distaste. He rubbed his chin, grizzled with early-morning stubble, deeply cleft as though a cartoonist had drawn the jaw of a superhero. "I wanted the kids to spend time with my parents."

"I thought you weren't seeing them."

He shrugged, "For a while we didn't. You know Rocky hates my mother. But since Dad's last stroke--I guess he's wants to make amends. . . ."

She knew the story. Rocky's hostility toward her mother-in-law had begun before the wedding, when she overheard Edwina tell her son, "You can take the girl out of the trailer park, but can you --?" Rocky had entered the room and in her best stage British told Edwina she was welcome to piss off permanently.

"Rocky didn't want you to take them?" Frankie sipped at the coffee, still shivering. Scents of pine and cinnamon mingled in the air.

"They have a right to see their grandchildren!"

Pretty defensive, she thought, but plunged on. "No, I'm glad. They should know their grandparents." The image of her own father, before liver cancer finally claimed him--a sour, depressed old man with little interest in his grandchildren--flashed through her mind. "You drove up to Marshalls Creek?"

"Yeah. Dad's back home. They put in ramps and an elevator."

He got up and took the bottle from the counter, poured several inches into his glass, and paced, heading into the den, where he stood looking out one of the huge windows that faced the lake. Gordon usually moved with the grace and carriage of one of his thoroughbreds, but now he seemed dazed, clumsy, oddly jittery. She followed him in, searching the room, eyes lingering on the fireplace where Rocky had supposedly fallen. It was huge, fieldstone, almost large enough for an adult to step into. It seemed, from a hint of embers and the smell of smoke, that a fire had burned there recently. A lordly Christmas spruce, adorned with white silk ribbons and red holly berries, dominated the room. Beribboned gifts in red and gold were stacked beneath its branches. Jeffrey wandered in, carrying the truck, and stood, awestruck, before the tree.

"Gordon, please tell me what happened." Frankie kept her voice carefully controlled. He's lying, she thought, lying.

"I told you what happened!" he snapped.

"Maybe you left something out. I. . .just want to figure out--"

"I've told you everything," he insisted, turning away. "We argued. Things got a little out of hand. I pushed her and she fell. She ran out to her car and drove off. I waited for a while, but I knew she had some sort of meeting before the show started at eight, so I took the kids and left. Dad was expecting us, and you don't keep him waiting."

He paused for a few moments, and just when Frankie was about to prod him again, he resumed. "I thought she'd be here when we got back at eleven, eleven-thirty maybe. She always lets me know if she's going to be later than that. I called her cell, but she never answered." He resumed his pacing before the windows.

"And she never called you?"

"No, she never called me."

"Did she take anything? A bag?"

"I guess just her purse. Her keys would have been in it."

"When you came back, what did you do?"

"I put the kids to bed and waited up for her. Called the Playhouse, but the box office was closed by then. Checked for messages. There was a call from the director, you know, Ken Werther, at about seven-thirty. He was pissed off, said if she wasn't there in five minutes one of the understudies would go on for her. I realized she'd missed the show and started calling people."

"Who?"

"Aphrodite, an actress friend. She wasn't in."

"Do I know her?"

"Wasn't she in *Gypsy* with Rocky last year? Gorgeous Black woman. You worked on that, didn't you?"

"No, I don't think so."

"She's staying at Shawnee for the run, likes to party after the show. I left a message." He paused for a breath, ran his hands through his thick blondish hair, and continued. "I called Lourdes--woke her up, I guess. She didn't know anything. Said the daycare was closed till the Monday after New Year's. Sounded pretty snotty too, considering all that we've done for her." Gordon gulped from the glass. "I watched some TV and fell asleep on the sofa. Woke up about two. When she still hadn't come in by two-thirty, I called you."

He put the glass down on the high mantle so hard that drops of it splashed onto Frankie's cheek, and then turned to look at her full in the face for the first time. His eyes had dark circles beneath them. "I've got to get out of here, make another search." He was suddenly moving toward the door. In the entryway he took a blue Thinsulate parka from a peg. "Waiting around is--"

"Call me if you hear anything."

"The kids will sleep for a few more hours." He punched numbers into the security panel by the door and went out. She heard the garage door glide open and the Suburban roar off.

For a moment her eyes searched out, and lingered on, the photos that decorated the den walls. There was a small framed snapshot of Rocky as a ten-year-old tomboy, arm protectively around Frankie at six. Her own young face had the dazed expression that she wore for years after their mother's suicide, while Rocky stared defiantly at the camera. Next was a small photo of their parents--a fair, sad-eyed woman, and a man with a coarse boxer's face. He'd raised his daughters as much like sons as possible, with surly neglect, an occasional cuff to the head, or, in a jovial mood, a boxing lesson.

A series of wedding portraits were artfully arranged to lead the eye along the little gallery, with Rocky and Gordon posing like film stars conscious of their glamour; a shot of Frankie, gawky in a pale green bridesmaid's dress, gazing at Rocky with shining eyes. Last were the photos of Rocky holding her babies, and a family studio portrait.

"Jeffrey, honey, come here," Frankie called. "Sit on the sofa and watch TV for a little while." She lured him away from the tree and settled him with an Elmo DVD on the huge, plush couch before the entertainment center. Thumb in mouth, he snuggled down, black curls matted, eyelids heavy, looking so much like Angelo that her heart constricted. She blanked out the thought as she always did when his memory intruded. Since Angelo, there had been no one. She'd closed and boarded up her heart like a house condemned. But she nuzzled her son for a moment, breathing in his sweet talcum-and-baby smell.

Maybe there was something—some clue to tell her what had really happened last night. Details, she thought, look for details. Making a quick sweep around the room, she noted that several candles on the mantle were disarranged, the greenery askew. She rubbed her fingers along the stone edge and they came away with a sticky pinkish stain. Lifting the small hearthrug, she found smears, as if wine--or blood--had been wiped up.

She picked up a poker and jabbed at the smoldering embers, dislodging the coals, and she saw what looked like pieces of cloth and a knotted cord with glass beads. She dragged it out and shook off the ashes. A friendship bracelet, she thought, like kids wore. There was a small scrap of a furry material, dirtied by ash. She wrapped both carefully in a piece of newspaper and placed it into her handbag. What am I doing? she wondered.

After checking that Jeffrey was still engrossed in the video, she made a quick search of the house. Upstairs, she peered into the children's' rooms. Autumn, tiny in a canopy bed, had tossed her blanket off, and Frankie replaced it, bending over her. Her mouth was open, and her thick lashes shadowed her cheeks. Gordie, in his own room, decorated with trains and planes, was sleeping on his back, arms outstretched as though he had fallen from the sky. They were both as golden as Jeffrey was dark.

Frankie tiptoed into the master bedroom. The heavy bedspread was rumpled, but the bed had not been slept in. She lifted Rocky's pillow and found a silk nightgown beneath it. She buried her face in it, and at the scent of her sister's perfume, felt the sting of tears. Rocky loved the feel of real silk. Frankie, who preferred flannel and jeans, teased her about her lavish tastes but often accepted her cast offs. which were far more luxurious than anything she could afford or was willing to buy for herself. And because Rocky still loved to play big sister and dress her younger sister up in her own lovely things.

She replaced the gown. Another silver-framed wedding photo sat prominently on the dresser--Rocky looking out, joyous and triumphant, while Gordon looked only at her.

She pulled open drawers in the dressing table and chests. Rumpled items of silk lingerie spilled out, as though someone had rooted through them. In the huge walk-in closet, clothing was arranged on hangers according to color and season, but stacks of cedar boxes had been pulled from the shelves and left open. The Vuitton luggage set had been left scattered, as though someone had conducted a haphazard search.

She opened the doors to Gordon's closet and patted the pockets of his finely made suit jackets and slacks. Ten pairs of shoes, dress boots, all of Italian leather, on shoetrees, six pairs of sneakers, neatly arranged. She quietly slid open drawers, heart thumping.

Gordon had a small office at the rear of the house. He often preferred to work at home rather than drive to Gardiner and Gardiner, Architects and Developers. Particularly fearful during her invasion of that retreat, she tripped over a leather golf bag propped against a desk covered by rolls of blueprints and architect's tools. A computer screen looked at her with a blank gray eye. Several drawers were locked. In one deep one, beneath old building plans, she found a stack of unpaid bills, crammed and wrinkled. She examined a few: final demands for payment, some for car leases and household expenses, some for bank loans, all with recent dates. An empty manila envelope had a slight residue of powder; an exploratory taste told her it was probably cocaine. "Shit!" she murmured. She knew there had been an early history of drug abuse, but Rocky swore those days were long over.

She heard a noise outside and rushed to a window that faced the lake, spread out like an immense sheet of sky. Figures were moving along the shore, indistinct behind the snow-covered trees. A spell of warmth had caused the ice to break and shift, and deer, venturing out on the unstable surface, would sometimes be trapped on a floe.

In the den, Jeffrey had fallen asleep, snuggled under the earth-toned afghan. With a glance toward the door, Frankie crossed to a small Queen Anne desk in a corner of the room. A slide-out revealed a notebook computer. I shouldn't be doing this, she thought, but doing something gave her a feeling of control. She couldn't bear to simply wait when Rocky could be in trouble. She searched through folders, papers, envelopes, until she found a leather day runner and flipped through it quickly. It appeared to be filled with dates, names, and coded entries, for bank accounts or computer files, perhaps. She slipped it into her pocket when she heard shuffling behind her.

CHAPTER 3

Autumn was standing at the foot of the stairs in a Barbie nightgown, sleepy-eyed and bewildered. "Aunt Frankie, what are you doing here? Where's Mommy?"

"I don't know, honey." Frankie scooped her up and wrapped her in her arms. "I was hoping maybe you could tell me something."

"Daddy and Mommy were yelling," she said, "and then Daddy took us to see Nana and Poppy."

"Did Mommy say goodbye?"

"Mommy was resting on the floor. But Daddy said to go out to the garage and wait for him."

"Are you sure, sweetie?" Frankie could feel her heart thudding against her ribcage, blood pounding in her head. "She didn't leave first?"

Autumn looked puzzled. "I don't think she did, 'cause Daddy said she was resting." She paused to think. "Will you make me French toast?"

"Are you hungry?" Frankie released her niece, noting the sweet smell of her breath and the little sandy grains at the corners of her eyes. She nodded solemnly.

"With strawberries like Mommy does?"

"How 'bout scrambled eggs?" Frankie offered. Rocky was capable of whipping up an extravagant dinner for six on the spur of the moment; Frankie, who favored take-out, invariably scorched the toast and dropped the omelet onto the floor.

"I   need   French   toast!"   Autumn   insisted, "Strawberries!"

"Come out to the kitchen with me. No, don't wake him!" Autumn had been poking Jeffrey with an exploratory finger but did as she was told but her son was already awake.

Frankie's French toast emerged burnt on the surface and raw inside, so she scraped it into the sink disposal and fed the children leftover pizza. Gordie had awakened and she managed to wrestle him into his diaper and a Barney coverall and allowed Autumn to dress herself in a fuzzy pink sweater and ballet tutu. She cleaned up the kitchen, and patience finally exhausted, she left them in the playroom below, where she could hear them running and shrieking.

Another sweep of the house failed to disclose anything. The security videotape had been reset only that morning, and Gordon's computer required a password to gain access. She called the Pocono Mountain Regional Police and spoke to the desk sergeant, who failed to reassure her. "Most of the time, people aren't really missing at all," he said. "They turn up in a day or so. But you can call the State Police Barracks at Swiftwater and there's a special number for missing persons."

She spoke to Ken Werther, the director of *Victorian Holidays* a tall, slim man with an ascetic face and a shock of silver hair with whom she'd worked on several previous shows. He apologized for his biting message but could only say that Rocky had not called or appeared. She left messages at the Happy Face Daycare for Lourdes McCoy and at the Shawnee Inn for the friend Gordon had mentioned, Aphrodite Antoine. Two days before Christmas was a difficult time to reach anyone.

Consumed with a nervous energy, she opened the little notebook she always kept in her handbag and made a list of things to do. Frankie was famous for her lists--for herself, her cast members, babysitters, friends. It gave her focus, a feeling of being in control.

Where had Rocky gone? Frankie sat at the computer with mounting anxiety, consulting the leather daybook for codes, unable to open anything except Microsoft Word files. Autumn appeared beside her.

"I can't find Wilby," she said, eyes tearing.

"Did you look in your bed?"

"I looked when I waked up. He wasn't there." Her fuzzy sweater was already smeared with something green.

"Maybe you left him at your grandparents'?"

"No, I didn't take him with me, 'cause I couldn't find him, and Daddy made me get in the car without him, and that's why I was crying." The computer screen caught Autumn's attention. "Mommy don't let anybody touch her computer."

"I'll help you look for Wilby in just a few minutes. Why don't you run back down and keep an eye on the boys for me?"

"Okay, Aunt Frankie." Autumn, impressed with her new responsibility, trotted off.

Inspired, Frankie typed in *Wilby* and was given sudden access to all of Rocky's files. She decided to start with *Calendar* and pulled up the file for *Victorian Holidays*, a repertory of three holiday musicals--*Babes In Toyland*, *The Gift of the Magi*, and *Goblin Market*. Although Rocky had given up an active career for motherhood, she was still in demand for local shows and relished each performance.

Her first acting role had hooked her for life, no longer "Tornado" Witokowitz's neglected kid with skinned knuckles and bony knees but Saint Joan with a sword. In her teen years she'd apprenticed at the Pocono Playhouse, bequeathing to Frankie her job of mucking stalls and grooming horses. But Frankie had followed.

She found a calendar notation for a cast meeting before Sunday evening's show and a note: *Chantelle/Cliff--Willowtree*. She assumed that Cliff referred to Cliff Thornton. A dark romantic lead in the early eighties, he had slipped to slimmer roles in regional theater. "He's a little high strung," Rocky'd said. "And he lives in the tanning booth--he's as crispy and golden as a KFC drumstick."

"I liked him in *Rouge and Rain*." She'd laughed at Rocky's deadpan expression. "He's not gay?"

"I doubt it. Married to wife number six. A Vegas showgirl he picked up a few years ago." Rocky's eyes had glittered with amusement. "Bianca Dulce. Isn't that sweet?"

"That's her real name?"

"Now she's Mrs. Cliff Thornton. Cast gossip says she's very good at spending his money, and he's already shopping for wife number seven."

Had Rocky made it to the dinner and cast meetings the day before? Why the note to meet Thornton? Who was Chantelle? She added them to her call list. Thornton would no doubt be staying at the Inn, but she couldn't find a number for a Chantelle. She added *Call Willowtree Inn* to her list. Perhaps someone had recognized the aging star or would remember her sister.

So far, the last verified sight of Rocky had been either slamming out the door and driving off in her little silver Mercedes SLK 230, or "resting" on the floor as Gordon hustled the children into the Suburban at about 4:00 the previous afternoon.

She opened the file labeled *Diary*, detailing personal events: Holiday Parties, Horseback Riding, Skytop--Jazz Night, Craft show, Paradise Bazaar, Courthouse--Carol Sing. She copied everything to an empty disk. The two boys tumbled into the room with Autumn straggling behind.

"I'm hungry, Mommy," Jeffrey announced. He looked sleepy as well. Gordie's face was smeared with chocolate, and his sippy cup was dribbling milk onto the floor.

"They won't listen," Autumn sniffed, "and I still can't find Wilby." Her lower lip trembled. "When's Mommy coming home?"

Reluctantly, Frankie popped out the disk, shut down the computer, and closed the desk. She stuck the disk into her handbag along with the scraps from the fireplace. Evidence, she thought, of what?

"We'll have lunch," she suggested. "And then everybody is going to take a nice long nap."

"Even you, too?" Autumn asked.

"Even me, too." Frankie realized suddenly how bone-weary she was. Cheese sandwiches, she decided. She could manage that. In the stainless surface of the top oven, she caught a glimpse of her reflection, hair wild as a brushfire, dark smudges on her cheek. She swiped at her face with a damp paper towel and patted her hair.

"You'd be really pretty, Frankie," she almost heard Rocky's voice, "if you'd just make a little effort." But Frankie had long ago conceded the role of family beauty to her, feeling most comfortable behind the scenes, in life as in the theater.

She put the children to nap in the room she always claimed during extended stays, designated the "nanny's room," although Lourdes had been the only nanny who survived for more than a year in that household. Autumn, curled next to her little brother in the big bed, was soon asleep. Frankie lay down beside her small son, who slept clutching his fuzzy blanket. The bed was comfortable, smelling faintly of lavender, but every exhausted muscle in Frankie's body remained tense. The children's demands were endless. Her brain felt full of sludge. She would rest for a few moments. Then she would think of what to do.

CHAPTER 4

Frankie woke to the sound of rain. She had been dreaming that she and Rocky were children, running in a summer shower. The children were sleeping deeply, the two boys with limbs entwined like puppies. It was already mid afternoon. She heard the rush of a shower running in the master bathroom. She jumped up. Rocky! Relief flooding through her, she hurried toward the sound. Hope died as quickly. Steam was billowing from the bathroom to where, just past the Jacuzzi, Gordon's dirty clothing lay scattered across the floor. She glimpsed his massive shoulders behind the steamy shower door and tiptoed quickly back to find her boots and go downstairs. In the garage she saw the Suburban and the Lexus van, but no sign of Rocky's little silver Mercedes.

She found the number for the Willowtree Inn near the kitchen phone. When a receptionist answered, Frankie asked if Cliff Thornton had been there for dinner the previous evening.

A bland voice refused to divulge any information but allowed her to speak to the owner. Frankie explained, ears attuned for steps on the stairs.

"There were several actors from the Playhouse for early dinner," an affected masculine voice told her. "My assistant remembers the young lady."

"She does?" A rush of blood made Frankie feel lightheaded. "About five foot seven, with reddish blonde hair?"

"Yes," he said after a moment. "There were two blondes and Mr. Thornton. And a tall Black woman. They dine here often."

"Thank you very much! Please, if Mr. Thornton or any of the actors come in today, have them call me?" He took her number. Gordon came down the stairs freshly shaved, dressed in a blue shirt, a blue sweater, and tan wool slacks, but red-eyed and exhausted. She searched his face.

"Nothing?" Frankie asked. He shook his head dispiritedly. "Where did you go?"

"Everywhere. All over Shawnee, The Playhouse, of course, the hotel. I talked to Ken--nobody saw her last night. I even drove over to Foxwood." Foxwood Stables was where they stabled their riding mounts. His first anniversary gift to Rocky had been a black thoroughbred named Zillah that she rode several times a week. Frequently the sisters rode together, Rocky, impeccably English in form and style, Frankie riding western, letting Satan know who was in charge.

"That's it?"

"The ski lodge, the daycare," Gordon continued, blowing out a long sigh. "Nobody's seen her." Frankie still thought he was withholding something or lying. She wanted to scream at him, demand answers--but knew that would merely ignite his temper.

When they heard the children stirring, he went upstairs and returned carrying Gordie and Jeffrey, one in each arm, opposites, blond and dark. Autumn followed, golden hair disheveled, dragging Jeffrey's blanket.

"Look what I found," Gordon said with mock gaiety. Jeffrey removed his thumb from his mouth and reached out to Frankie with both arms. His face was creased from the pillow. She took him and kissed his sleepy face. He put Gordie down, and the little boy immediately headed toward the Christmas tree. Autumn followed behind him.

Frankie didn't mention the computer files or the restaurant call. "You look beat," she said. "If you want to sleep, I'll take charge of the kids."

"I can't sleep! How can I sleep?" he demanded, eyes flashing.

"I made sandwiches," she offered.

"I can't eat either." He noticed that Autumn and Gordie were crawling under the branches, making it tremble. "Get out from there!" he shouted. "I'll kill you if--!" He caught himself and stopped.

"I'll take them," she said, wondering how to keep the three of them occupied. Perhaps if she threw herself on Lourdes's mercy. . . .

The phone rang in the kitchen. They both went for it. He got there first and listened, making noncommittal sounds.

"Uh-huh. . .hmm, uh. . .thank you." He hung up, looking puzzled. "The hostess from the Willowtree. She said that she made a mistake, that Rocky was there Saturday, not last night. . .you called them?"

"The cast goes there--"

"Why don't you let me handle things?" A loud crash sounded from the den; Frankie rushed back in to see that a small side table had been overturned and a Chinese lamp lay in shards on the floor, its shade smashed. The children stood frozen before the mess. Gordon was beside them in a moment, screaming, his face twisted in fury.

"Who did this? Who the fuck *did* this?" Jeffrey let out a startled sob and began to wail. Gordon grabbed Autumn by her upper arms, shaking her, shouting into her face, "Why can't you watch your brother for five goddamn minutes?" Autumn whimpered, clearly terrified.

"*Stop it, Gordon!*" Frankie shouted, putting her arms around the girl and prying at his powerful fingers. "You're scaring them all! *Stop it!*" He shoved the child away. When he turned back a few moments later, there were tears glittering in his pale blue eyes.

"I'm sorry," he murmured, "It's just--everything's so fucked up." He bent down to Autumn's level. "Come here, sweetie. Daddy's sorry he scared you." Autumn buried her face against Frankie, but he tugged at her, planting a wet kiss on her half-hidden cheek. This display, even more than his violence, filled Frankie with rage. She wanted to do him physical damage, kick him, slash his face with a broken shard.

She took a deep breath and asked him for the keys to the van. He reluctantly pointed to an extra set near the security monitor. "I don't like you taking them out. The roads are bad." She rocked her small son against her shoulder.

"I'll take the highway to the mall. We'll go see Santa." She needed to put distance between her and Gordon. She turned to the still frightened children. "Want to go find Santa?" Gordie clung to her knees, and Autumn slumped to the floor.

"I want my Mommy," she sobbed, and Gordie chimed in, "Mommy! *Mommy!*" His little face was desolate, fat tears rolling down his cheeks. She found snowsuits and hats in the breezeway and bundled them up. She hauled Jeffrey's car seat from her Honda into the Lexus van.

The dark of the threatening storm made it feel like evening. In the van she fumbled, unable to find the controls for lights and windshield wipers. She made a left turn and found herself on Burnt Shanty Road, which looped in a circle back toward the lake. She recognized the one-lane bridge and was soon on Route 940, headed toward the development of Pinewood Trails and Lourdes's daycare. The roads were growing more treacherous. She should have called ahead; her cell phone was buried in her purse on the back seat. "We're going to stop at Lourdes's," she announced, looking over her shoulder.

"I want to see Santa!" Jeffrey whined.

"After I talk to Lourdes. Maybe Kiki will be home." Seeing that Autumn was digging through her handbag, she asked, "What are you doing?"

"Why do you have Wilby's collar in your pocketbook, Aunt Frankie? Do you have Wilby?" Autumn had found the little bracelet remnant, and was examining it.

"No, honey, I don't. That's Wilby's collar?" She tried to focus on her driving, but her heartbeat had suddenly become more rapid.

"Yes." Autumn was starting to sniffle again. "Mommy made it for Wilby!" Frankie popped in a Barney song tape.

"I *hate* Barney!" Autumn   pouted, "He's only for babies."

Frankie pulled up near a low ranch house with a Smiley Face Daycare sign, bright swing sets, and monkey bars half buried in snowdrifts. Lourdes appeared in the doorway dressed in a blue silk tracksuit--a short, solidly packed young woman with thick black hair that hung like a cape around her shoulders and huge dark eyes like those of an exotic night creature. Her plump face, as she approached the van, wore a stricken expression.

"*Ai, pobrecita!*"

"What? What is it?" she asked.

"*Dios mio*! You have not got the news?" Lourdes looked confused. "Larry heard this on his police radio. They have found Rocky's car!"

"Where?" Her heart jumped. "Where did they find it?" She demanded.

"It is in the river," Lourdes said. "Just behind the Shawnee Playhouse." Lourdes was still speaking, but Frankie's knees had gone weak and the words no longer penetrated.

CHAPTER 5

Minutes later she was again speeding over slippery roads through fast-falling snow. Route 80 was clogged with shoppers, and skiers heading out for an evening run. Frankie stabbed at the radio buttons, hoping for an official report, but Christmas music was blaring with relentless cheer from every station, and she angrily snapped it off. She felt as if some robot had taken over her body, edging the van through traffic, honking in fury at slower drivers. She finally turned onto Route 209, then onto Buttermilk Falls Road, a left onto River Road, and down into the valley. At the entrance to the Shawnee Resort, the Playhouse hulked on the right, its marquee proclaiming: *Victorian Holidays, Starring Cliff Thornton and Rochelle Gardiner, December 12 through Jan 1.*

She continued over snowy ruts for about two miles, and then, ahead on the right, saw the red flash of police lights. A tow truck was in position on the shore, and various smaller trucks and vehicles were parked about. A park ranger engaged in conversation with a state trooper was gesturing toward a big yellow raft with pontoons on the broken ice. She pulled the van up next to one of the state police cars and was soon picking her way across the snowy wooded banks. The blowing snow inhibited movement and made visibility difficult. Rocky must have gone to the Playhouse early, she thought, inexplicably driven past it and down along the river, and then lost control of the car. Or maybe Gordon's blow had left her dazed.

A policewoman with a ruddy face and wispy tendrils escaping from beneath her cap, who had been speaking into a walkie-talkie at the open door of a cruiser, stopped Frankie as she stumbled toward the lake. "You can't go out there." She extended a gloved hand with automatic, bored authority.

"It's my sister's car!" Frankie struggled to get past her.

"How do you know that?" Now the officer was interested.

"The police radio! They said it was a silver Mercedes! My sister's been missing since yesterday!" Frankie tried to pass, driven by the need to know even the worst, but the cop restrained her.

"They're just getting it hooked up," she said, looking into Frankie's eyes, her voice softer. "It's going to take a while. Sit inside and keep warm."

But Frankie stood there shivering and tried to make out what was going on. A chain was being attached to the rear bumper of the partially submerged car, but progress was incredibly slow. Men in heavy jumpsuits were edging out from the raft.

She remembered another such snowy day when she was twelve and Rocky sixteen. Their father had ordered them, just as they were about to leave for school, to shovel his car out of the snowdrifts where he had lodged it after a night of drinking. They had worked in the snow together, cold and hungry and late for school. The school bus had come and gone without them. Hands and toes numb, they had gone inside to warm up. They had found Teddy slumped at the kitchen table, drinking black coffee, trying to rouse himself to go to the job he loathed.

"You got that car free yet?" he'd asked Rocky.

"We can't work till we warm up." She had extended her frozen hands over the coal-burning stove.

"I'm gonna be late," he'd told them, rubbing a black nailed hand over his morning stubble. "Get the hell out there, and don't come in till you're damn sure I can drive it."

Rocky had met his angry stare with one of equal intensity. "We already have to walk to school. And we're gonna be late."

"School ain't putting any bread on the table, now is it?" he had remarked.

"All I see is coffee and beer on this table."

She'd known it was dangerous to respond when he was on a mean drunk, but even then she'd been reckless. He had lumbered up from his seat and cracked her hard across the face. She'd staggered back outside to the old green Cougar with Frankie following, where she picked up her shovel and, swinging it like a baseball bat, smashed every window in the car.

After a half hour, Frankie was numb from the cold and little progress had been made. A station wagon with the legend *County Coroner* made its way toward the police cars and stopped. A television news van arrived, and despite pleas, shouts, and angry gesticulations, the reporter and cameraman were prevented from moving in on the action. The reporter, a perky blonde in her mid-twenties, climbed back into the van where she could be seen retouching her makeup.

Frankie returned to the van for her cell phone and called Gordon. He answered on the third ring.

"What? Hello?" His voice revved into alert concern when her recognized her voice. "Where are you?"

"I'm by the Delaware River, behind the Playhouse." She choked on the words. "They've found a car in the river."

"Oh, no! Christ! Is it--"

"Yes, a silver Mercedes," she told him. "They're hooking it up now."

"I'm on my way," he said. "Where are the kids?"

"Lourdes has them." She went back to where the action was. Or wasn't. The excruciatingly slow operation was being hampered by the weather and balky equipment. At the yelp of another siren, Frankie turned to see an ambulance jouncing along the rutted road toward them. Pointless, she thought, if Rocky had gone off the road before yesterday's show. She imagined her sister's body frozen behind the wheel, her eyes turned to ice, and shuddered.

When Gordon approached, stomping through the snowdrifts in his blue parka, she was almost pleased to see him. His face, under his fisherman's hat and blue hood, looked ghastly, eyelids swollen, the scratch on his face infected looking. He reached out to her, but she directed his gaze toward the river.

There was a sudden commotion and shouts from the shore. The tow truck was moving with great lurches and spinning of wheels, dragging its burden toward the group, which surged forward. Gordon and Frankie picked their way closer and saw the Mercedes being dragged onto the bank, water and chunks of ice streaming from it. Her fingers dug into Gordon's sleeve as they struggled to see and were shunted aside by emergency workers carrying a stretcher. The driver's door was open, a figure slumped on the passenger's side of the little car.

They tried again to force their way past the cops, but the heavy, dark-browed one turned ugly. "No one is allowed past this point." He brandished the walkie-talkie.

"It's my wife's car!" Gordon shouted into the cop's face,

"There's only one body," the trooper said dryly, "and it's not your wife's--unless she's a middle-aged male."

CHAPTER 6

Frankie and Gordon waited while a police photographer took videos of the car and its occupant. The coroner moved in to pronounce the frozen body officially, and detectives stomped through the snow, taking notes. Men marked off sections of the shore with yellow tape. Finally the corpse was removed, shoved into a body bag, and loaded into the ambulance. Rocky's car was impounded to be searched for clues.

Frankie and Gordon were pulled aside by a heavyset trooper who, although unable to reveal the identity of the dead man, listened to their concerns. He wrote down their names, information about Rocky, their phone numbers, and said they'd be called if a search seemed warranted.

Although it was nearly dark, Gordon insisted he would search the area on his own. She agreed to pick up the children, wondering if he planned to hike or merely drive around the park.

Lourdes had the foldout in the den ready for Frankie when she returned. "You will sleep here tonight," she told her. "The *ninos* are already asleep."

Frankie checked on the children before collapsing. Kiki and Autumn were in Kiki's bed, one dark, one pale, like Snow White and Rose Red; the two little boys were in portable cribs from the daycare. "I don't know what I'd do without you, Lourdes. I'm too exhausted to think," she sighed. Lourdes had brewed herbal tea, but Frankie hadn't even inhaled the scent of mint before her head slumped toward the table.

"Maybe things will look better in the new day." Lourdes put her arm around Frankie's shoulders and led her toward the makeshift bed.

I've got to get hold of myself, she thought. Removing only her scuffed boots and heavy sweater, she climbed under the sheet and pulled up the comforter.

But sleep eluded her. How many times had Rocky played the hero to her little-sister-in-distress? Rocky, her protector, more of a parent than the weak mother who'd abandoned them or the bitter father who'd ignored them. She remembered a fifth grade incident--Rocky had found her sobbing after school because Normie Thompson had called her a freckled face giraffe.

"Don't listen to idiots," Rocky had hissed, kissing her freckled nose. "You're strong, like me. Nobody makes us cry!" The following week, when Norman started to tease her again, she'd turned and without a word landed a solid right to the astonished boy's jaw.

When she was twelve, it was her sister who'd rescued her from the police station after she'd been caught stealing a necklace from J.C. Penny's. Shame had burned more deeply for having intended the cheap trinket as Rocky's birthday gift-- though it hadn't prevented her from hanging out behind the Dairy Queen with other kids from the trailer park and making minor forays into delinquency--cutting school (where she felt constantly measured against her sister's perfect record), drinking beer, and smoking pot.

She remembered Rocky's angry warning when Angelo Lupino began to pursue her. He'd been nineteen and on parole for breaking into summer cottages, but she'd shivered under his hot-eyed stare. She'd defied Rocky, slipping out to meet him at every opportunity, amazed to find him charmed by the very things boys her own age labeled weird--her fiery hair, the freckles that dusted her cheeks, her notebooks full of angst-ridden poetry and dark sketches. His first kisses, wet and urgent as he pressed her against the kitchen cabinets in a summer cottage they'd broken into had been followed by an equally urgent exploratory hand beneath her plaid schoolgirl's skirt, and, in time, by--everything, knowing everything was wrong, but lost in the sweet intensity of first love.

There had been no recriminations when she discovered she was pregnant; Rocky'd been maid of honor at the city hall wedding and beside her at the hospital when she lost the baby. (Angelo couldn't be located.) Later, when Jeffrey made it safely into the world, damp and squalling, she and Rocky had examined and cooed together over her tiny, perfect infant.

Rocky had taken her in when Angelo's always-smoldering anger turned violent. Frankie, swearing the first time he hit her that *she* would never be like her mother, never like Rocky in this--no man would ever control her life again--had vowed to care for her son alone, and had. Rocky'd encouraged her to finish night school and hooked her up for crew jobs, providing the foundation of Frankie's career. Now it was *her* turn to help, she thought.

She drifted off to sleep just as morning broke.

At six she heard Larry, Lourdes husband, preparing to leave for work; the Christmas season was big business for the ski resorts. The smell of coffee lured her, still in her rumpled clothing, to the bright kitchen, where she found him pouring. She had known him when he'd worked as Rocky's gardener years before he'd met and married Lourdes and he greeted her with a grim smile.

"You want coffee? Cream?" he asked. He had the homely face of a child's puppet, with a large balding head, pasty looking skin, and a tiny mouth beneath a prominent nose and bristly mustache.

"No, just black, thanks." She took the mug he proffered and sipped it with silent gratitude.

"Me, too." He indicated a brown bag on the table, taking gulps from a metal carry cup and heading toward the door. She saw concern in his eyes, but he made no mention of the previous night's events, merely waved and bolted, leaving in a cold blast.

The bag contained fresh bagels, a pint of cream, and that day's *Pocono Record*, featuring the biggest story to hit the area in years. The headlines screamed out at her: *Well-Known Actor Dead in Accident, Local Woman Missing.* She felt unreal, dislocated, heart thudding as she read the account of the car pulled from the river and the identity of the body: Cliff Thornton.

There was speculation about the relationship between the car's owner, Rochelle Gardiner, and the dead actor-- including a quote from the hostess at the Willowtree, who claimed that Rocky and Thornton had been a frequent twosome--dining together and often returning for a post-show drink. Frankie felt her stomach twist and knot. She sipped hot black coffee, eyes heavy from lack of sleep, body quivering with exhaustion. She reread the story, looking for any detail she had missed.

Lourdes appeared in blue chenille bathrobe and fuzzy slippers. She leaned over Frankie and, seeing the headlines, snatched the newspaper out of her hands.

"Dios mio! Ai, Frankie!" she gasped, reading slowly, pointing to the words.

Frankie watched her. "Do you know anything about this guy Thornton?"

"Only he acted with Rocky." Lourdes poured a cup of coffee and looking into the bag, sat down at the table.

"What was he doing in her car?" Frankie looked at the paper again. "Some woman at the restaurant claims they came in together late, after the show."

"This man?" Lourdes rolled her eyes. *"Por favor!"* She thought for a moment. "When she meets him, then she says he is a very sweet man. But not for the kissing. *Estube uno viejo!"*

"Do you think she's--"

"I think *he* was driving the car," Lourdes said. "She is lending it to him."

"But why was he on the passenger side? The driver's door was open. She could have jumped out."

"We must hope to find her," Lourdes said, spreading butter on a bagel and thrusting it toward Frankie. "I am praying last night she will be fine. Now, you must eat."

"I've got to *do* something. I wonder if the police will talk to me."

Lourdes looked at her darkly, "I am sure they will talk to you. And to Gordon, too! They are always looking for the husband first, *sí*? Larry told me this."

"Do you think she ever filed a report with the police?" Frankie asked. "About Gordon?"

Embarrassed, eyes sliding away, Lourdes shrugged. "I do not think so," she answered. "She tried to keep to herself these things." She nervously fingered a dark mole on her neck.

"Who is Chantelle?" Frankie asked. "Rocky had a note to meet someone named Chantelle."

"I saw her one time," Lourdes said. "When I have gone to see Rocky's show, this woman was there. She sees me talking with Rocky, and then she sits by me and asks me questions. Not like Rocky. *Ordinario*. And hungry."

"Hungry?"

"She is wanting for something--greedy. I see in her eyes."

"Do you know her last name?"

"This I do not know."

"I want to go back to the house before Gordon gets back," Frankie said. "Look through Rocky's files some more."

"Be careful."

"Do you think he. . .did something to Rocky?"

"He is many times losing his temper." She had lowered her voice to a whisper. "But I think, after, he is always sorry."

"Could you keep the kids for a few more hours?"

"*Sí, sí, de nada.* Do not think about that. *Por favor.* I must help. But please, Frankie, be careful." She covered Frankie's hand and gave it a gentle squeeze.

"I'll be back before the kids are awake," Frankie promised, grabbing her parka from the peg near the door.

CHAPTER 7

Without showering, Frankie drove back to the lakeside house. The gates slid open when she pressed the remote. It was still dawn, with a hint of pink, as a pale sun struggled to climb into a heavy gray sky. She punched in the security code. Her footsteps echoed on the flagstones of the breezeway. In the nanny's bathroom, she scrubbed her sleepy face, stripped, and swiped at strategic areas with the warm washcloth. As she dressed in clean jeans and pulled on a warm blue sweater, she caught an unexpected glimpse of herself in the full-length mirror. She moved closer to look. Eyes like Rocky's looked back, and there was the familiar full mouth and wide cheekbones. But the smattering of freckles, the bright red hair, and her lean figure confirmed the physical differences. No one ever doubted they were sisters, yet in her company Frankie had often felt a candle flame to Rocky's sun.

In a few moments she was accessing Rocky's files again. She found phone numbers for Aphrodite Antoine and for Gordon's parents. Could she call and probe for information about Gordon's state of mind when he'd showed up with the children? But Gordon's mother believed that Rocky had driven a wedge between her and her son. That avenue could wait.

She opened the file labeled *Financial* and perused the record of cash flow, noting as she read that the joint checking and savings accounts had been down to minimal balances for the past six months. The other accounts, labeled *Professional* and *Children's College Funds*, were nearly empty, too, after numerous ATM withdrawals.

When the telephone rang, Frankie started, almost jumping from the chair and grabbed the receiver.

"Mr. Gardiner, please." An official masculine voice.

"He's not here. Can I help you?"

"Detective Ransome, Swiftwater State Police. We need him to identify some items found in his wife's car."

"He's at his parents' home in Marshalls Creek. You have news? I'm Mrs. Gardiner's sister."

"Maybe you better come down, too," he suggested.

She gave him the number for Gordon's parents, rushed outside, and climbed into her Honda. The door stuck and the driver's seat was freezing, the windshield covered with ice and snow. When she turned the key it choked and sputtered. She opened the glove compartment, looking for an ice scraper, and spotted the card the state trooper had given her. She stashed it in her purse, scraped the icy windows, and tried the engine again. It started.

The state police barracks was a low brick building on a slight hill across from the Leisure Lakes Souvenir shop. She was confronted first by a young woman in civilian clothing, busy with paperwork behind a glass partition, and a pudgy, gray-haired man who sat at a desk talking on the phone. The woman ushered her into a small windowless office in the back, where the trooper she had seen at the river was sitting at a metal desk. Gordon, rigid in a chair across from him, glanced up.

The detective, a slightly heavy man with golden skin, sleepy hazel eyes under heavy brows, and dark jowls, introduced himself as Trooper Ransome. Gordon nodded to her. He wore a striped blue shirt and matching tie and looked rested, but a muscle just below his left eye was twitching. On the desk lay a damp Givenchy handbag, its contents scattered: waterlogged wallet, make-up case, checkbook, hairbrush, cell phone, pens, and other small articles.   There was something unbearably intimate about the collection; Frankie wanted to whisk everything back into the privacy of the handbag.

"They found this in the car," Gordon said in a strained voice, adding unnecessarily, "It's Rocky's."

"I know." Frankie reached toward it.

"It's evidence," said Ransome, stopping her.

"Evidence of what?" Frankie's heart was choking her, grown so large that she could feel it expanding like a balloon into her throat. "Have you found. . .anything?"

"We haven't found your sister yet," the trooper said, "but a full search is underway."

"Thank god!" Frankie sat in the empty chair. "Can they search underwater?"

"We've got some divers, but the ice makes it difficult. Two hundred troopers, park rangers and volunteers are sweeping the area.   Meanwhile, I have a few questions." He flipped open a small pad and seemed to refer to notes.

"Are you through with me?"

"Not quite, Mr. Gardiner."   Ransome's tone was deferential. "Just a few more minutes if you don't mind." The Gardiner influence, Frankie thought bitterly as he continued, looking at him. "When did you first report your wife missing?"

"About 3:00, the twenty-third--Monday morning."

Ransome looked at his notes. "You call *this* station?"

"No, I called Pocono Mountain Regional. I know the guys there. And it's closer to Lake Nakomis." Gordon twisted his wedding band nervously. His pale blue eyes looked moist, almost colorless, their whites red-veined.

"So the last time you saw her was about 4:00, Sunday afternoon?" asked Ransome. Gordon nodded.

"She missed her show that night?"

"Yes. And some meeting she had first."

"You left the house right after she did?" Gordon nodded. "Where were *you* going?" Ransome's voice was low-key, simply gathering information, but Frankie felt Gordon's discomfort.

"To visit my parents up by Marshalls Creek."

"I know where your parents live." Ransome paused. "How long did you stay?"

"All afternoon. About five hours. We had dinner. The kids opened presents."

"And you got home by. . .?" Ransome was still looking at his notebook.

"Eleven. She--my wife--should have been home about the same time, but she never came in."

"When did you realize she'd missed the show?" Ransome asked.

Frankie answered without thinking, "He *said* from the messages on the answering machine when he got home."

"I'm asking Mr. Gardiner," Ransome snapped. "Anything unusual before she left? Had she been upset?"

"No, nothing," Gordon said. "She was in a rush."

Frankie felt herself torn. Should she jump in again about the fight, the fall, her suspicions?

"You called the local hospitals? Why?"

"I thought there might have been an accident."

"Mr. Thornton was friendly with your wife?" Ransome was looking steadily at Gordon, who shrugged.

"They were both in the show."

"Well, we've got searchers, with dogs, combing the whole area, spreading out from the spot where the car went into the water. It's tough in this weather to find any trail, though. You can go out there if you like. It's under state park jurisdiction, so report to the head ranger." The detective rose, moving lightly on his feet; he extended his hand to Gordon. "I know this is rough on you, holidays and all," he said. "We'll find something soon." Gordon turned to leave. Frankie stood up, too.

"Mrs. Lupino," Ransome interrupted, "You mind staying for a few moments?" Gordon gave her a questioning stare as Ransome escorted him to the door, closed it, and turned to her. "Something you want to tell me?" he asked.

"Yes," she spilled out what she knew. "Gordon hit my sister, knocked her against the fireplace! She was hurt. She may even have been unconscious when he left!"

"You know this, how?"

"He told me himself when he called me all upset yesterday morning. And it wasn't the first time. He's always upset after he hits her." Frankie heard the bitter tone in her voice but couldn't soften it. "And their daughter told me her mommy was *sleeping on the floor* when they left!"

"How old is this kid?"

"She's four."

"Your sister ever sign a complaint against him?"

"I don't think so," Frankie said. "She covered for him."

"Any ideas about where she might be?"

"No." Frankie thought for a moment. "But she would never have left the kids alone with him. I'm staying at the house because someone needs to be there. His temper is dangerous!"

Ransome's blue eyes narrowed. "You making an accusation?"

"I should have heard from her by now."

"What about friends? Other relatives?"

"I'm her only close family. I have names of friends, but so far I've only been able to reach one, the babysitter."

"Let's see what you've got," he said. She fished out her notebook and opened it to the numbers, embarrassed when he took it, and skimmed through the pages, stopping to scrutinize the pages of lists, rough sketches, and notes to herself. He copied the numbers on a yellow sheet.

"What about a--male friend? A boyfriend?"

"No! Not a chance. She's totally in love with that--"

"This actor, Thornton? She ever talk about him?"

"They worked together! Period!"

"You're sure?"

"She's not like that!"

"They never are." He gave her a cool glance, thanked her, and then, still sitting at the desk, dismissed her with a nod. He didn't shake her hand or escort her to the door as he had Gordon.

CHAPTER 8

Frankie half expected to find Gordon waiting for her, but his Suburban was not in the parking lot. He must have gone to join in the search, she decided. It was nearly noon. As she passed the Playhouse, on impulse, she pulled into the parking lot. Draped across the marquee a banner now read: *HOLIDAY SHOW TEMPORARILY CLOSED.* The theater looked deserted. It was an old stone-and-wood building dating to the 1800s, and although a fire had gutted it several years before, it had been carefully restored.

She climbed up the front steps and pulled at the heavy wooden door. Surprisingly, it opened. The box office and house were dark. She marched down the center aisle. A few work lights illuminated the stage, curtain up and set for the opening number of a lighthearted romp in which Rocky had played the ingénue, set upon by Thornton as the mustache twirling villain. Rocky had sent her the musical numbers, and a lilting tune now rippled incongruously through her mind. A Victorian Christmas scene had been created--fireplace, leather armchairs, a rocking horse, oversize dolls, and trains, from a bygone era. A Christmas tree, bedecked with candles and old-fashioned ornaments, rose center stage. Giant toy soldiers and candy canes served as set pieces and a jack-in-the-box mocked her with its manic grin.

"Is anyone here?" she called out. She moved through the dark house, onto the stage, and behind the set into the dim recesses where props were stashed. She glanced over the call sheet for familiar names. All was quiet and dark.

She took the dark stairs leading to basement dressing rooms and entered the communal dressing area for the female cast, where costumes hung in giddy profusion. Lockers were built into the walls, and several old-fashioned chests slumped like tired animals against each other. A damp, musty smell mingled with the scent of sandalwood. Nothing stirred. As Frankie turned to leave, she was startled by movement behind her. Both she, and the woman who was suddenly facing her, gasped. Aphrodite recovered first. "My Lord, you scared me!" And then, "I thought for a minute you were Rocky!"

"I'm Frankie, Rocky's sister."

"I knew that right away! I'm Aphrodite Antoine." She took Frankie's hand and held it warmly in both of hers. She looked like a dancer, lithe, almost six feet tall with burnished café noir' skin, huge dark eyes and a model's pouty mouth. Her hair was long and worn in a tangled profusion of snaky braids. In jeans, boots, and a gray faux fur parka, she looked ravishing. "Rocky and I do a number in *Babes* together and we're the sisters in *Goblin Market.* Have they. . .found her?"

"They? Who?" Frankie asked. She appeared, Frankie thought, remarkably serene despite the death of the star and her friend's disappearance.

"Anyone. The police, I guess. I've been sick with worry. I read in the paper that no one's seen her since--since-- she missed Sunday's show."

"You didn't hear from her at all on Sunday?"

"No, the last time was Saturday night. I've been calling Gordon, but only getting his machine." Her expression darkened. "It's so awful about Cliff!"

Aphrodite brushed past her into the dressing room where she flicked a switch. Brilliant light flooded the small, mirror-lined room.

"What do you think he was doing in Rocky's car?" Frankie was struggling for the words. "They weren't. . .?"

"Cliff? And *Rocky*? Lord, no! I mean, he was a real sweetie! That man sure liked to party! Threw his money around like water!" A half smile flickered across her face. "But him and Rocky? Nah!" She opened a locker and pawed through its contents. "I just came to get a black dress."

"You're leaving?"

"We're taking a limo into the city for the service. Cliff's funeral. Bianca, his wife, came up for the last week of the show, and now this happens." Aphrodite turned luminous eyes on Frankie, the pupils huge and dark. Her bottom lip was quivering. "I can't believe it. It's like we're all in some Shakespeare tragedy."

"When is the funeral?" Frankie asked.

"This afternoon. Five o'clock." Aphrodite continued pulling garments from the locker.

"So soon? It's Christmas Eve!" Frankie protested. "Don't they have to do an autopsy or something?"

"I guess the police were satisfied. They released his body."

"But still. What's the rush?" Frankie asked.

"He's Jewish."

"Jewish? Cliff Thornton?"

"Yes. Who knew? It's like a law, I think; he's got to be buried right away. Before sundown. And then they have this shiva thing for a few days."

"In Manhattan?" Frankie asked.

"Long Island. He's got family there. Bianca asked me to go back with her." She paused. "I'm sorry I can't tell you anything. Like I said, I haven't talked to Rocky since after the show Saturday." She slammed the locker closed and seemed anxious to leave, stopped, glanced at Frankie's face again. "Are you all right?"

"No, I'm not all right! How could I be all right when Rocky's still missing?" Frankie fought back a surge of panic. The actress was looking at her with real concern.

"Want to come back to my room at the hotel for a few minutes? Bianca won't be ready quite yet." A half smile turned up the left corner of her sulky mouth. "I've got some Xanax and some Elavil. Smooth you out a little?"

"I don't *want* to be smoothed out!" Frankie snapped, and instantly regretted her tone. ". . .Will you be back after the funeral?"

"Well, I have to see if they're going to finish the run, and if not, talk to my agent. I probably won't have anything till after New Year's. But yeah, of course." She moved closer and gave Frankie a hug. "I'm worried, too! But I'm sure she's all right. They'll find her."

"Do you know someone named Chantelle?"

Aphrodite made a sour face. "I'd stay away from *that*."

"Why?"

"Because Chantelle is one fucked-up, crazy bitch if you ask me!" She hoisted up her huge leather tote and turned. "I've got to go."

"What do you mean?" Frankie asked. "Weren't she and Rocky friends?"

"Not really. They knew each other but Rocky mostly avoided her."

"I found her name in Rocky's planner. She had a note to meet her and Cliff Thornton."

"Well, they had some sort of--misunderstanding, I guess." Aphrodite was edging toward the stairs.

"What's her last name?"

"It's Rojas, I think. Yes, Rojas."

"Take my cell phone number." Frankie found a pen and tore a piece of paper from her notebook. "Please, call me if you think of anything. Or when you get back?"

"Sure, okay." Aphrodite stopped suddenly, a puzzled expression furrowing her brow. "Now that I think of it--I saw Rocky's car in the parking lot when I got in."

"What parking lot?"

"Here. At the Inn." She gestured vaguely in the direction of the Shawnee hotel.

"When? Sunday night?"

"Yeah——well, it was Monday morning by then. I noticed it because she'd missed the show, and of course she never stayed at the Inn."

"Have you told anyone?" Frankie asked.

"What? About the car? No. I guess I forgot about it till now." She gave an ironic little shrug. "We'd been doing a bit of partying. And it *could* have been someone else's. I didn't actually check it out."

"Which is Rocky's locker?" Frankie asked.

"Oh, yes, I guess you could take her stuff. Since the show's probably cancelled. Right here, next to mine." She slipped out of the door and headed up the stairs.

Frankie went to open the locker. It had a small combination lock on it. Using the numbers that Rocky had favored since high school, she popped the lock open. Inside, costumes were hung in order, scenes and numbers pinned onto the stuffed hangers. The scent of her sister's spicy Allure perfume rose from the fabrics. She pulled out a frothy green gown and stared at it, overwhelmed by dark foreboding. Rocky believed a green costume brought bad luck, and yet she'd probably worn it. "Where the hell *are* you, Rocky?" she leaned into the locker for a long moment.

She found a large tan duffel at the bottom of the locker and stuffed the Victorian dresses and petticoats into it. She snatched up everything, including a small jewelry chest, a makeup kit, Rocky's well-thumbed scripts, and a thick manila envelope. When there was nothing left but a dusting of powder, she slung the bag over her shoulder and started out. As she passed through the hallway toward the box office, she noticed someone moving between the aisles. She recognized Eddie, one of the security guards, making rounds. The man was nearly seventy and half blind but a fixture around the Inn.

"Eddie, hi," she accosted him. "I was wondering if you happen to remember seeing Rocky on Sunday?"

"I guess that means she hasn't turned up yet?" He removed his cap and ran his hand tenderly over his smooth gleaming head as though searching for long-departed hair.

"Aphrodite says her car was in the lot on Sunday."

"Not that I remember," he drawled. Before that Thornton guy turned up in the river, I didn't really pay much attention to what car she drove. I did notice them big shots in the fancy limos." She thanked him and retreated.

Before she started the car, she called Ransome. "Did you know Rocky's car was seen in the Shawnee Inn parking lot early Monday morning?" she asked.

"Are you doing detective work, Mrs. Lupino?"

She refused to be intimidated. "Someone saw it late after Sunday's show."

"And your informant was?"

"Aphrodite Antoine. One of the actresses."

"I'll be sure to talk to her. Meanwhile, how 'bout you let us conduct our investigation?" He sounded mildly impatient.

"Why did you release Thornton's body so soon?"

"We know what we're doing." His voice was dry.

"Then where's my sister?" she demanded.

"We're doing all we can," he repeated. She signed off and called Lourdes, who might have been waiting by the phone so quickly did she respond.

"How are the kids?" Frankie asked.

"Gordon came for them a while ago," Lourdes, told her. "But they were fine. Jeffrey ate Coco Puffs for breakfast. He said you do not give them to him?"

"*Gordon took them?*" Frankie asked.

"Is that okay?" Lourdes asked. The thought of the children alone with Gordon in a bad mood made Frankie anxious.

"I'm sure it's fine," she said. "Thank you for last night." Why hadn't he gone to help with the search? she wondered. Perhaps because he knew exactly where Rocky was.

A thought occurred to her. "Have you ever heard of a guy name Roman Sarvonsky? A private detective?"

"No," she said, "But Larry might know of him. He knows of everybody. Are you...?"

"I'm getting desperate. The police don't even suspect Gordon. I'm sure he knows *something.*" After hanging up, she searched through her handbag, found the card for Sarvonsky, and dialed the number. When an answering machine clicked on she snapped her cell phone closed without leaving a message.

She felt suddenly very alone. She and Rocky always spent the holidays together. How could she face Christmas Eve

without her? She tried to start the old Honda; it sputtered, and
died. On the third try it roared back to life

CHAPTER 9

Frankie drove up to the Shawnee Inn proper, a half-mile from the theater. The broad verandahs were decorated for the season with greenery wrapped around the columns. The lot was filled with upscale cars--BMWs, Jaguars, and Mercedeses. Several limousines were parked at the far end, engines running. She wondered if others besides Thornton's widow were being driven to the actor's funeral. She waited until Aphrodite and a blonde woman in a long fur coat emerged from the Inn. The latter, who was almost as tall as Aphrodite, with masses of thick blonde hair, was clinging to the actress as though for support. A dark Cadillac limo pulled up. The woman turned her pale face in Frankie's direction as she waited for the driver to open the door. The driver loaded their luggage and they sped off.

It was late afternoon when Frankie headed back toward Lake Nakomis. Christmas lights did little to relieve her sense of gloom. She'd had nothing to eat since her morning coffee with Lourdes.

Outside the gates, two television location trucks were parked on the edge of the roadway; an exhaust plume was rising from the closer one. Visions of fire, burnt bodies, and blood splatters leapt in her mind. But there were no fire trucks or police cars.   She slammed on the brakes and, frozen with indecision, sat unmoving several hundred yards away.

A figure suddenly blocked the driver's window, and a light blinded her. A man holding a shoulder videocam tapped sharply against the glass; snow blowing into his face and sticking to his eyebrows gave him a menacing look. He shouted at her through the glass, "What do you know about the murder of Cliff Thornton? Can you give us a statement? Were he and Miss Gardiner lovers?"

Another figure approached the front of the car, and a flash of light assaulted her through the windshield. Then she leaned heavily on the horn and stepped on the gas; the engine roared and she inched forward, forcing the reporters to retreat a few steps. She pressed the remote and the gates opened and closed behind her. Voices followed, screaming questions. She entered the house through the side door, which was opened as she reached for it. Warm air enveloped her. Gordon was standing just inside, fuming, his eyes glittering. "Those fucking bastards!" he exclaimed, "Vultures! Who the hell do they think they are?"

She shuddered as she slipped out of her coat and gloves. Empty bags from McDonalds, and white cardboard boxes with thin silver handles, littered the kitchen counter. The smell of food made her stomach rumble. She could hear the TV and children's voices from the den. "They said Thornton was murdered?"

"Ransome called me. He told me before it hit the news." Gordon stood in the breezeway looking into the surveillance monitor. His flesh looked pallid; beads of sweat dotted his upper lip. His hair was disheveled and he seemed barely in control.

"How?" she asked.

"He was strangled."

"Strangled!"   Her hand went to her own throat. "Nothing about Rocky?" Gordon shook his head, his eyes flickering nervously.

"They haven't turned anything up yet." He looked out the window. "I thought of going back when I saw them waiting, but I didn't know where *you* were." He indicated the evidence of a fast-food orgy. "The kids were starving."

"They're okay?"

"Yeah. Cranky as hell. Excited about Christmas and upset. . . .Jeffrey wet his pants. They're driving me crazy."

"I'm sorry," she said.

She hung up her coat and hat, popped a cold French fry into her mouth, and chewed on it as she turned toward the den. Gordon kept muttering. She heard "shotgun" and "goddamn hyenas."

"You didn't join in the search?"

"The ranger sent me home. Anyway, I already covered that whole area myself." When? she wondered. Last night, in the dark? Early this morning?

The children were playing with train sets while *Winnie the Pooh's Christmas* flickered unwatched on the huge TV screen. At the sight of her, Jeffrey's face lit up. He ran to her, shouting, "Mommy! Mommy!" As she swung him up, he began unaccountably to sob. Autumn and Gordie ran toward her as well, shouting, "Aunt Frankie!" Her heart tightened as she hugged them.

"Up! Up!" Gordie demanded, and she tried to hold the two small boys together while they squirmed and pushed one another.

"How are my pumpkins?" she asked.

"We're not pumpkins," Autumn told her.

"Then how are my little bunnies?" she asked, regretting her choice of words before they left her lips.

"My Wilby didn't come back. And I want my mommy!" She wailed in a thin voice. Frankie led them into the kitchen where, settling Gordie on one hip, she put on a pot of coffee, cleaned up the clutter, and sat at the table to finish the cold hamburger and French fries. Gordie's shirt was smeared with ketchup. He reached a sticky hand into her hair and grabbed a lock to twirl around his fingers. She removed it, feeling the gooey residue. God, she needed a bath. Maybe after she settled the kids for their nap.

"Aunt Frankie, when is my mommy coming *home?*" Autumn told her in a serious voice, "I'm not *happy*." Frankie cupped the small face and looked deep into the troubled eyes.

"Honey," she told her, "We're trying to find out." She looked to Gordon, but he had turned toward the den.

"But Santa is supposed to come," Autumn persisted. "Mommy has to help me put out cookies and write a note."

"If your mommy doesn't come tonight, your daddy and I will help you," Frankie promised, then, looking at Jeffrey's drooping eyes, added, "Has anyone taken a nap this afternoon?"

"I don't have to take a nap, because I'm four," Autumn said.

Frankie suggested cocoa with marshmallows on top, and popcorn, followed by a nap and later Christmas carols and setting out milk and cookies for Santa. She kept thinking of the tan duffel in the trunk of her car.

When she took the children upstairs a short while later, she passed Gordon snoring loudly on the sofa with a newspaper over his face. How could he sleep while strangers scoured the snowy woods and fields searching for signs of his missing wife?

Children finally napping, she turned on the taps and undressed in the nanny's bathroom, leaving the door slightly ajar in case one should wake. Violet jars and bottles of scented bath oils, soaps, and shampoos coordinated with the pale violets and grays of the décor. Fluffy gray-and-violet towels hung from the silver fixtures and were piled in baskets.

She poured bath salts and oil into the steaming water. When the bath was nearly full, she turned on the whirlpool and lowered herself in. She closed her eyes, drifted, the same images replaying in her brain: Rocky falling against the fireplace; Rocky driving through the snowy night; Rocky's car slipping into icy water, Rocky lost somewhere in a hospital ward, unclaimed.

She heard a sound and opened her eyes, expecting one of the children. Gordon was standing in the doorway with a glass of wine. "I thought you could use this," he said, advancing.

"What the hell?" Startled and embarrassed, she slid deeper into the foam. "What are you *doing*?"

"I always bring Rocky a glass of wine in the tub."

"*I'm not Rocky! Get out!*" She felt herself flushing, hot with confusion and embarrassment, anger mixed with residual guilt--for the girlish crush she had once harbored for the man. She was overreacting and waking the children as well. On cue, she heard Autumn's sleepy voice from the room outside.

"Christ!" Gordon said, "I didn't *mean* anything! Calm down!" He backed out of the room. She heard him talking softly. Her pulse was racing as she got out of the tub and closed the door hard. Overreacting, hell! The stupid fuck! How *dare* he! She should have thrown one of the heavy jars at him.

CHAPTER 10

Twenty minutes later, Frankie was calm --- dressed in one of Rocky's cast-offs, a soft velour sweat suit in muted carnation that she had given her the previous year. Autumn had drifted back to sleep, and Gordon had retreated downstairs. She ran a brush through her wet hair and pulled it back into a ponytail. The children looked like angels, but she knew they would soon wake and resume their demands. It was Christmas Eve. They expected Mommy to come home and Santa to visit.

A sudden wave of sadness engulfed her. She could either melt down or persevere. Rocky would persevere. She took a deep breath and went downstairs.

Gordon was on the telephone in the den. She could hear his voice rising and falling, arguing with someone. He spoke for a few more moments in a harsh, low tone before slamming down the phone.

"My mother wants me to bring the kids up for the rest of the holidays," he said as he turned around.

"Is that a good idea?" Frankie asked.

"We couldn't get away from the jackals anyway. Reporters are calling her, too," he observed, "and. . . ."

"And?"

"My father. . .scares them."

"How?"

"The last stroke left his face paralyzed. . . ." His voice trailed off. He looked at her balefully for a moment, then took a deep breath and said, a little too loudly, "Look, I'm sorry."

"No. Forget it. We're both frantic." She forced a slight wry smile. "I could use that glass of wine."

"I drank it," he admitted, "but I'll pour you another one." He rose unsteadily and went to the small bar refrigerator for the opened bottle. He poured two glasses and handed one to her, then sat heavily on one of the deep suede chairs. He'd lit a fire in the fireplace. It crackled and sputtered. The huge windows mirrored the room back to them in the early winter dark.

"Frankie, please listen to me." He turned the full intensity of his pale blue gaze on her, his voice deep with emotion. "You know how much I love Rocky. I would never hurt her. You do *know* that, don't you?"

"No, I don't! You *have* hurt her," she stammered. "I've *seen* her after--"

He emitted a low moan. The scent of the burning logs filled the room. When he looked at her again, his eyes were moist. "I know I've lost my temper with her," he said slowly. "I know I've shoved her or fended her off when she was attacking *me*. But any bruise or injury was. . .accidental. Rocky is my life. I'd never deliberately hurt her!"

Frankie swallowed, took a sip of wine. It was Christmas Eve. There were the kids to consider.

"I know you love her," she conceded finally.

"And you know how infuriating she can be!"

"Yes? Well?"

"Stop *blaming* me!" His voice was hoarse.

She met his eyes with an unyielding stare. The room was quiet except for the crackle of the flames. "You swear you don't know anything?"

"You don't believe me?"

"Autumn said she was on the floor when you left to go to your parents. You said you saw *her* leave."

"You've been pumping the *kids*?" His voice throbbed with fury.

"No, of course not. I just--"

"Autumn is four years old! She gets confused!"

"You said she hit her head--"

"Okay. She fell down. But I'm telling you, Rocky *walked out of here*!" There was another pause. Finally he continued, "I've talked to everyone. Werther. The cast. The police are already sick of hearing from me. I've driven around the whole damn mountain. I'm at a loss!" His words dissolved, but she felt only cold suspicion and a dizzy sense of dislocation.

Christmas Eve, which should have been full of festive activity, progressed like slow torture. Gordon remained in the den, drinking steadily. Frankie cajoled the children through a meal of instant macaroni and cheese and frozen peas. The boys ate, but Autumn complained that her tummy hurt.

Later she tackled the stocking ritual. Autumn refused to hang the one labeled *Mom*. When the phone rang again, Frankie dashed for it. It was Lourdes. Frankie told her about the TV crews.

"But it is Christmas Eve," she protested. "Larry was going to come over and bring you *un cordero*, a leg of the lamb, for tomorrow. And cookies."

"I wouldn't want him to come out tonight," Frankie told her. "The roads--"

"What will you do tomorrow?" Lourdes asked her. "You got to eat the feast on Christmas. I know you are not the cook but you got to feed the kids."

"That lamb does sound good." Frankie admitted.

"I'll drive over," Gordon's belligerent voice broke in. He'd picked up the extension in the den. "If those bastards are still out there, they can get the fuck out of my way."

Lourdes drew in her breath. "Larry could come in the morning."

"I need fresh air," Gordon announced. "I'm on my way."

A short time later, they heard the Suburban drive off. Without Gordon, the heavy cloud lifted a little. The children wrote letters to Santa. The boys lay on the floor and scribbled with crayons on large sheets of paper. Autumn printed carefully, with Frankie holding her hand and forming the letters.

"What do you want to say?" she asked her.

"Dear Santa," Autumn said quietly, "please bring my mommy back. I don't want the Barbie dollhouse any more." Frankie stroked the little girl's red-gold curls, fighting her own tears, remembering her own childhood.

The cheerless Witokowitz house, even on Christmas, had had only a sour smell of desolation. The year after their mother's death, in a feeble attempt to create a holiday spirit, their father had dragged home a small crooked tree, and the girls had decorated it with tinsel and popcorn. He'd even wrapped up a few inappropriate gifts. Frankie remembered a used hair dryer and a worn tennis racket. For Rocky there was the small gold locket that had been their mother's. Frankie's favorite gift had been a pair of well-worn Everlast sparring gloves. She remembered Teddy's look of sour surprise when, during her first lesson, purely by luck, she'd bypassed his defensive block with a blow to his twice-broken nose. She remembered also how her exhilaration later gave way to misery, how she'd sobbed under the thin blanket on her bed.

Finally the letters were written, the milk and cookies placed on the table, the children asleep. Gordon was out of the way; she could examine the contents of the tan duffle before he returned.

CHAPTER 11

Frankie slipped out through the winter night to retrieve the bag from her car. The storm was increasing in intensity, a combination of snow and sleet driving down hard. *Rocky*, she thought, *where are you? Please, help me to find you.* The icy wind bit her cheeks and coated her hair with crystal. Lugging the duffel, she retreated to the security of the house.

Inside, she sat at Rocky's desk to unzip the bag and pull out the clothing she had stuffed inside, then the scripts, the jewelry box, and the manila envelope, from which she dumped out a stack of photos and papers. The photos were dark, grainy, taken in poor light and enlarged. She couldn't make out the subject of the first one until she turned on the desk lamp to study it: a man and a woman, the man's face half obscured and the woman nearly naked. She recognized Gordon's profile. "You bastard!" she whispered under her breath. "You fucking bastard!"

She went through the stack. There were eight photos taken in a bar or club and showing Gordon in close contact with various topless dancers in glittery outfits. Six featured a heavily made up blonde with large eyes, penciled brows, and round breasts, who seemed to be gazing past Gordon's head directly at the photographer. A man with a shaved head, small ratty beard, and massive shoulders, professionally evil looking, was visible in the background in several photos. "Bastard," she muttered again, tossing the photos face down on the desk. Rocky's pride could never have endured such an insult! Maybe she'd found the photos and confronted him, precipitating their most recent battle.

Shaking with fury and disgust, Frankie examined the papers, bills from local restaurants and motels, legal documents concerning development properties and loans from an Allied Mortgage Company, with signatures that including Gordon's. Why would her sister have stashed these papers, she wondered, when she had never concerned herself with the Gardiner family business?

She opened the jewelry box and dumped its contents out on the desk--necklaces, bracelets, earrings of ebony and diamonds, Victorian style costume jewelry for the show. She sorted through them, clutching each piece like a talisman, trying to conjure up some essence of Rocky. In a little drawer, she found a silver key with a tag attached. The tag bore hand-printed initials *MBD* and the number *209*.

She hung the clothing in a downstairs closet, laid the jewelry box on her dresser, and slipped the thick envelope into her own suitcase. She put the small silver key on her own key chain before she returned to the desk and went through the phone numbers she'd found in Rocky's book. There was a number for a C. Rojas.

She started with that. After a few rings, someone answered. She could barely hear the voice that said, "Hello?" A party seemed to be in high progress, with laughter, loud Christmas music, and off-key caroling in the background.

"Is this Chantelle Rojas?" she asked.

"Who?" somebody asked several times before a woman's voice came through clearly.

"This is Chantelle. Who wants to talk to me?"

"I'm sorry to bother you," Frankie said. "I'm Frankie Lupino. Rocky Gardiner's sister."

"Oh." There was a moment's pause. The voice turned hard. "How did you get my number?"

"I found it in Rocky's address book. I thought maybe you could tell me--"

"Listen, I read about them finding your sister's car. I'm real sorry she's missing, but I don't know anything."

"Did you see her on Sunday? She had a note in her calendar to meet with you."

"I don't remember the last time I saw her. I only know her through Aphrodite, cause me and her both work at Skytop," the woman continued in a rush. "I can't talk now. I'm sorry." The line went dead. When Frankie called back she got a busy signal.

She fished out the card for the private investigator, Roman Sarvonsky. She dialed it and, at the same time the answering machine started, a gravelly voice said, "Hello." The machine message obscured Frankie's voice, and she heard swearing and fumbling. "Let me shut that damn thing off. . .okay, who is this?"

"I'm sorry to bother you on Christmas Eve." She tried to sound businesslike. "I was given your card by a state trooper." She read the trooper's name. "Stanley Chernyakov."

"Oh. Yeah? What do you want?"

"Is this Roman Sarvonsky?"

"Yes."

"You're a private investigator?"

"Yes. What's the problem?"

"My sister is missing. Her car was found yesterday in the river--"

"In the Delaware, with that actor, what's-his-name--Cliff Thornton?"

"Yes. But she disappeared on Sunday evening. Nobody's heard from her. And then they found--"

"It's not my kind of case. The police are already involved. Let them find her."

Frankie started to cry despite herself. "You don't understand. Everybody knows her husband and his family. The Gardiners own half of the Poconos. He's friends with the local cops." She held her keys in her hand, studying the initials on the disc – *MBD* – a bank deposit box, she wondered.

"More reason they'll make the effort."

"But maybe *he's*--done something."

". . .What makes you think that?"

"They fight a lot. He hits her. He admitted he--hurt her the night she disappeared."

"Hurt her?"

"He claims she fell, hit her head, but that she drove off in her car. There was something, maybe blood, on the mantle and the floor. And I have proof that he was fooling around."

"A girlfriend?"

"I don't know. Hanging out in clubs, pictures with lap dancers."

"That doesn't prove he's done something to his wife. She's only been missing for, what, two days?" He paused, "She knew this guy they found in her car?"

"They were in a show together."

"Why not give the cops a little more time?"

"Maybe time is important. Maybe she's hiding. She might be hurt, or in danger!" Frankie broke down, sobbing.

"Where are you?" he asked after a moment.

"I'm at her home," Frankie explained trying to stifle her sobs, "On Lake Nakomis."

"Where's the husband?" he asked.

"He went out about two hours ago."

"Why are you there--if you suspect *him*?"

"I'm looking out for her kids. And hoping somehow she'll show up," she sniffed.

"Give the cops a chance. If they don't find her in the next few days, call me again." She hung up the phone and put her head down on the desk, berating herself for losing control.

CHAPTER 12

Frankie realized she had fallen asleep only when several sharp cracks from outside startled her awake. It was nearly midnight. Stiff from sleep, she rose to switch off the one burning lamp. The flames still sputtering in the fireplace, reflected back in the windows, seemed like a second fire.

The noises, she thought, had come from the direction of the lake. The world outside was absolute white. Small trees had bent almost double from the weight of the snow, branches tipped with ice. The skylights, too, were heavily blanketed. She wished for curtains or shutters to close, but Rocky had been adamant about an unobstructed view of the lake. She heard the wind and the splintering of tree limbs.

There was another snap. Ice shifting and fissuring on the lake, Frankie assured herself. Yet fear dragged its fingers along her spine and whispered into her ear. *Was* there a murderer on the loose? A mass of snow fell from an overloaded branch near the window. Perhaps that was all she'd heard. Just as she had begun to relax a bit, a small, whining noise, like that of a snowmobile, broke the night. She turned to the window again and saw--or imagined she saw-- shadows moving through the shifting blow at the edge of the lake, disappearing into further shadows near the boathouse. Her heartbeat was loud in her ears.

Could someone have come by way of the country club grounds adjoining the property, following the rocky lake path to the house? No vehicle could cross the lake, she was certain, and not even the most persistent reporter would spend Christmas Eve skulking in a snowstorm. Wouldn't the security system have sounded if anything had crossed the perimeter? Perhaps she was hallucinating.

The phone rang. She picked up in Rocky's room and whispered a hello. It was Lourdes. "Gordon has come back?"

"No. Not yet. When did he leave?"

"Maybe twenty minutes. He was drinking, angry. And the roads, too, are very bad. I am worrying," Lourdes told her.

"About him?"

"For you and the kids." Lourdes's voice faltered. "He was talking of shooting people. Reporters."

"He's been drinking all day," Frankie said. "The kids are asleep. It's midnight."

She listened for a moment. "He might be coming now," she said. "I hear a car."

"Should I wait? Until you see how he is acting?" Lourdes asked.

"Maybe the drive sobered him up." Frankie gripped the phone. She heard the garage door below open and close. But an engine continued, to hum just below the window. She looked down; through the driving slant of snow, she could see a black-and-white police car. "Gordon just pulled into the garage, but. . .there's a cop car in the driveway."

"*Dios mio!*" Lourdes whispered. "Call me when you find out--anything."

Downstairs a solicitous young patrolman was supporting Gordon as they crossed the cobblestone breezeway.

"Here you go, Mr. Gardiner." The boyish officer, face mottled with the cold, deposited Gordon at the kitchen table and looked up, startled, as Frankie entered.

"What's happened? Have you found her?" she demanded.

"Mrs. Gardiner? No, ma'am, I'm afraid not. But Mr. Gardiner shouldn't be out tonight." He looked her over, embarrassed and curious.

"I'm Mrs. Gardiner's sister," she explained.

"Oh, yes. Of course." He seemed to be reassessing. "Mr. Gardiner was driving erratically. Under the circumstances," he shrugged, "I decided to bring him home to sleep it off."

"Thank you." She stopped him as he turned toward the door. "Before you leave. . .I thought I saw something down by the boathouse. And I heard noises. I know the storm--and I'm probably imagining things--but--"

"No problem," he said. "My partner's in the patrol car. We'll take a look."

Gordon's head was resting on the table. He looked at Frankie. "Lourdes sent a lot of food. It's out in the Suburban," he said. "I should bring it in." He sat, however, with his head down, unmoving.

"I'll get it." From the garage she could hear the two cops stomping toward the lake. In the rear of the van she found an old-fashioned hamper so heavy she had trouble carrying it into the kitchen. As she was unpacking, she heard the police radio crackle and the excited voices of the officers. There was a pounding at the back kitchen door. The young policeman stood there, his uniform coated with snow, face grim.

"I've called for backup," he told her. He'd adopted a stiff formal manner as though he needed to employ professional calm to manage the situation. "I'm very sorry, ma'am, but I think--" He stopped and looked desperately at Gordon, who was slumped, eyes closed, at the table. "We've found something in the lake--down by the boathouse."

"Found what?" Frankie searched his face. His impassive demeanor faltered.

"I'm not sure. We've called in Homicide, the crime unit--"

"Oh, god! Is it--?" Frankie tried to push past him but he stopped her.

"We can't be sure until. . .it looks like a——a bundle half in the water."

His partner appeared in the doorway, a snow-covered hulk, radio crackling.

"They're on the way," he said. "We'll have to set up right here." The radio in his hand barked, and Frankie was able to make out the rasping words that penetrated her panic: Responding to report of female cadaver. Possible tie-in with missing person report. Gardiner residence on Lake Nakomis.

"*Rocky!*" Frankie wailed. "Oh, god! *Oh, god!*" She fought to get past him again, and he grabbed her and held her by her shoulders.

Gordon raised his head and looked about, dazed. "What happened?" he asked.

Frankie turned to his puffy face, the bloodshot eyes. "They've *found her!*" she screamed at him. "She's *dead!* They found her *body* in the *lake!*" And before anyone else could react, she flew at him, punched at his face, clawed at his eyes. She was still tearing at his hair as the two of them pulled her away.

"You bastard! *You fucking bastard!*" She broke into hoarse sobs as she was being dragged to the other side of the room.

Gordon, dazed, staggered to his feet. "What? Rocky's dead?" He started toward the door, but the second officer, a large man who looked to be in his forties, with a bit of a paunch and a pudgy face, intervened.

"You can't go out there. Nobody can touch anything. The crime unit's on its way." It seemed only moments before there was the buzz over the intercom, the sound of sirens, and the red whirl of lights as police cars raced up the hill and halted in the driveway.

CHAPTER 13

In minutes the property was overrun, lights flooded the place, and loud voices resonated through the night. The crime unit tramped through Rocky's garden, taping off sections all the way down to where the body had been discovered. Others, one in a sports jacket and tie who seemed to be in command, took measurements and photographs. The local police chief arrived and assigned the young cop who'd escorted Gordon home to stay in the den with Frankie. Ransome's name came up and there was a brief argument about jurisdiction.

The local chief, a heavy man with a large stomach and a florid complexion, disappeared into the basement with Gordon and the second patrolman. Frankie felt she was going to pass out or throw up. The young cop, unable to sit still for more than a few seconds, walked back and forth to the windows. They heard a sound from above.

"I've got to go upstairs. The kids--"

"Kids?"

"Rocky's kids. And my son. They're babies. The oldest is only four. If they wake up--"

"Let me see if it's okay." He stepped into the kitchen and spoke to a trooper. "It's okay," he told her when he returned. "But I have to stay with you."

She hurried up to the bedroom to look in. Autumn stirred and sat up.

"Is it Mommy?" she asked sleepily.

"No, honey. Go back to sleep." Frankie sat on the edge of the bed.

"Did Santa come?" The girl spotted the officer, who was standing just outside of the bedroom.

"No. Shhh."

"Why is a policeman here?" There was fear in Autumn's whisper, as though some understanding had penetrated. Her sniffles escalated to sobs. "Mommy! I want Mommy!"

Frankie tried to rock her, but her wails increased, waking Jeffrey. He, too, crawled into Frankie's lap. At that moment Ransome appeared on the stairs, spoke a few words to the other, and entered.

"I need to ask you a few questions." He seemed taller but as calm and sleepy-eyed as when they'd talked hours earlier. She tried to read his bland, noncommittal expression.

"It's Rocky, isn't it?" she demanded.

His eyes took in the children. "Could we talk in another room?"

"Yes. Of course." She tried to disentangle herself. "It's real important for me to talk to Detective Ransome for a minute. I want you to stay here with this policeman. I'll be right back."

They went into Rocky's bedroom. Frankie saw his eyes automatically sweep the room, lingering on the wedding photo. His dark overcoat was open.

"You've found her, haven't you?" she asked.

"We need a positive I.D.," he said shortly. "But--" he paused for a long moment, and his voice was low--"we think it's likely. Any idea what she was wearing?"

"No."

"You'd recognize something that belonged to her?"

"Probably, yes. Does she look so. . . ?"

"She don't look like that photo. When did you last see her?"

"Two weeks ago. But we talk on the phone. We email every day."

"She say anything--"

"I told you. Gordon beat her two nights ago. And then, according to him, she disappeared right afterwards. I don't buy his story."

"What do you think?"

"I think he hit her and cracked her head on the fireplace like he said, only a lot harder! And——and then he panicked!"

"Well, before we talk theories, we need an I.D. You feel you could do that before they take her away?"

"Where will they take her?"

"To Allentown. The morgue there."

"Oh, god!" Frankie wailed. "Yes. I want to see her."

"You can't touch her," he said in a flat voice. "We need a--a formal determination on the cause of death. You understand?"

"Yes." She followed him out of the room. "Where's Gordon?"

"In the basement. Too drunk to be any use."

Downstairs, the detective who had taken charge earlier was taping off sections of the kitchen and den. Outside, an ambulance squatted in the snowy night, doors open to accept the lumpy bundle waiting on the gurney. A photographer moved away as they approached. The snow was icy, blowing slantwise, sharp as needles, and the EMS workers huddled, collars up, against it. Frankie stifled a cry when she saw the long red-gold hair streaming from under the blanket; droplets splattered as ice melted under the police lights. She recognized the brown-and-tan afghan, a twin to the one in the den. It was thick with ice, enclosing the rigid figure like a marble shroud.

"Rocky!" she murmured. "Oh, god, Rocky!" The blanket had been peeled back to reveal a face washed in the harsh glare of police lights. It was discolored--a greenish white--contorted, eyes and mouth frozen open, but, to Frankie, still recognizably her sister's face. She saw that the hands were protruding from the blanket as well, encased in plastic bags. A rush of blood made her lightheaded; her knees went slushy, and her sight momentarily dimmed. Afraid she might pass out, she reached out to steady herself. Ransome put an arm around her, supporting her weight. She looked at him and back at the gurney. The scene shifted in and out of focus, as though she were viewing it through a ratcheting lens.

"You recognize her?"

"It's Rocky." She choked out the words.

"You're positive?"

"Yes." She nodded and closed her eyes, allowing herself to lean against his bulk. He signaled to the two shivering men. They closed and zipped up the body bag and loaded the gurney into the ambulance. One slammed the back doors and they got into the cab. The motor revved, lurched to a start, and the tail lights disappeared into the swirling snow.

Frankie pulled away from Ransome's support, wanting to run after them, to cradle the body and warm it back to life. A vision flashed, taking her back to a scene Rocky had played in college--the drowned Ophelia, still and pale, starkly beautiful in counterfeit death, so unlike the grotesque reality. Frankie had been crying for days; now, no tears came.

She saw figures still moving down by the lake, faintly discernable through the blowing whiteness, and heard faint voices through the storm. "What are they doing?" she asked Ransome.

"Looking for tracks, footprints. They'll make some casts. One of my guys thinks he's got some skimobile tracks, if the wind hasn't already buried them. This goddamn storm...." They moved back into the house. Frankie remembered that Lourdes was waiting to hear from her.

"I've got to call Lourdes!"

"Who?"

"Rocky's friend. The kids' sitter. I promised I'd let her know as soon. . .as we found out anything."

"I'll need her name and number, and a list of all your sister's friends," he said. "Anybody you think might tell us something."

"Lourdes will tell you the same thing I'm telling you. He did it! Arrest that fucking bastard!"

"There's got to be an autopsy. She might have--"

"Killed herself and then crawled under the ice? He *killed* her! And then he tried to hide the evidence!"

"Call your friend. This whole area is officially a crime scene, off limits 'til we're through checking it out!"

"Well, check out the fireplace first!" Frankie said. "Don't you have some chemical that shows where there was blood?"

"We'll do that. Meanwhile, you've got to vacate the premises for the next few days. Let me know where you'll be," he said. "Can you and the kids stay with that friend for a while?"

"I think so, yes."

"Pack what you need. An officer'll drive you."

Frankie made the call. Lourdes listened, moaning under her breath as Frankie gave her the barest details.

"Bring my *ninos* and come," she said, as Frankie had expected. "We will wait for you."

In a daze, Frankie packed; she handed the bags to Officer Clarke.

"Where are we going?" Autumn asked her.

"To stay with Kiki and Lourdes for a little while."

As they started down the stairs, Autumn pulled away and ran back into her bedroom. When she emerged she was dragging a stuffed toy, a monster-like creature half as large as the little girl, with yellow horns, bulging yellow eyes, blue shaggy fur, and terrifying fangs and claws.

"It's Clarence," she told Frankie. "I need him, 'cause my Wilby's gone."

Officer Clarke led them through the confusion, past the police cars and the activity inside and out.

Lourdes and her husband were waiting for them, robes thrown over pajamas. Larry's hair stood up in a dark corona; a bulging Adam's apple moved like a mechanical device as his hazel eyes blinked in consternation. Lourdes chewed at her lower lip, tears dripping steadily as she lifted Gordie from the back seat.

The children, disoriented by the midnight trek, were put to bed but, with the flexibility of the very young, were soon asleep, the boys in daycare cribs and Autumn hugging her monster in the bed she shared with Kiki. The three adults sat at the table in the small kitchen, drinking cup after cup of coffee, numb with disbelief.

CHAPTER 14

Later, Frankie could barely remember Christmas Day.
When she heard noises in the house, she stirred and glanced at
the watch that she had failed to remove. Ten-thirty: A cold
winter light was streaking through the blinds. Rocky is dead,
she thought. She felt as though a bowling ball had been
dropped on her chest. Her head was aching with the hint of an
incipient migraine, and the light when she turned on the small
table lamp felt like icicles jabbing into her eyes. She rose and
stumbled out to the kitchen. Coffee had been brewed. She
needed some, but she needed the bathroom even more. She
could hear the indistinct children's voices from the playroom.
She stumbled to the bathroom, where she washed her face and
made an attempt to look presentable. She pressed a cold
washcloth to her face. She had once again fallen asleep in her
clothing. Where was her suitcase? Somewhere in the den, she
thought. She used one of Lourdes's brushes to subdue her
tangled hair.

Before she was finished, there was a frantic knock at
the bathroom door, and Lourdes's panicked voice: "Frankie,
you are dressed?"

"Sort of."

"You must come out here."

"What's wrong?" Frankie emerged into the hallway, still barefoot and dazed. Lourdes looked anxious, her eyes still red rimmed and more than usually protuberant.

"Gordon's mother is here. Gordon, too. They came to take the kids."

"Oh, god!"

"What can we do?"

"Gordon's their father, and nothing's been--where are they?"

"She is waiting in the living room. Gordon stays outside in the car. I asked her to talk to you before I. . ."

Frankie took a few more swipes at her unruly hair and again pressed the washcloth over her swollen eyes. She brushed at her rumpled sweater and jeans, and followed Lourdes out. The children had littered the room with wrappings torn from Christmas packages and toys.

Mrs. Edwina Gardiner was sitting on the edge of an armchair, back straight. It was Frankie's first glimpse of her in several years, and her initial impression was that the slim, stylish woman bore no resemblance to her son. However, as Edwina rose and came forward, hand extended, she noted a similarity in the intense blue of her eyes and the determined line of her chin.

She was wearing a simple dark wool dress and a single strand of pearls, exuding careless elegance. She was perfectly groomed--gray hair cut into a becoming frame for the pale angular face, subtly made up, remarkably unlined, and perfectly composed. Taking Frankie's hand in her cool, well-manicured grasp, she met her eyes with apparent compassion.

"I'm so sorry, dear." Her voice was low.

"I can't believe it."

"No, of course you can't. None of us can. Gordon is quite distraught. He's waiting in the car." She indicated the window through which Frankie saw a long dark limo parked in the snowy driveway with a liveried driver. The back windows were too darkly tinted to reveal any occupant.

"He needs his children with him, she said. And, of course, his father and I want them, too. "

"They like it here. Lourdes and Kiki—"

"And we do so appreciate her taking them in these past few days." The older woman glanced at Lourdes, who was standing in the doorway, shifting uneasily from foot to foot. "I'll send you a check for the extra duty."

"Rocky was my friend!" Lourdes protested. "I do not want money for caring for the children now!"

But Edwina Gardiner had gone on to the next item on her agenda. "Could you gather their things and call them upstairs, please? " It was clearly a command.

"Let me talk to them first, to explain. . ." Frankie glanced toward the stairway; looking back, she caught an unguarded expression of cold contempt as the older woman studied her.

"That won't be necessary." There was icy metal in the voice now. She glanced at Lourdes and then, pointedly, at her slim gold watch.

Lourdes turned to Frankie, who nodded. They soon heard her calling the children and the shuffle of small feet.

"You and your son are welcome to stay with us as well. " Edwina's generous invitation was belied by the coolness of the voice that offered it.

"I think we'll just stay here for the time being."

"Yes, I suppose that might suit you temporarily. " Edwina reached for the dark, fur-lined coat that had been thrown over the arm of the sofa. "We hope to be able to hold services Friday evening or Saturday morning. If the police. . ."

"Rocky always said she'd be cremated."

"Oh, no. No. We've already made arrangements. There's space in the family plot in Laurelwood Cemetery. Generations of Gardiners are buried there. The wake will be held at the Thomas Funeral Home and a funeral service at First Presbyterian just as soon as we get permission. I spoke to Reverend Taylor this morning."

"She wanted her ashes to be scattered over the Nakomis Falls."

"Young people say foolish things when death seems a long way off. She deserves a dignified farewell--as Gordon's wife. As a Gardiner."

"As my sister, she deserves whatever she wanted!" Frankie's voice had veered up into a thin, high-pitched wail.

"I know you're upset, dear, but could we skip the drama? It's her husband's decision to make, in any case."

The children appeared at the top of the stairs. Jeffrey was holding a huge red fire truck; Gordie was tugging at it, whining that it was his. Autumn carried her monster in a chokehold and was rubbing its fuzzy hair against her cheek. Kiki began to arrange several small stuffed animals beneath the branches of the Christmas tree.

Lourdes padded back upstairs for their luggage while Autumn approached Frankie and Edwina.

"You remember your grandmother, don't you?" Frankie asked. Autumn nodded, looking shyly at Edwina while Gordie took advantage of the moment to secure his grasp on the truck.

"Are you *my* grandmother?" Jeffrey asked.

The older woman ignored the question until he repeated it, tugging at her coat. Then she replied in her mild, controlled voice, "No, dear, I'm not *your* grandmother. I'm Autumn and Gordon Junior's grandmother." She gave Autumn a thin smile. "Dear, leave that toy for the children who come here to play."

"He's Clarence," Autumn told her. "He's mine. I want to keep him, cause I can't find Wilby."

"I have some lovely dolls for you to play with at my house," her grandmother told her.

"I want to stay here and play with Kiki." Kiki's head popped from beneath the tree, and the two girls exchanged conspiratorial giggles. "We're making a tea party."

"We're going to spend the day with Poppy," Edwina informed her. "Your daddy is waiting for you in the car."

Autumn's face lit up. "Is Mommy waiting in the car, too?"

"No, dear. I'm afraid your mommy has gone very, very far away, and she won't come back any more."

Frankie gasped. Anger as hot and furious as an eruption of lava flooded through her. She glared at Edwina, wanting to strike her.

"How could you tell her like that?" she sputtered, her face suffused with color. Edwina returned her gaze, unmoved.

Frankie knelt and held the little girl in a close embrace. Autumn's confused face turned up to her.

"My mommy didn't go away!" She looked at Edwina and back to Frankie. "My mommy didn't go far away, did she, Aunt Frankie?"

"I believe in telling children the truth," Edwina said, her voice calm and competent. "Fantasy and lies only confuse them." Frankie pulled her attention back to the child.

"I'm afraid it's true, honey. Your mommy can't come back. But she loves you, and she will always be close to you, inside your heart." Frankie held the little girl's troubled gaze. "Your daddy wants you to go with him now."

"I don't want to go."

"I'll see you again very soon. I promise you."

"But I want to *see* her!" Autumn sniffled, and Gordie let go of the truck and came over to her. Lourdes and Frankie dressed the two protesting children while Jeffrey and Kiki played under the tree. Edwina waited at the door, slipping her fingers into fur-lined gloves, an eyebrow impatiently raised.

"I don't *want* to go!" Autumn was on the verge of hysterics. She looked at her grandmother. "I *hate* you! I want Aunt *Frankie*!"

"Honey, your daddy's waiting," Frankie said to soothe her.

"I don't *want* my daddy! I want *Mommy*! I want to stay here with you and *Kiki*!"

"Autumn, stop that right now! Put down that disgusting toy and come with me. Miss, do you think you could help get them out to the car, since Frances isn't wearing shoes?"

Just as they got the children and their luggage to the door, Gordon appeared. He was wearing a topcoat over a conservative suit. His face looked pale, freshly shaved, calmer than Frankie had seen him in days, but his eyes were flat and dull.

"Frankie," he stammered, standing in the doorway while the cold wind blew in on them. "I'm so sorry. I can't believe--." He stammered." Tears welled in his eyes. Frankie stared at him, cold-eyed, her hands at her sides in white-knuckled fists. Oblivious, he picked up his little son. "I want the kids with me."

Gordie went to Gordon willingly, and Edwina took Autumn firmly by a hand and led her out; the little girl pulled back, crying for the stuffed monster lying just inside the door.

The driver opened the door and assisted them into the limousine. Gordon came back for the last of the bags and looked at her helplessly. "You know you and Jeffrey are welcome, too," he told her. He looked so bewildered that she felt a rush of confused emotion before she remembered the photos and hardened.

"Bastard!" she muttered under her breath as she turned away. She came inside, shivering, and sat at the kitchen table, her head in her hands. Jeffrey toddled over to her and put his small hand on her knee.

"Mommy, why are you sad?" he asked. "Don't you know it's Christmas?"

CHAPTER 15

Lourdes and Larry accompanied Frankie to the Thomas Funeral Home early on Friday afternoon. After the autopsy, the police had released Rocky's body. Frankie, numb with shock and grief, had been unable to talk to the coroner's office or the police. But she *had* seen a front-page story, quoting "official sources" that stated that Rocky's death had been ruled a homicide; police believed that both Cliff Thornton and she had been murdered near the Shawnee Playhouse. Gordon Gardiner, Rochelle's husband, "was not a suspect at this time."

That story threw Frankie back into anger. No doubt the Gardiners' influence had colored local press coverage, could even have had stories planted to benefit Gordon, although their prominent name generated intense media scrutiny as well. The *Pocono Record* devoted an entire page, highlighting the connections between this and Cliff Thornton's murder.

Reporters and television crews were lying in wait in the cold December afternoon as mourners made their way into the funeral home. The three pushed past, heads down, ignoring the shouted questions.

Inside, a portly, middle-aged man with gray hair like the pelt of a beaver greeted them with a scented hand and a professionally somber expression, and handed each a gold-edged card and program directing them toward an inner room.

They were immediately enveloped in the sweet, heavy fragrance emanating from the enormous bouquets that banked the closed rosewood coffin and lined the walls of the room. A large framed picture of Rocky at her loveliest sat on an easel. At least, Frankie thought, no one would see her sister's face, prettified and painted in death.

Her own last glimpse was burned into her brain. No, no--she had an endless store of memories of Rocky smiling, laughing, talking, teasing, but against her will hideous images rose up: Rocky's face bruised and swollen from a beating, Rocky's face frozen and distorted in death. A low moan escaped her, and Lourdes reached to squeeze her hand.

They stood like intruders at the back of a room filled with Gardiners, Gardiner relatives, Gardiner friends, and Gardiner business associates. Even Gordon's father, with his ravaged face, had been dressed in a dark suit, propped upright in his wheelchair, a nurse beside him, and stationed at the front of the room, where Edwina and Gordon were accepting condolences.

She recognized several officers who had been present the night Rocky's body had been found standing near the back in dark suits. She wondered fleetingly if they were there in a professional capacity or closing ranks around someone they considered their own.

She thought of the envelope she'd found in Rocky's locker. She would have to give it to someone but could she trust these people? And what about the key? She'd been unable to find any clue to what it might unlock. She'd even done a search on the internet for matching initials but came up blank.

Edwina was icily regal in a charcoal Chanel suit and small dark hat with a hint of veiling; Gordon, pale, in a dark suit, head bowed, was the classic picture of grief. His eyes were lowered, and his voice drifted back to Frankie, a low murmur. Now and then he gave some mourner a manly hug.

"We should go up," Lourdes whispered after a moment.

Larry grimaced, nodded, and reached to take their coats. The ranks of composed and elegant Gardiners made Frankie suddenly conscious of her appearance. She had borrowed a dark purplish shift, the only dress in Lourdes's closet that even remotely fit her; it was too short and hung loosely on her inches above the heavy boots. Her hair, skinned back and pinned with a metal barrette, had partially escaped, forming a wispy halo of wild red frizz. She thought wryly of Rocky's love of style and her frequent attempts to inflict those standards on her, how she pressed her to borrow one of her designer outfits for opening or closing night parties. "Sorry, Rocky," she whispered.

Moving through the crowd, Frankie recognized a cousin she had not seen for years and others she knew: Ken Werther, the director, who hugged her for a long moment; some of Rocky's school and college friends; actors Rocky had studied or worked with; a young man Rocky had once dated; and Ritchie Shames, the director from the Playwrights' Theater. He was a tall, reedy man who stood nearly a head taller than anyone else in the room. She hadn't called him or arranged for coverage beyond the three days they had agreed on, yet here he was, with his boyfriend Jorge, waving and giving her a wan smile.

She noticed Detective Ransome paying his respects. He bent down to speak to Mr. Gardiner, who responded with loud guttural noises that caused Edwina to place a hand on his shoulder.

When Frankie reached the front, she felt Edwina making a quick, merciless appraisal, whispering to Frankie in icy tones, "You should be standing next to Gordon." Then Gordon was hugging her, and she choked back her fury as he pressed her hard against his chest. Murderer, she thought. Bastard! She was left standing beside him, observing him from the corner of her eyes, as Lourdes and Larry moved off.

In a flurry at the door a group of latecomers, as exotic as peacocks, staged an entrance. Aphrodite drew all eyes, tall, dark-skinned, and dramatic, in an elegant black floor length dress, and with her several young men and woman in subdued colors but with a flair that bespoke costume design. But when Aphrodite reached her, Frankie saw that she looked truly anguished. She enfolded Frankie in a warm embrace. Tears trickled down her dark cheeks leaving salty streaks.

"I'm so sorry. I can't believe this is real," the actress whispered. "Bianca sends her sympathies."

"Bianca?"

"Cliff's wife. She's still too upset to leave her room." She leaned even closer and whispered in Frankie's ear, "Talk to me later."

Several of the other actors introduced themselves with murmurs and whispers, hugging Frankie, pressing her hand.

"Oh, my god," a slight young man with spiky orange hair whispered, "aren't you the image of Rocky!"

Ritchie explained that a mutual friend from the cast of Rocky's show had called him, and assured her that Jorge would cover as stage manager of her own production, *A Child's Christmas*, until her return. The production was well into its run, and Jorge was relatively untried. He'd depended on her quiet control and synchronization of the backstage elements. There would have to be adjustments. Still he hugged her warmly, his bony arms poking out like sticks.

She was operating on automatic, thanking people for their kindness, accepting murmured words of sorrow, attempting to place some of faces she dimly recognized.

A flashy blonde in a dark, form fitting dress and three inch heels stopped directly in front of Gordon. Frankie thought at first that she recognized her. The woman stood waiting while Gordon's attention focused on an elderly man. She didn't look at Frankie.

She was perhaps in her mid twenties, heavily made up but striking, with strong even features, large hazel eyes, and an attitude that demanded attention. Her spicy perfume drifted toward Frankie like a mist. Gordon, who seemed to be deliberately ignoring her, greeted several others as the line moved forward around the woman.

The blonde woman caught Frankie looking at her and seemed to start a little, then returned her stare, even looking for a moment as though she might speak to her. But then Gordon acknowledged her, leaned toward her, and there was a low

murmuring exchange before she moved off abruptly, dress
swishing.

The Reverend Taylor offered a long, sonorous prayer,
then extended his hand to Gordon, who stepped forward and,
choking back tears, made a rambling speech, proclaiming
Rochelle's sweetness, gentle nature, and endless maternal
patience, painting such a cloying picture that Frankie felt her
gorge rising. Liar, she thought, phony, cheat!

When Reverend Taylor invited her to speak, she was
momentarily overwhelmed by self-conscious confusion as all
eyes turned toward her. But then, as though Rocky had
imparted some of her confidence, she stepped forward,
forgetting her ill-fitting dress and usual awkward shyness, to
speak with simple eloquence of her strong, feisty sister, her
friend and mentor, who, despite the early loss of their mother,
had never allowed her to feel orphaned. Audible sobs reached
her as she stepped back into place.

Frankie kept an eye out for Aphrodite but she was not
with the group she'd come in with. Finally, the crowd
dispersed; Frankie stood alone beside her sister's coffin. The
nurse guided Mr. Gardiner's wheelchair down the ramp while
Gordon gathered coats. Edwina, about to follow her husband
out, came back to Frankie.

"The church service tomorrow starts at ten o'clock.
We'll head directly to the cemetery afterwards. I'd like you to
ride in our car."

Frankie merely nodded. She could endure their
proximity for a few moments in order to hide her anger and
suspicion.

"Afterwards there will be a reception at our home."
Edwina glanced down at the purple dress and the worn boots.
"Perhaps you could find something a little more suitable to
wear," she suggested. "Out of respect for the occasion. I know
Rochelle gave you many of her lovely clothes but if you don't
have anything more presentable with you, please choose
something from her closet."

Frankie cringed, yet she knew Edwina was right.
Rocky would have been mortified to see her looking so
unkempt, and how she had loved to dress her little sister in her

own designer outfits. She would swallow her pride for Rocky's sake.

"Isn't the house still sealed?"

"They're almost finished. According to Captain Matthews, Rochelle's death occurred somewhere else entirely. Officer Clarke will escort you into the house."

Gordon was approaching them, and Edwina glanced at him. "Something simple," she continued. "And a coat--there's a Donna Karan that should fit you."

"How are the children?" Frankie asked, but Edwina was already retreating.

"Gordon will take care of the arrangements," she said indicating her son.

For a moment Frankie almost believed in Gordon as heartbroken widower. His brows were drawn together, eyes downcast, lashes damp. His deep voice trembled. It seemed he had forgiven her attack on the night of the gruesome discovery, or perhaps been too drunk to remember it. His breath smelled of peppermint, and he was wearing a heavy cologne. To mask the smell of alcohol, she thought.

"Autumn and Gordie were asking for you."

"How are they?"

"Pretty bad. They want Rocky." His breath was ragged. "And you."

"When can I see them?"

"Come after you pick out clothes for tomorrow. I'll tell Bobby to drive you."

"Bobby?"

"Clarke. Officer Clarke. His brother Mark was in my class at Barton Prep."

"They'll be at the house during the reception?"

"Yes. Mom wants Autumn to come to the church." He seemed to be struggling to say something else. When he moved to embrace her she stifled a small "no" and stepped away. Oblivious to her response he left.

Frankie made a last search for Aphrodite and thought she saw her with a group near the door. She started to move toward them but was intercepted by a tall man emerging from the dim hallway.

She felt a brief moment of panic as a bulky form moved toward her, with a slight but unmistakable limp, silhouetted against the light. Emerging from the shadow, she saw he had dark eyes shadowed beneath hooded lids, heavy dark brows, and a full sardonic mouth. He was, perhaps, in his mid-forties. Frankie's eyes were drawn to a thick-ridged scar that ran from just under his left eye to the corner of his ear. His sudden appearance had startled, even frightened her. There was something dark about him, something compelling, too.

"Frances Lupino?" he asked.

"Yes?" She looked about warily.

"I'm sorry about--your sister." His voice was full of gravel with an unfamiliar accent. He wore, in what appeared to be a casual arrangement, a dark suit with a blue shirt and loosened tie. He took her hand, holding it and standing so close that she was forced to breathe in his woodsy, leather scent. His eyes radiated a dark intensity so unnerving that she pulled back. Despite the damaged face and the limp, his tall broad form exuded strength.

"I'm Roman Sarvonsky," he told her. "You called me Christmas Eve." He appeared detached, an observer, but for that spark in his eyes.

"Sarvonsky," she said foolishly, eyes riveted to his. Recovering herself she withdrew her hand. "You're the detective. I still need to talk to you," she said. "No one's even looking for the truth."

"I can't get involved in an open homicide," he replied, his gaze still steadily holding hers. "But we can talk. Call me."

CHAPTER 16

Officer Clarke kept a distance while Frankie tried to choose a funeral outfit. They'd picked their way through the house, avoiding the yellow crime scene tape around the back entryway and parts of the kitchen and den. As she entered Rocky's room, the young officer took up a spot at the top of the stairway.

She stepped into the walk-in closet and surveyed racks of clothing, a profusion--cashmeres, silks, chiffons, arranged like an artist's palette. Her throat ached; her eyeballs felt like burning glass. Absorbed, Frankie was conscious only that each item had been chosen and worn by her sister. She hoped that her sister's hunger for beauty had finally been satisfied. Officer Clarke shuffled impatiently and cleared his throat.

"I'll only be a few minutes," she called out, and quickly chose an outfit that Rocky had insisted she wear to an awards ceremony the previous winter, a long velvet dress in a dark chocolate, a pair of dark brown suede boots with half-inch heels, and a black cashmere sweater. She added a long wool coat with a velvet collar and cuffs and as an afterthought chose from one of the jewelry cabinets, a slim Cartier watch and a string of pearls.

Rocky would approve, she thought. As she held the garments close, she breathed in the faint, lingering scent of Rocky's perfume and felt her sister's presence. She followed Clarke down the stairs and out to the black-and-white. He drove silently, looking ahead as though she was merely a package to be delivered.

Lourdes and Frankie arrived late for the church service the following morning and squeezed into the pew behind the Gardiners. Autumn, looking like a pale porcelain doll in a blue, lace-collared dress, sat stiffly between Edwina and Gordon. She had removed her navy blue coat, but a blue velvet cap still framed her elfin face. When she saw Frankie, her glum expression brightened. She lifted her arms to her and then tried to climb over the back of the pew.

Edwina placed a firm hand on her granddaughter's shoulder, but she wriggled away and had clambered halfway over before Gordon caught and held her. At this she began to screech, drowning out Reverend Taylor's gentle monotone, and her father relinquished her to Frankie. The little girl buried her teary face against Frankie's coat and snuffled.

After the service, Frankie submitted, primarily for Autumn's sake, to riding with Edwina and Gordon in the limo that followed the hearse to the snowy slopes of the Laurelwood Cemetery.

Although the windless day was cloudy and dim, the temperature had risen into the forties. The press and television cameras, still in pursuit, had been contained behind latticed screens erected at a protective distance from the funeral tent, their presence reduced to mere background nuisance, like seagulls that circle, squawking, over a beachside cafe.

The frozen earth had been broken open, the coffin poised for lowering. Frankie prayed that her niece was too young to understand the connection between her mother's corporeal form and the long, dark box. The loss of her own mother had been softened by Rocky's protection. Who would protect Autumn and little Gordie? The icy grandmother who wanted them only out of some sense of family entitlement?

The father who had beaten and almost certainly killed their mother?

She would be there for the children, she vowed. She would do for them what Rocky had done for her--prevent them from ever feeling friendless in the world. He won't get away with this, she thought fiercely, eyes drifting to where he and his mother stood, heads together, whispering and nodding.

She searched the crowd for Rocky's friends, hoping to see Aphrodite, but she was unable to catch even a glimpse of her.

As the limo approached, through huge sentinel pine trees, the reception at the sprawling Victorian mansion built by Gardiner forebears, she took in the wide verandahs, the cunning balconies and cupolas, and the sparkle of stained glass in the immense oak doors. Even the wheelchair ramps had been integrated into the overall design and softened by strategically placed shrubbery.

The catered reception was flawlessly executed. Edwina, a most gracious hostess, welcomed the mourners and effortlessly presided. Gordon, somber in his dark suit, cut a tragic figure, his expression blank, making an effort but apparently still too distraught to be fully present. A plump, brown-skinned woman in a pink uniform whisked Autumn away from Frankie almost the moment they stepped into the house.

A lavish buffet had been arranged in the long dining hall with a serving staff ready to provide the choicest cut of rare roast beef or tender morsel of squab. Young waiters circulated with trays of hors d'oeuvres and canapés. There was a bar at one end of the dark-paneled room, and most of the men gathered there quickly. The room itself was furnished in muted hues, with stiff antique furniture, the only brightness provided by gleaming wood, faded Persian carpets and bouquets of fresh flowers.

Frankie, responding to the succulent aromas, accepted a baby lamb chop as tiny and delicate as a sparrow's wing, ate it in one bite, and deposited the bone on a passing tray. She wanted to see the children. Unobserved, she made her way down a corridor, searching for the nursery. She found them in a room that must have once been their father's. Gordie was sitting on the floor near an open toy chest.

The young woman in pink, who introduced herself as Fiona, was rummaging through a high wooden dresser while Autumn stood listlessly beside her on a chair. Fiona looked to be about twenty, with thick dark hair in a short spiky cut. Her cheeks were as pink as her uniform, and she exuded an air of cheerful efficiency. The little girl clambered down and ran to Frankie. Gordie got to his feet and toddled over to be picked up as well. Instead, Frankie sat on the floor with the two of them, her velvet dress making a chocolate circle around her on the blue carpet.

"Autumn, let's put you in play clothes," Fiona suggested, approaching with a pair of flowered coveralls, but the little girl clung to Frankie.

"Don't want to," she said.

"I can stay for just a little while," Frankie told her, "but you know I'll come back soon."

"Can't we go home now?" An anxious tone had crept into Autumn's voice. "I don't like it here. I want to sleep in my own bed. I want Clarence."

"You'll be back home soon, I promise."

Gordon appeared at the door. She felt every muscle tighten, a shiver at the back of her neck. He seemed unaware of her reaction. "How are you, Frankie?"

She shrugged and a small, undefined sound escaped from her. He came into the room.

"I can't believe this," he murmured. And then, his voice hoarse, "You look--like Rocky--in that dress."

Fiona fluttered nervously near the dresser, still holding the little outfit for Autumn. Gordon seemed to notice her for the first time. "Take a break, Fiona. Go get something to eat, a cup of coffee." She went out, squeezing past him. He sat down on a low chest of drawers that looked too fragile for his bulk. His son went over to him, carrying some blocks, trying to get his attention, but Gordon was gazing distractedly off.

"We're going to offer a reward," he said. "For information leading to an arrest."

"Your idea?"

"My mother's, but of course, mine, too. She has all the money--"

"Someone has to have seen something," Frankie said. She focused her attention on the little girl, unbuttoning the many tiny pearl buttons on her dress. Perhaps, under stress of the moment he would make a slip, reveal something. "You know the tall African-American actress, Aphrodite?"

"Yes. She likes--liked--to shop with Rocky."

"She said she saw Rocky's car parked at the Inn early Monday morning."

"They think Thornton's the reason it ended up in the river."

"Who told you that?"

"I have my sources."

"Who put Mommy's car in the river? Is Mommy in the river?" Autumn's eyes searched her father's face.

"We shouldn't be talking here," Frankie warned. "No, honey." At a loss she said, "Remember what I told you. Your mommy's in your heart now," but feeling that she had only Disney philosophy when she needed Shakespeare. "Let's change out of this pretty dress before you get it dirty, okay?"

Gordon rose to his feet. "When can we talk?"

"How long are you staying here?"

"I don't know, a few days maybe. Until we can get back into the house. My mother would like us to move in permanently. It depends on--what happens."

"Tomorrow?"

"Sure. You *could* stay here."

"No, I couldn't." Frankie lifted her shoulders in a shrug. Gordon turned and walked out.

Frankie was dressing Autumn in her play clothes when she heard the sound of angry voices drifting up from the driveway below the window. Her view, somewhat obstructed by the roof of the porch, revealed a bulky figure being roughly escorted toward a limo by three men in dark suits. The man being dragged and pushed into the car was bellowing, and Frankie heard the Gardiner name intermingled with obscenities and threats. Doors slammed and the car drove off.

CHAPTER 17

When Fiona returned Frankie extricated herself from the children and went to find a ride back. She spotted Detective Ransome near Mr. Gardiner's wheelchair. The old man's mouth was twisted entirely to one side, and he needed constant attention from his nurse, to wipe the drool, and lift him upright in his motorized wheelchair, but his eyes were alert and he made grunts that denoted understanding. She watched the detective pat the old man's shoulder, then take Edwina's hand in his. She waited until she saw him head toward the door and slipped out into the hallway to intercept him.

"You heading back towards Swiftwater?"

"Need a ride?" She nodded, and he made a jerking motion with his head. In moments, she was seated beside him in his dark, unmarked car heading west on Route 80. Shivering in the late afternoon cold, she snuggled deeper into the cashmere coat. Ransome drove automatically, his sleepy eyes sweeping back and forth from the highway to her face.

"How are you holding up?" he asked her.

"I'm still numb. Maybe it'll sink in when you arrest that snake." Another shudder ran through her, and he responded by pushing a button for heat, looking at her with an impassive expression.

"You still suspect Gordon?"

"Yes, I do."

"Oh what evidence?"

"On the evidence that he beat her, on the evidence that he hung out in clubs with topless dancers and scum."

"Not enough. What about the actor?"

"Well, *he* didn't kill her!"

"How does he tie in?"

"Gordon must have killed him, too."

"Why?"

"I think Thornton got in his way. Maybe he was planning to leave Rocky's body in her car near the Playhouse so it would look like she made it there the night she disappeared. And Thornton interrupted him."

"Maybe she and Thornton were fooling around."

"Rocky wasn't fooling around. She loved that bastard. Gordon. Christ, I warned her--"

"How come you hate the guy?"

"You've never seen my sister's face after one of their 'spats'!"

"There's nothing on the books."

"So it never happened?"

"I said there's no record."

"What about hospital records?"

"Nothing that couldn't have had another explanation-- the one she gave. An accident. A fall from her horse."

"She's ridden since she was nine! She's had Zillah for six years, and he's tame as a kitten. Would a trained dancer--a great horsewoman--be so accident prone?"

"A few stitches here and there. Bruises. No broken bones. And if we're accepting your scenario, why would he take Rocky's body back to their own home?"

"I don't know. Panic, maybe."

"If he drove her car there, how'd *he* get back?"

"Oh god, *I* don't know." A painful throbbing blossomed at the base of her skull; she rubbed her temples. "What now?"

"Bring in experts. Examine physical evidence, DNA, phone records."

"Is there DNA evidence?"

"I can't give specifics."

"Was there blood in the car? Could you tell after it was pulled from the water?"

"You're still trying to play detective?" She felt his irritation despite the blandness of his tone.

"I'm not *playing* anything." Her voice choked. "What should I do? Forget she was murdered?"

"Not at all. We got some questions for Gordon."

"Like what?"

"Like why the security system was turned off on the twenty-second. Don't mention that by the way." He glanced over to measure her reaction. "But if you're wrong about him, there's *another* dangerous man out there. He's killed two people and we don't know why." They drove in silence for a while. Ransome cleared his throat. "You'll be called in for an interview."

They aren't even considering Gordon, she thought. Should she turn over the contents of the duffle or the silver key? But what if her evidence just conveniently disappeared--if it was evidence?

"What happened outside, the shouting?" she asked. "I saw some guy being shoved into a car."

"It was nothing," Ransome assured her. "One of the limo drivers had a little too much to drink."

"He wanted Gordon, didn't he?"

"He was drunk," Ransome replied curtly. "And no, he was asking for Mrs. Gardiner."

Ransome dropped her in the church lot near her car. Frankie had never believed in coincidence or serendipity but suddenly she had reason to ponder the forces of the universe that unexpectedly converged. She'd driven past the Maarz Bus Depot several times in the previous days and had again passed the large sign with *MBD* entwined in large letters before their import suddenly struck her. These were the same initials she had been pondering, trying to guess their meaning. She slammed on her brakes and turned back.

Inside the depot behind the ticket counters, she discovered a bank of metal lockers. She had to squat on her heels to insert the key into the lock on number 209, being careful not to let the long coat sweep the dirty floor. She yanked open the stiff metal door and reached inside. She had to struggle to pull out a heavy cardboard box, close the door, relock it, and pocket the key.

At the daycare center, she walked into the kitchen, dumped it on the table and asked for scissors. Lourdes and Larry watched her cut away the cord. As she raised the lid of the box, they all gasped. It was packed with cash--layered stacks of fifty-dollar bills held with thick rubber bands.

"My god!" she and Larry said at once.

"You have to turn it over to the police," Lourdes said.

"Why?" Frankie asked.

"It's evidence," Larry stammered. "Rocky was murdered. You can't hold onto *evidence*."

"What is it evidence of? It doesn't tell us who murdered her. Anyway, I don't trust the police," Frankie protested. "I want to talk to someone else before I turn it in. What did you find out about that detective?"

Larry told her what he'd learned. A former New York cop, detective grade, Sarvonsky had been assigned to the 44th Precinct, in the Bronx, for ten years. He'd worked undercover for five of them, been injured in a shootout, and retired on disability.

"I'll talk to him before I go to the cops," she said.

CHAPTER 18

Frankie met Sarvonsky on Monday afternoon. He suggested the Jubilee, a local landmark restaurant and tavern.

Her Honda struggled up the steep, icy slope to find her way back to Route 940 heading east.

The diner was warm inside with a long counter, and two rooms of tables and small padded booths. He waved to her from a back booth, where she joined him. There was an empty plate on the table. He was drinking coffee from a thick, old-fashioned mug.

He looked up as she slid in across from him. He was dressed in a blue flannel shirt and jeans, and in need of a shave. He studied her with dark, serious eyes. "Want some lunch?"

A waitress appeared, wiping her hands on her stained white apron. She was a plump maternal type with a round potato face, wispy hair pulled into a knot, and thick bifocals.

"Just a cup of coffee," Frankie said.

"Just a cup of coffee? Honey, you need to put some meat on those bones. Special today is home-made pot roast."

"Just coffee," Frankie repeated, mustering a thin smile. When the cup was before her, he leaned across the table. Her attention was drawn to the scar that marked his face, like a plate that had been broken and glued back together. There was about him an air of power held in reserve.

"What do you think I can do that the cops can't?" he asked.

"They *could*, but they won't--go after Gordon. It's too late to help Rocky," she said. "But he's not going to get away with it. I need absolute proof. Something even the police can't ignore."

"You believe her husband killed her?"

"Yes."

"Why?"

"I don't think he meant to. It's his goddamn hair trigger temper. He's hit her, hurt her, before. But the cops--" Frankie's eyes burned, and her voice caught in her throat. "I don't trust them."

"Why not?"

"The Gardiner family has too much influence. They're the power in this county. The cops won't even treat Gordon like a suspect. I'm afraid it will just be a. . . ."

"A cover-up?" A sardonic grin seemed to tug at the corner of Sarvonsky's mouth.

"Maybe they just won't look very hard. People like that get special treatment, special justice. They treat the cops like personal errand boys."

"Some cops can be owned, and some can't."

"What type were you?" she asked.

"I was a stupid cop. That's why I'm out of the business." His eyes focused on hers with the intensity of a beam of light.

"You worked undercover?"

"For five years."

"Why?"

"Hard to explain. It seemed important. Or because the rush was addictive, like a hit of crack. Take your pick."

"But?"

"I took one chance too many." He looked at her, measuring. "What do you expect me to do?"

"Make sure the truth doesn't get lost." Frankie hated the note of pleading in her voice. "Don't let Gordon's family connections--"

". . .You know that he's been taken in for questioning?"

"No. I didn't! When?"

"This morning. And he was still there a half hour ago." He glanced at his watch, a leather-strapped Timex. "That's a long time for a friendly chat."

"But I saw how they treat him."

"How?"

"Like he's doing them a favor just to show up!"

"You're sure he's guilty?"

"Who else would hurt her? They should have arrested him already. . . ."

"You reported seeing someone down by the lake that night?" She was faintly surprised that he knew that.

"I saw some *thing*, yes. But there was a storm. I couldn't really see much. It could have been deer."

"Or someone dumping a body." There was a long pause before he asked, "Or do you think she was there from the night she disappeared?"

"I don't know. I'm not a detective. That's why I need your help."

"Give me your best scenario."

"I think they fought. He hit her, she fell against the fireplace like he said, only harder. There were some stains on the fireplace stones, like he wiped up blood. But he claims that she left first, in her own car."

"The little Mercedes that ended up in the Delaware with Thornton's body in it?"

"But there's--"

"But there's no proof that she actually drove off in it because the security system--"

"How did you know that?"

"I've got my sources."

"Sources? What sources? Everybody has sources but me."

"So give me the rest of your version." He took a gulp of his coffee. The waitress paused at the table to refill their cups. When she moved off, Frankie continued.

"I think she was unconscious or already dead when he left. He took the kids to his parents and came back. When he

realized what he'd done, he got scared, so he dumped her into
the lake and drove her car to the Playhouse."

A pair of elderly women in a booth ahead of
them stopped talking. One of them turned to look over the
back of the booth. Frankie waited until she turned back and
resumed, her voice now a whisper. "To cover his tracks."

"Like it happened there?"

"Yes. Next he choked Thornton and put *him* into the
car and pushed it into the river."

"Because Thornton saw him with her car?"

"Yes. He could point the finger at him. Maybe he
hadn't planned to dump the car in the river——he only thought
of that after he'd killed Thornton. Then he went to pick up the
kids, like nothing had happened."

"How did he drive back?" Frankie had no answer to
that. "And where was Rocky's body until Christmas Eve?"

"In the lake."

"It's a stretch to make it work."

"How is it a stretch?"

"Well, time and method. For another thing, her car
was seen late Sunday night, early Monday, at the Shawnee Inn."

"*Maybe* it was her car. Aphrodite wasn't sure."

"A couple of other problems. Number one--Thornton
was in the Christmas show that night and he was seen at the
Stone Bar afterwards, so he had to have been killed much later.
Number two--Rocky died from strangulation, same as
Thornton. She did have a cut on the back of her head. There
was blood on the headrest in her car. And they found a bloody
scarf in the snow. So she must have driven her own car there."

Frankie felt dizzy. It had to have been Gordon. She
was lost in thought for several minutes. He sat there, calmly,
his dark eyes piercing.

"I might be wrong about the scenario," she said, "but I
still think he did it. Maybe when he came back she was still
alive and they fought--he strangled her, then put her in the car,
and late at night, when the kids were sleeping, drove it out to
Shawanee. He could have put her in the driver's seat, then
wrapped her head in the scarf and moved her over. If it was
Thornton who caught him, he'd have a reason--"

"Why does it have to be Gordon?"

"If you'd ever seen her after one of their battles. . .the man is out of control. And I have other evidence."

"Other evidence?" He waited while her mind raced. A cop had given her his card. A state trooper. Maybe he had police connections too. She took in a deep breath. She had no idea why she felt that he could be trusted, that trusting him was her only choice.

"Gordon burned something——clothes, I think, and Autumn's favorite stuffed toy--in the fireplace just before I got there. I saved the scraps. And I found some stuff," she said hesitantly. "Papers and pictures. Gordon with strippers. . . lap dancers, I guess. Legal papers, about loans and mortgages. They were at the Playhouse in Rocky's locker."

His eyes narrowed. "Who released them to you?"

"Well, nobody released them exactly. They were with her clothes. I just took them."

"Have you mentioned this to Ransome?"

"No. I was afraid to."

The brackets around Sarvonsky's mouth deepened and there was suppressed amusement in his eyes.

"Is there anything else you forgot to mention to Ransome?"

"Yes. I checked out Rocky's bank records. Every account, even the kids' college savings, is almost empty." In a rush, she added, "and, and the last thing--this little key. I found out--it's for a locker at the bus station."

"And you found the locker?"

"Yes." Her voice was a whisper.

"Anything in it?"

"A shoe box filled with cash--"

Finally, the crinkles around his eyes and the look of amusement vanished. "How much cash?"

"A lot. Thirty-five thousand dollars."

"Fuck!" He whistled softly. "You found thirty-five thousand in cash?" He picked up his glass and took several gulps of water. "Why do you need a detective? You seem to be doing pretty well on your own." He put down the glass. "What did you do with it?"

"I--still have it. It's in the trunk of my car."

"Shit!"

Neither spoke for a few minutes. After a while she went on. "So if the police release him today, we have some evidence to take to the media, right?"

"*That's* your strategy?"

"I don't have a strategy. I just gathered up whatever I could find."

"And hid it from the police."

"I just didn't turn it in yet. How do I know they *want* to find the truth?"

"And when they arrest you for withholding evidence? And charge me with conspiracy?"

She studied his expression. "Would they do that?"

"They might. When they interview you, they'll ask for anything you have."

"What if I don't have anything? What if I gave it all to you? They won't call *you* in, will they?"

"You got a devious mind."

"I never needed one before."

He rubbed his chin. "And you're driving around with it in your car?"

"Yes. Could you hold onto everything for me? Until I figure out what to do?"

He rubbed his chin. "The money too?"

"I'm afraid to keep it."

"You trust *me* to hold it?"

"Yes."

"Why?"

"I don't know. Should I get it?"

"No, no. Don't bring it in here. Christ!" He thought for a moment. "You can follow my truck. We'll stop someplace less conspicuous, and you can hand everything over. If you're sure that's how you want to handle it."

"Do you need a check?" Frankie pulled out her checkbook and scrutinized the balance column. She had five hundred dollars in her account.

"A check?"

"A retainer?"

"I'll tell you what," Sarvonsky said, his eyes traveling over her face and body as though trying to assess her resources. She flushed; she must look pathetic. She wore no makeup and there were dark circles under her eyes. She was dressed in her old parka, a worn sweater, jeans, and the shabby boots. "Let me see what I can find out, and get back to you after we see what comes of Gordon's interrogation. I can't really take the case officially," he told her. "Let's just put the payment issue on hold for now."

"I can afford to pay you," she insisted, the color hot in her cheeks. The litany that had run through her childhood, *we can't afford it,* ran through her mind. She could take out a loan. She could run up her one credit card that wasn't already maxxed out. When she looked up, she saw that his eyes were glittering again.

"You're ready to hand over thirty-five thousand dollars to me, and you're concerned about a retainer?" He shook his head, picked up a worn leather jacket from the back of the booth, and headed outside. She followed him out. He got into a battered red truck with a small snowplow attachment. When she turned the key, the Honda sputtered but started up on the third try.

CHAPTER 19

As Frankie had predicted, Gordon was not held after his day of questioning. He called her at Lourdes's, where she and Jeffrey were snuggled on the lumpy sofa, watching a Snoopy DVD. Lourdes had transformed the den into a makeshift guest room, and Frankie was spending a quiet afternoon with her son. When she answered the phone, Gordon's voice was an intrusion.

"Frankie, could you stay with the kids for a while?"

"Where? Up there? At your parents'?"

"We'll be back at Lake Nakomis tomorrow. The house is being unsealed." Her heart began to race at the thought. Go back to Rocky's house? Stay there with him, now? Was he oblivious to her suspicions and her determination to prove them? She stalled, trying to think.

"What about the media vultures?"

"Well, they found us here anyway. Dad's caretaker caught one trying to get a shot through the kitchen window, and he turned the dogs loose. You should have seen them stampede back to their vans." There was a crackle; his voice returned louder in her ear. "I'm thinking of getting a couple of dogs myself. Pit bulls, or Dobermans."

"How did your interview with Ransome go?"

"He just wanted to go over everything, get the details straight." Another crackling pause. "You know I'm not a suspect?"

"That's what the paper said."

"Ransome had the preliminary autopsy report." Gordon's voice faltered. There was a rasping sound, as though he was having trouble breathing. "He told me--he said--Rocky was--raped before--before she was strangled." He was sobbing now, hoarse ragged sobs, and for the first time Frankie felt sympathy for him--as well as a violent sense of shock and disorientation.

If she'd been raped, that meant--what? Perhaps it had happened just as he'd said. They'd fought, she'd driven off, and she'd met someone else who had killed her.

"They're sure—a-about the rape?" she stammered.

"They're doing DNA tests," he said. "Results take a while." She remembered her sister's hands, bagged in plastic, as she lay on the gurney. She knew that they commonly scraped under fingernails for incriminating DNA, and she recalled the scratch on Gordon's face. Chills rippled through her, making her feel feverish and icy at once.

"Oh, god! I can't stand it!" Had it been someone else? Some stranger? She imagined Rocky attacked and brutalized, thick hands gripping the slender throat. She would have fought, Frankie knew that. She imagined her sister's body, defenseless on a metal table, medical examiners handling, probing, cutting, and photographing, reducing her to a specimen. She rocked in anguish, squeezing her small son against her. The images her mind conjured up were almost worse than the last sight of her sister's body. Jeffrey squirmed in her lap and looked up with concern. She kissed his head, and he turned back to the TV screen.

"Frankie, please come. We need you. We can't stay here. My mother's driving me crazy, the controlling bitch--she's keeping the kids--"

". . .How are the kids?"

"They're unhappy, confused. They miss their own things."

"They miss their mother." Her voice was as hoarse and shaky as Gordon's.

"Yes. Of course."

"I can't fix that."

"But they feel safe with you."

"And Lourdes?"

"Well, yeah, Lourdes, too," he conceded, "But if you could stay at the house for a while, till we get a grip on things. Just for a month or so."

"I can't afford not to work for that long. Ritchie took me on for the run of the show and he promised he'd use me for his next production. Jorges has been covering for me."

"Couldn't you take a break? You could work here again at the Playhouse, for the summer season. Ritchie will understand."

"I'd be letting him down."

"You could be here for the kids."

Frankie thought about being back with the children in their own home. She could observe Gordon. Maybe there were clues she'd missed. But, no, no, she reminded herself, she had to start thinking in another direction.

Still, she could not free herself of her certainty, that, whether Rocky had been raped or not, he was somehow involved, somehow to blame. She would have to face him daily. Did he expect her to be a permanent nanny? He didn't know the meaning of boundaries.

Rocky's kids, of course, were the most important consideration. She could endure anything for them. She heard his voice. "Even for a week?"

"I'll think about it," she said. "When will you be at the house?"

"About two."

"Okay," she told him, "I'll meet you there. But I'm not promising to stay. I have to talk to Ritchie."

He sounded immensely relieved. She asked to speak to the kids, but he was outside on his cell phone.

"I'll meet you at the house tomorrow at two. I have to go. I'm scheduled for my interview with Ransome this afternoon," she told him.

CHAPTER 20

Ransome was working on New Year's Eve. Frankie was led to the same small interview room as before to strains of "Silver Bells" drifting in faintly from a radio somewhere. Ransome lumbered in and sat down across from her. "Is it true," she demanded, "that Rocky was raped?"

A flicker of annoyance crossed his face. His heavy eyelids lifted a little. "Who told you that?"

"Gordon. Didn't you tell him that?" It was as though another part of her, a determined, relentless, previously unknown part, had elbowed diffident Frankie aside and taken over.

"My interview with Gordon was confidential," he said, "like this one better be."

"But it changes what--"

"It's not your job to figure out what happened," he said. "The way you can help is to tell us everything you know. We'll put the pieces together."

A whiff of stale smoke made her stomach clench, and the back of her neck felt sweaty. Ransome had picked up a notepad and a pen, and she noticed a small recording device on the desk as well.

"Are you taping this?" she asked.

"You got an objection?"

"No."

"So let's get started."

He asked her to recall everything concerning the events of the twenty-third, starting with the first phone call from Gordon.

She did her best to recount it all--the call, the drive from New Jersey, the scratch on Gordon's face, his lengthy disappearance that morning, her drive to the Delaware River after she heard the news of the submerged car. She omitted her own efforts and what she'd uncovered. He finally thanked and dismissed her.

It was nearly six when she left the low brick building and got into her car. Her breath turned into steamy plumes in the air, and the seat felt like a chunk of ice, but the cold revived her. For once, despite the cold her car started up without a sputter.

Traffic on Route 611 was clogged and slow-moving, people preparing for a night of New Year's revelry. She ought to head back. But Jeffrey would be cozy with Lourdes for a few more hours.

There had been no response to the messages she left for Aphrodite. She made a right turn toward the Playhouse.

The media blitz had proved a tonic to the Playhouse, especially after several actors (ignoring official pleas for privacy and respect for their murdered fellow cast members) had granted TV interviews. Better-known stars had filled the roles left vacant by Thornton and Rocky, and the production, instead of closing after Christmas Day, was scheduled for fourteen additional performances. If it hadn't been for the holiday theme, Frankie thought, the Playhouse could have parlayed the tragedy into a year-long run.

Aphrodite's image had been prominent in the coverage. A front-page photo had caught her comforting a blonde woman, her face obscured by a veil, presumably Bianca, Cliff's widow.

The Playhouse parking lot was full, and a crowd was already milling about outside. The marquee now read: VICTORIAN HOLIDAYS STARRING JERRY ALISON AND CATHERINE DU PLESSY. ADDITIONAL PERFORMANCES SCHEDULED.

A line formed somewhat haphazardly; people bunched on the wide steps and sheltering verandah, blowing steam into the air and stamping to keep warm. Frankie ducked past the line automatically appraising them; a good audience, she thought, ready to be entertained.

Most were clad in furs and overcoats, and the conversation level seemed to indicate an unusual level of camaraderie and excitement. Frankie and Rocky had often jokingly assessed the evening's assemblage, as either, "rogues, rascals, thieves, cutpurses, the very scum," or alternately as "gentlemen, earls, the Queen's own knights." This group was definitely the latter, although some had already begun to cheer in the New Year. No one objected to her cutting past the line to pull at the huge wooden doors.

"It's not open yet." An Asian woman with a shiny cap of dark hair indicated a sign. Box Office Opens at 7:00.

Frankie ducked around to the actors' entrance, taking the stairway to the basement dressing room where pre-performance chaos reigned; garments were hanging from racks, protruding from lockers, flung over trunks. Women in every state of undress crowded before the mirrors. She found Aphrodite at her locker, squeezing into a frothy green gown.

"Hi, Frankie."

"You're wearing green, too?"

"Werther laughs in the face of superstition."

"Maybe he won't after this show. You wanted to talk to me?"

"I do. But not right here." Aphrodite eyed the other women elbowing for space. Caught up in their frenzy of preparation, no one paid them notice. "Come with me."

She led Frankie through the hallway to a door that opened into a smaller, more private dressing room evidently reserved for the star.

"Catherine?" She knocked and called out again but got no answer. "I think she's already backstage." They slipped into the dressing room, and Aphrodite closed the door. Her face had been made up for the performance; close up, she looked almost grotesque in heavy pancake, thick dark eyeliner and green eye shadow, her full mouth brilliantly outlined and painted red. Her own hair had been covered with an ornately styled wig, featuring knobs of hair over her ears and dangling curls.

"I don't know if this means anything," she whispered, "but I got something else." She blinked huge, false lashes and swallowed. "Something that happened the night Rocky disappeared--we were all at the Willowtree, having dinner before the show. Not Rocky. She hadn't shown up. Cliff was in the john when this big guy with a shaved head stopped by our table, said wasn't I in the show at Shawanee, and then asked for an autograph. Then he asked about Rocky."

"Asked what?"

"Where she was."

"He knew her?"

"I don't think so. I just figured he wanted her autograph, too. Nobody knew she was missing yet. Turns out he's a limo driver. He drove Bianca and me to Long Island for Cliff's funeral. Kept the divider up the whole trip, but I caught him staring at us in the rear view. What made me think of it--at Rocky's wake I happened to see Chantelle get out of a black BMW. And that guy was driving."

"Chantelle came to the wake?"

"Sure. You must have seen her--the tall, leggy blonde? Looks like a poor man's version of Bianca, Cliff's widow."

"Cliff's widow? I haven't met her."

"Yeah, well. Chantelle used to be just as pretty before she got heavy into using. I saw her talking to Gordon. You were standing right next to him."

Frankie recalled the young woman in the sparkly dress whose face had seemed vaguely familiar at the time.

"But you say she and Rocky weren't friends?"

"They were at first but Chantelle, um, came on a little too strong for Rocky's taste."

"How did she know her?"

"My fault, really. We ran into her one night at Skytop Lodge. I have a steady gig there--Jazz Night. Chantelle had been a cocktail waitress at another club where I perform, so we knew each other by sight. She came over and I introduced them. But she and Rocky were never close."

"But Rocky had her number in her phone book. And a note about meeting her and Thornton on the night she disappeared."

"Really? Seemed to me she'd been trying to avoid her. But Chantelle couldn't take a hint. She'd just show up and hang out with us."

"Hang out where?"

"Skytop, the Martini Bar, wherever I had a gig. If Rocky came to hear me, Chantelle would invite herself to join our table. And since the holiday show opened, she's been coming to matinees--always sits in the front row. Started inviting herself to the Willowtree, too. She'd squeeze right in between Rocky and Cliff. It pissed me off."

"Why?"

"She was making a fool of him."

"How?"

"Flirting with him. It was just an excuse to get close to Rocky but his big ego never let him pick up on it. People who knew Bianca said she looked a lot like her. And when I met her, his wife, I saw it was true."

"Was there a chance there was something between Chantelle and Cliff Thornton?" Frankie asked.

"Naa, she wanted to be close to Rocky. But she did seem to get some perverse little thrill from teasing him, leading him on. He'd be hanging all over her right there in the restaurant. It was embarrassing. She'd promise to meet him after the show, but I doubt she ever did."

"This was before his wife came up?"

"Yeah, but it didn't stop even then. I met Bianca during the last week of the show. She and Chantelle may be the same type—tall, blonde, gorgeous, but Bianca is high maintenance and Chantelle is low rent, if you know what I mean. I couldn't figure out why Cliff was digging that tough little bitch when he had a finer version waiting for him at the hotel."

"Did you ever see them together?"

"Naa. Nobody saw much of Bianca. She kept to herself, stayed at the Inn, except for coming to see the evening show."

"This bald guy who dropped Chantelle off at the wake--you're sure it was the same one who asked you for an autograph?"

"Yeah. He had a sort of wispy little goatee. And then I saw him again at the theater. He came to the show last night, sat down front and stared at me. Gave me the creeps."

"You told the police?"

"I called that detective, Ransome. Handsome Ransome with the sexy eyes. He grilled me for an hour. Wanted to know all about Cliff and Rocky. Who they hung out with, any enemies, all that. I felt like I was in a Humphrey Bogart flick." She smiled, teeth flashing white against the dark skin.

There was a knock on the door, and Aphrodite looked around. "I gotta go," she whispered. At the door she turned, shrugged, and offered an apologetic smile. She turned back to give Frankie a hug. "You know--the show must go on."

"Yeah, break a leg," Frankie offered automatically. She left, taking the stairs and passing unnoticed through the crowd.

CHAPTER 21

New Year's Eve was somber, with no attempt to create a holiday mood. Kiki asked for Autumn before contenting herself with Jeffrey for a playmate. Frankie helped in the kitchen as Lourdes prepared an early dinner and then put the children to bed. Later, the two sat in the quiet kitchen. Early fireworks boomed in the distance. Larry would not be home from the ski lodge until after the celebrations ended.

Frankie no longer wondered at the friendship that had grown between her sister and Lourdes, whose gentle manner made Frankie comfortable, letting her talk, merely murmuring assent. She accepted Frankie's erratic emotional shifts, grief like physical pain surging through her, causing her to sit and stare, to lash out in impotent fury, or to compile lists---pages of lists-- people who had known Rocky, people who had worked with her, socialized with her and Gordon, questions to ask, details known and details to find out, connections, possible suspects.

Meanwhile Lourdes baked, filling the kitchen with the smell of homemade bread, cake and pie; she made fresh coffee and saw to it that Kiki kept Jeffrey entertained.

"I've got to do something!" Frankie pushed the table so hard that the coffee cups rattled. Lourdes rested a hand on her shoulder.

"You are doing something." Her large eyes were moist.

"What? What am I doing?"

"You are mourning for your sister."

"But I've got to know what happened!"

"Yes, maybe you will know, later. Now you must feel the sadness of letting go."

"How can I let go until I know? Was it Gordon, or could it really have been someone else? If she was raped. . . ? Did she try to escape, talk her way out? Was she thinking of her kids?"

"This is not good to think about," Lourdes told her. After a few moments she added, "Have you talked again to this man, this Sarvonsky?"

"No. Do you think I can call him on New Year's Eve?"

"Why not? If you think he is not out having the party."

Frankie dialed his number but got his machine. She left her cell phone number and asked him to call.

She said goodnight by ten-thirty and settled down on the foldout bed. She imagined walking along the seashore, releasing and letting go of her tensions. She'd drifted into a restless sleep when the phone woke her, blending with shrieking sirens and the frenetic boom of fireworks. It was midnight. She fumbled for her phone.

"Frankie Lupino?"

"What? Who's this?"

"I take it you didn't stay up to see in the New Year!"

"No. Mr. Sarvonsky?"

"Roman."

"What do you want?"

"You called me." She sat up, struggling to remember what she had meant to ask him. "Did you learn anything?"

"I got some information."

"Me too. I talked to Aphrodite today. She remembered some details about the night Rocky disappeared."

"Can we talk at my office tomorrow morning?"

"Your office?"

"The Jubilee Diner."

"Will they be open on New Year's Day?" Frankie asked.

"They're open three hundred and sixty four days a year, closed Christmas, open Easter, and Yom Kippur."

They agreed to meet at ten a.m. Frankie finally fell back to sleep, and troubled dreams.

Sarvonsky was sitting in the same booth in the back. The plump waitress, both hands occupied with hot coffee pots, nodded to her. The aroma of hotcakes and bacon filled the air. Wearing a blue work shirt and jeans, freshly shaven, he looked much too alert to suggest a night of partying. She unzipped her parka and hung it up, feeling herself flush under his gaze.

Frankie had taken pains with her appearance, merely, she assured herself, to avoid looking pathetic. Her hair was subdued; she wore jeans and her old boots but had borrowed a soft turtleneck in a pale celery color that intensified the green of her eyes, and she'd applied gloss to her winter-chapped lips.

Sarvonsky indicated the leather seat opposite him, and she slid in. Two old men turned to look at them; one of them grinned, showing tobacco-stained teeth. There was a thick envelope on the table near Sarvonsky's plate. He continued to demolish the stack of hotcakes, eggs, bacon, and hash browns as though it were an assignment, waving to the waitress for a coffee refill. Frankie ordered coffee and toast, and the woman went off shaking her head.

"What did you find?"

"It's in the folder. Don't look now. Have a little breakfast. You talked to the actress?"

"Aphrodite. Yes."

"She's been ducking me. What did you learn?"

"She claims there was some big bald guy, a limo driver, asking for Rocky at the Willowtree the night she disappeared. And he showed up at the theater last night. Scared her."

"Sounds like the bouncer."

"What bouncer?"

"Dominick Maggoti. The big guy off to the left in the photos you gave me. With that hooker from the Paradiso--and Gordon."

"Hooker? Oh, the blonde exotic dancer?"

"Same thing. She keeps the gentlemen happy while they lose big bucks on booze and gambling. He throws them out if they get unhappy."

"But why would he be looking for Rocky?"

"Good question. Lou Loucasto owns a couple of those gentleman's clubs. Maggoti works for him, mostly at the Paradiso." He'd lowered his voice and she leaned forward to catch his words. "They're officially private clubs, which basically means you buy a membership to get in."

"Gordon's hangout?"

"Yeah. That's where some of the shots were taken. A front for deals, gambling, prostitution. Magotti drives a limo for Loucasto's Limo Service part time. Spends his day off, rumor has it, busting kneecaps."

"But what connection could he have to Rocky?"

"A message from Gordon? Checking up on her after their fight?"

A thought struck her. "Chantelle!" she exclaimed.

"Chantelle?"

"Chantelle Rojas! In the photos! She's the connection!"

"Works at the club as Velvet Lee?"

"I don't know about that. If she's the one in Gordon's pictures. She used to work as a cocktail waitress at some of the resorts. Aphrodite hinted that she got pretty heavy into drugs. Do you have the pictures?"

"They're at my cabin with the other stuff," Sarvonsky said.

"I'd recognize her if it's Chantelle. A kind of hard looking blonde, came to Rocky's wake. She tried to talk to Gordon in the reception line."

"You've met her?"

"Not personally. I talked to her on the phone Christmas Eve. Before we found Rocky's body. I gave you her number."

"It's disconnected."

"Well, it wasn't on Christmas Eve. There was a party going on when I called. Aphrodite says that she introduced them. And she stalked Rocky after that."

"Stalked her?"

"Well, maybe that's too strong. But she said Chantelle tried hard to be friendly and Rocky froze her out. But here's the part I don't get--I saw a note in Rocky's calendar about meeting Chantelle and Cliff. And Aphrodite claims she saw some big guy, maybe the bouncer, drop her off at Rocky's wake."

The waitress reappeared with a pot of coffee, filled their cups, and looked askance at the untouched toast on Frankie's plate. "You skinny girls," she sighed. "In my day a man appreciated a woman with a nice plump figure."

"In your day?" Sarvonsky said. "Your day isn't over yet, sweetie." She giggled and put down the check.

"I've got some pretty bad stuff to show you," he said quietly after she'd had moved away. "Why don't you follow me when we go out. I'll take you up to my cabin and we can check out the photos again. And look through the folders."

Frankie whispered under her breath, just loud enough for him to hear her, "Gordon told me Rocky was raped."

"Gordon told you that?" His voice was probably louder than he'd intended, and he glanced around. The old men at the counter had gone, and the waitress was wiping a booth. "Let's get out of here."

Frankie followed him outside to his truck. The day was bright, a cold sun had escaped from the clouds, but an icy wind was blowing. The huge heaps of snow were already growing gray.

They drove west on 940 and exited in Whitehaven winding through the small town, up a hill, following a street that passed by an old church and various dilapidated Victorian houses, then turned left and wound its way out of the town proper and into the countryside. The paved highway turned into a dirt road that had hardly been improved by the snowplow, and Frankie's car lurched and shuddered over the ruts. Sarvonsky pulled over near an old-fashioned mailbox on the side of the road and turned his truck into an even smaller lane that led up a steep hill. She stopped behind him; he got out of the truck and came back to her window.

"Why don't you pull over and leave your car here? I'll take you the rest of the way."

"Where are we?"

"Just a few miles outside of Whitehaven," he said, pointing. "My cabin's at the top of that hill."

She clambered into the truck. It was surprisingly snug and neat. He removed a stack of audio book tapes from the seat and tossed them into the back. The little road seemed no more than a winding path. There were open fields on one side and dense forest on the other. They passed an old barn, squat and shapeless, that looked as though it had been slowly sinking into the earth. Finally they emerged at the top of the hill, where a chunky log cabin sat sheltered by tall pines. A shivering herd of deer, huddled against the wind, raised their noses to sniff as the truck stopped. First one, and then the others, raised white tails and bolted.

They could see for miles--snowy hills and forests in the distance and, below, a small lake. A wind was blowing icy cold, but Frankie paused to look around before following him. "It's wonderful up here. So quiet."

"Not quiet enough. At night I can still hear traffic from Route 80."

She heard the barking of dogs; when he opened the door a thick-furred shepherd-and-rotweiler mutt and a low-slung yellow lab came bounding out, jumping and sniffing first at him and then at her, circling, checking her out.

"Down, boys!" he told them. After he patted each of them, they bounded off in the direction the deer had taken.

"Won't they chase the deer?"

"Never catch them," he said. "They'll run off a little steam and be scratching to come in in ten minutes."

Inside the cabin was as snug and neat as the truck, utterly simple, life pared to the minimum, she thought: a small galley-like kitchen, a light maple table and two chairs in a sort of nook, and across the one open room, a dark sofa with a plaid blanket thrown over the back. The winter light streamed in through a small skylight. Against a brick-lined wall squatted a wood-burning stove, with a crooked black chimney, emanating a circle of warmth.

Another wall was lined with shelves and loaded with utilitarian objects and books. A chessboard with a game in progress sat on a small table. There were several photos of a young woman with a round face and long, lustrous hair. In one she had an arm around Sarvonsky, her cheek pressed to his. He caught Frankie looking at it and grinned. "My daughter, Clarissa."

He had a computer and telephone but, apparently, no TV. A circular wooden stairway led to a loft. Frankie looked about with the sensation of being in a tree house.

"This is so clever. Everything you need."

"Built it myself," he said. "It took me three summers." She noticed his good physical condition--strong upper body, muscular shoulders and arms beneath the work shirt.

"You cut down the trees?"

"No." He glanced at her with the look of suppressed mirth she had seen before, crinkle lines radiating out from his dark eyes. His skin was smooth and tan except for the stubble and the raised ridges of the scar. "It's from a kit. A company specializes in pre-cut packages, everything from the blueprint to the stove. I assembled it."

"Like Legos?"

"You could say that." He pulled out the desk chair and sat down, indicating the couch.

"What I have here isn't pretty. You'll have to tell me how much you want to see."

She felt her limbs suddenly grow cold; her head felt as though small insects were buzzing inside. She realized she'd been postponing the moment of truth. "What do you have?"

"Copies of the autopsy reports. Rocky's and Thornton's."

Her gasp was instinctive and audible. "How did you get them?"

He ignored the question. "Summaries of the police interviews with Gordon, Larry and Lourdes McCoy, Edwina Gardiner, Bianca Dulce, Aphrodite Antoine, and about six of the other actors."

She looked at his face. There was no change of expression, the dark eyes steady on hers. Her hands were trembling and she felt a pressure in her chest that made it difficult to breathe. "Do you have the summary of my interview?"

"Not yet."

"But you can get it?"

"Eventually."

"How?"

"You want to hear what I got so far?"

"Yes. The autopsy reports? What do they say?"

"Here's the basic stuff. Both of them, Cliff and Rocky were strangled, manual strangulation by someone with very strong hands, probably the same person--hyoid bone fractured in each. Cliff may have been killed earlier than Rocky, even a day earlier."

"You mean she could still have been alive when... they found her car?"

"Possibly. Someone could have been holding her. More likely she was killed the same night but--her body was frozen."

"Christ!" She covered her eyes.

"In this weather. . . ."

After a moment she looked at him, not ready to go on, but needing to know all of it. "Was she raped?"

"Every indication's there. Abrasions. DNA reports take a little time, but yes. It looks like she fought her attacker. Cuts and bruises, lacerations, skin and blood under her nails, traces of blood in the car--"

"She fought with Gordon. Scratched his face. . . ."

"He could be implicated by DNA even if he wasn't the murderer."

"But who else? Why? Isn't there supposed to be a motive?"

"Well, we know it wasn't robbery. Thornton's wallet was found in his hotel room and Rocky's purse was in her car when they brought it up."

"It still could be Gordon."

"But why would he rape her?"

"If he was trying to make it look like someone else--" she suggested.

"The police believe that she and Thornton were both attacked near the Playhouse," Sarvonsky said.

"Why couldn't she have already been dead in her car?"

"Maybe. But the lab found bits of gravel from the parking lot on her boots and in the blanket she was wrapped in, and some blanket fibers on Thornton's clothes."

"If Gordon killed her at the house, wrapped her in the blanket and put her into the car--fibers would have been left--"

"But where was she until they found her Christmas Eve?" Sarvonsky asked.

"He could have hidden her and gone back to his parents' house. . . ."

"Improbable."

"I--I know we're missing pieces!   Frankie felt her frustration building.

"One piece we do have," Sarvonsky told her, "thirty-five thousand dollars in fifty-dollar bills.   That's what I'm pursuing."

"She'd been moving money around. Or he had. And making a lot of ATM withdrawals."

"Maybe she was planning to leave him?"

"Maybe. I wish. But I doubt it."

"Blackmail?"

"Who would want to blackmail Rocky?"

"You tell me. Anything in her past?"

"No. Nothing I know of. Gordon could probably be blackmailed--he loves the ponies. He had some drug problems in college.   And there was some trouble he got his father's company into last year."

"What trouble?"

"I don't know exactly. Rocky told me a little about it. His dad threw him out of the firm over it but then set him up in a sort of independent company. Something with one of their developments."

"Those papers with Gordon's signature--second mortgages with a company, Allied Mortgages, that's under investigation. An inflated appraisal scam. Looks like he was in it with a hidden partner. But the question is, why did Rocky have them, and the photos?" Roman's finger idly traced the scar that marked his face.

"And the money."

"Yeah, of course, the money."

She looked at the thick envelope they had been avoiding. "Can I see the autopsy report?"

"You're sure you want to?"

She nodded and reached for it; he reluctantly turned the packet over to her. Just then there was scratching and yipping at the door. As he moved to let in the dogs, Frankie noticed his odd grace, despite the limp.

She forced her eyes to focus on the papers, skimming the paragraphs. Ugly words jumped out at her: "strangulation," "hyoid fracture" "asphyxia," "post mortem lividity," "rigor mortis," and "stomach contents." Sarvonsky pointed out that there had been a mark, as though a wire or a chain had left a thin line around Rocky's throat.

"Not the cause of strangulation, though. More like a necklace was ripped off."

"Our mother's locket," Frankie said, her eyes filling. "She always wore it, except on stage."

"Why not on stage?"

"Bad luck. No real jewelry on stage, ever."

"It's not on the list. Here, items of clothing, pantyhose, watch, rings, no necklace," Sarvonsky said. Frankie checked the itemized list. She closed the folder and tossed it onto the small rough-hewn barrel top that served as a table, put her face in her hands, and cried, the first time since Rocky's body had been found. She sobbed like a child; she wailed, shaking and unable to stop.

Sarvonsky let her cry until the huge lurching sobs began to dwindle to shudders and sniffs. He put his hand on the back of her head and stroked her hair as though trying to soothe a child. He handed her a napkin. She lifted her tear-stained face, sniffing and wiping at her running nose, and he moved beside her onto the couch and gently pulled her against him so that her face rested against his chest. He held her like that for a few moments. After a while she pulled away and, embarrassed, straightened her clothing and hair.

"I'm sorry," she said. The rotweiler came over to her, nudging at her knee with his brown masked face.

"Don't be," he said. "I shouldn't have let you see it."

"No, no. I had to."

"Let me get you something to drink," he suggested, standing up. "Scotch?"

"Please."

He went into the small kitchen and rummaged about, finding a glass, pouring. She stroked the dog's head, rubbed between its eyes, and it wriggled with pleasure, attempting to lick her face. In a few minutes he brought a glass and handed it to her.

Her hands were shaking as she put the empty glass on the table and wiped at her face. "Gordon's bringing the kids back at two. I promised to be there."

"Is that smart?"

"I don't know." She shook her head, blew her nose.

"One question we didn't ask," Sarvonsky said. "How much life insurance did Rocky have?"

"You mean how much insurance did Gordon have on her?" she asked. "I'll find out."

"You shouldn't be staying there. Involved or not, he's sounds like a powder keg." The intensity of his gaze suggested more than professional interest. She turned away, flushing under the warm concern in his eyes. She was imagining things, she told herself.

"It's the best way to find out if he is or isn't. Meanwhile, the kids need me."

The dogs accompanied them to the door, attempting to follow, but he ordered them to lie down and they skulked off. He drove her back to her car and led her to the center of Whitehaven before giving a goodbye honk and turning back.

CHAPTER 22

Frankie reached the Lake Nakomis home moments before Gordon and the children. The media had decamped, and it appeared that Gordon had eluded the stakeout at his parents' home. He pulled up behind her Honda and approached.

"Thanks for coming, Frankie." He was standing awkwardly with his hands in his pockets, his large frame stooped, blue eyes peering through her window. "You haven't been inside yet?"

"I waited for you." She eyed him warily, wondering if she should have come after all.

"Pull into the garage," he said, pointing the remote. When Frankie opened the rear door of the van the children squealed, reaching to be lifted out. They were bundled up in snowsuits, faces almost hidden by hats and scarves. She turned back to her own car to retrieve her son and Autumn's monster. The child clutched at her ugly toy with surprised delight. "My Clarence missed me!" she announced. "He was crying for me."

Gordon, loaded down with bundles and diaper bags, fumbled with the new security code. With Jeffrey on her hip, Frankie entered the house. Her niece clung to her as she tried to move.

The house looked thoroughly ransacked. The kitchen was littered with paper coffee cups and cigarette butts in saucers, and in the den and living room furniture was misplaced, drawers open, and various objects d'art, stacks of books, magazines, and clothing littered the floor. Frankie noted that the little desk was open and Rocky's computer missing. Christmas gifts had been opened and tossed back in disorderly heaps beneath the tree.

Autumn sat on the floor to pull off her coat and boots, and then began to rummage through the packages. Jeffrey and Gordie, amazed to find it Christmas again, shrieked, extracting toys from half-opened wrappings.

Gordon brought in giant-size garbage bags and began tossing boxes, wrappings, and even some of the opened gifts into one while the children scavenged and protested. Frankie, too, having removed her parka and gloves, stuffed dirty paper cups and remnants of yellow crime scene tape into the bags. Gordon paused for a few moments when he found one of the gifts that Rocky had intended for him——a silver bracelet with an engraved message - Love forever growing. Sorting through crumpled paper and boxes, he stopped to pick something out. He advanced toward Frankie with a small Tiffany box, which he thrust at her.

"This was for Rocky," he said. "Please--keep it." His eyes looked glassy. She reluctantly opened the blue box and found two tiny rainbows blazing at her from one-carat diamond earrings in a delicate platinum setting.

"Oh, no!" Her voice was a startled wail. "I couldn't wear them!" She pictured the diamonds sparkling in Rocky's earlobes, Rocky laughing delightedly, shaking back her hair to show them.

"Why not?" Gordon's eyes were a glittery blue. "She never made a will, but--she'd want you to have them."

"Save her jewelry for Autumn. She'll want it someday." Autumn heard her name and abandoned the Barbie dollhouse she'd been exploring.

"I want it now!" she said, coming toward them and reaching for the blue box. Frankie kissed her soft cheek, smoothed back her fine golden hair, and despite the little girl's protests, put the box into the pocket of her own jeans.

After most signs of the invasion had been eliminated, Frankie changed Gordie's diaper and popped a bottle into his mouth. While the children played with their newfound booty, Gordon made a pot of coffee and poured them each a cup.

It was difficult for Frankie to look at him and speak calmly. Her eyes slid to the large fingers holding the cup, looking as if he had snatched it from his daughter's tea set. Had those thick fingers closed around her sister's throat, squeezed while she fought for breath? Or was he, despite his violent nature, as truly bereaved as she? She forced her eyes away. He was rambling about the reward money when his bitter tone caught her attention.

"Now she's ready to open her checkbook, when it's too goddamn late."

"What do you mean?"

"That bitch has taken over everything. She got power of attorney after Dad's last stroke. What does she know about business? She's controlling all of his accounts, makes me hold out my hand like a kid waiting for his allowance." His voice was almost a whine. "I'm not ten years old! You think she really gives a damn about my kids? She just wants to keep her hold over me. I should be handling all of the accounts. This is all her fault, the grasping--"

Frankie had felt a tingling at the back of her neck. What did he mean? Did Edwina have a role in Rocky's murder? His money problems? Why was his formerly indulgent mother now denying him access to even his own accounts? "What do you mean?" she asked.

"Nothing," he said, suddenly wary. "I just wonder why she's so generous with a reward after she treated Rocky like shit."

"What?" she repeated, her voice too loud. She glanced at the children. Autumn was trying to shove Clarence inside the Barbie playhouse; the boys were crawling on the floor together. Under her breath she asked, "What aren't you telling me?"

"Don't grill me!" His face darkened. "If you're going to start giving me shit too, get the fuck out!"

"You beg me to come, then you tell me to get the fuck out. Believe me, if it wasn't for the kids. . ." her voice caught in her throat. If only she could take them with her. She looked about for her coat. Gordon stopped her.

"Wait a minute, wait! Frankie, come on. I don't know anything. No more than you do. We're both hurting so bad, that's all." She looked at his contorted face. "We need you," he pleaded. "The kids need you. Stay! Please."

Autumn heard his tone and ran over dragging Clarence. She clutched at Frankie's hand with a frightened look in her eyes. Frankie relented.

"I'll stay tonight," she told him. "Beyond that, I can't promise." He thanked her and, pouring himself another cup of coffee, wandered upstairs. At least he wasn't drinking tonight. She heard the door to his office close and then the muted sound of his voice on the phone.

She hadn't listened to the news and had avoided reading the newspapers for two days, but after she'd fed the children and they were napping, she switched on the TV. A local channel was presenting a special update.

There was a bit of back-story on the Gardiner family, emphasizing their historical ties to the area, their wealth, and—surprisingly--focusing on Gordon now as "a person of interest." Much was made of his youthful drug use, stints in rehab, and minor run-ins with the law during college years. He was shown leaving the church next to Edwina, head bowed, but then he had been caught glowering at the camera with pure malice.

Frankie caught a glimpse of a familiar, elegant figure behind him, bright hair like a halo around her face. Her heart jumped before she realized it wasn't Rocky, of course not. It was her own image.

There was a glimpse of Cliff's widow, a tall curvaceous blonde of about thirty-five, wearing a dark suit and a hat pulled low to shadow her face. She appeared more a beleaguered star than the Vegas showgirl she was rumored to have been as she evaded the rabid press.

Frankie zapped the TV off, thinking about Thornton and the connection between his murder and Rocky's. She'd assumed that Thornton's accidental proximity to Rocky had caused his death. But what if it'd been the other way around. . .Rocky's proximity to Thornton? She couldn't imagine Rocky, even in death, as a minor player in someone else's tragedy. Had Sarvonsky uncovered anything about Thornton's wife? Too bad Rocky's computer was gone.

She heard Gordon's tread on the stairs, the closing of a door, the sound of his Suburban driving off. He might at least have mentioned his plans, she thought.

She heard the upstairs office phone ring several times and assumed that the machine had picked up when it stopped. But when it rang again, she crept upstairs and, allowing the machine to pick up, she listened. A masculine voice expressed interest in the "chestnut gelding out of Secretariat's line that you're selling," and left a number.

She replayed all of the messages and heard several similar requests for information on the thoroughbred, several calls from the media asking for statements or interviews, weirdoes warning about the wrath of God, and psychics claiming to have information about Rocky's death. There was, as well, a low threatening growl in an obviously distorted voice: "Listen, creep, don't think you're off the hook."

There were no messages for any date previous to the 28th. The crime unit must have cleared or taken that tape. Were they monitoring the phone lines now? she wondered--and then another thought struck her. She dialed Rocky's line. After the third ring she heard a click and her sister's greeting. "Rocky here. I'm out, busy, or screening calls." A beep. She redialed and listened to it several times, her eyes brimming.

At first, nothing in Gordon's folders seemed pertinent; most likely the police had confiscated anything of interest. The drawers that had previously been locked were open and empty. But on a last sweep, in a file she had overlooked among the blueprints on his desk, she found copies of several insurance policies.

Her heart thudded as she skimmed through them. Gordon had taken out two policies the previous April, one on Rocky and one on himself. Each was, if she was reading it correctly, for half a million dollars and doubled for accidental deaths. There were also policies for both of the children for lesser amounts.

She started downstairs to call Sarvonsky but remembering the little box in her pocket, detoured towards Rocky's closet and opened the jewelry chest to put away the diamond earrings. The drawer, full of expensive baubles on the day before the funeral, was now empty. She slid out several other drawers and found them empty as well. The crime unit would hardly have taken watches, rings, and necklaces, all the expensive gifts Gordon had showered on her during their seven-year marriage. She slipped the box back into her pocket and went downstairs.

From her cell phone she called Sarvonsky's number. He picked up on the second ring.

"It's Frankie."

"How are you doing, kid?"

"Hanging on, I guess. I'm back at the house."

"You know what you're doing?"

"I'd do anything for Rocky's kids. He and his mother are pulling them to pieces, using them against each other."

"Well, don't put yourself in the middle."

"Somebody has to protect them." She took a deep breath.

"Anything new?"

"Rocky had a life insurance policy worth half a million. Gordon took it out last April."

"Half a million? Any special conditions?"

"I'm not sure. Will he get it?" Frankie looked through the desk as she cradled the phone on her shoulder; it was devoid of the papers and folders she had previously examined.

"Probably. Unless he's convicted for her murder."

"He needs money. I told you about the bills. Now all of Rocky's jewelry is gone. And he's already trying to sell her horse."

"Blackmail? Extortion?"

"And there was a threatening call on his answering machine."

"Threatening what?"

"The voice sounded distorted, weird. It said you're not off the hook. It sounded like a threat."

"Maybe just another nut. But don't take chances. Let me know if you're going out."

"His mother is managing all of the business accounts. He said he has to ask her for money."

"Interesting. . .I got a hold of Chantelle. She agreed to talk to me tonight at the Paradiso. Goes on break around midnight. And something else."

"About her?" Frankie slid the small empty drawer closed.

"Yeah."

"Well? What?"

"She and Cliff's widow Bianca Dulce worked at the same club, Cheetah's, in Vegas for three years. Did a sort of sister act together--Bianca and Velvet--The Brazen Blondes. Before she met and married Thornton, natch. According to a matching social security number, Chantelle was working under the same name she uses now--Velvet Lee."

"So they did know each other!"

"It's a link. Bianca's a blank, but Chantelle has a record, prostitution, fraud, forged checks," he said. "Can we get together tomorrow? Eleven too early? My office?"

"I'll be there." She wondered what it was that made her trust him. Rocky had always urged her to believe in her gut feelings. But hadn't Rocky's trust been terribly misplaced?

Frankie called Aphrodite next.

"I do want to see you before I leave," she told Frankie.

"You're going back to New York?"

"Yeah, tomorrow afternoon after the finale. But I'll be back for Jazz Night. And a gig next Friday at the Martini Bar."

"I want to ask you about Bianca."

"You're not coming to the show?"

"I've got the kids."

"Bring them. They'd love it!"

"Gordie's too young. And it could upset Autumn."

"I found a few little things of Rocky's in my hotel room."

"Anything important?"

"I don't know, notes, letters and stuff, but I'd like to give them to you. Could you meet me before the show? If you get here before seven, I could run out to the car for a minute."

"If Gordon gets back in the next hour or so. Or else it means loading up three kids."

"It's not snowing."

"Well, I don't know what to feed them anyway. We could hit McDonalds and then meet you at the Playhouse."

"Take down my cell number. I'll have it with me. But I have to turn it off by seven."

"I'll call you from the parking lot. Look for Rocky's Lexus van." They signed off. The clock read 4:50.

CHAPTER 23

There was no sign of Gordon by five-thirty, so Frankie packed up the children and headed for McDonalds. They gorged themselves on French fries, burgers, and milkshakes. Each kid whined for a happy meal with a toy, and then they squabbled over which was the favorite. Autumn insisted on sharing her milkshake with Clarence and spilled sludge onto his blue fur.

An hour later, Frankie finally got them, thoroughly sated, faces wiped, smelling of ketchup and fries, back in their car seats. By 6:40 she was driving toward the Playhouse. The children chattered behind her until, first Gordie, and then Jeffrey, drifted off. Autumn carried on a two-part conversation with Clarence, making him respond with a growl.

Ten minutes later, the van was idling in the half-empty parking lot; she dialed Aphrodite's cell phone number. A few moments later she saw the tall, slim figure, wrapped in a hooded coat, moving through the evening darkness, breath steaming in the cold air. She was carrying a small box that she handed in through the window. In full stage makeup in the semidarkness, her beauty looked exaggerated and almost eerie.

"Hi, Autumn." She leaned past Frankie toward the back seat. "You remember me, don't you, honey?" The little girl, mesmerized by her exotic looks, gave no response. "Jesus! She looks just like Rocky, doesn't she?" Autumn hugged Clarence close, her expression awestricken.

"Yeah. Her little clone," Frankie replied. "About Bianca?"

Aphrodite bent into the car, emanating sandalwood perfume. "There's something weird going on. She came back to clean out Cliff's room at the hotel today. The door was open so I poked my head in. She was packing his stuff up. I offered to get a bellhop to help her, but she said she wanted to do it herself."

"Didn't they seal up Thornton's suite after--?"

"Yeah. I figured they must have unsealed it."

"So they must have known she was there."

"Yes. That cop, Ransome had called me for her phone number and address in New York."

"You gave it to him?"

"I just had a cell phone number. I gave him that."

"So what happened?" Frankie asked.

"Well I saw her on the way to my room. But then when I was leaving the door was wide open and Cliff's stuff was strewn all over the room. She and some woman were screaming at one another but I couldn't see who was there. I heard a thump, like something fell or got thrown. I wasn't about to get into any of that shit, but I told the concierge about it on my way out. He didn't even know Bianca was back. He said he was supposed to notify the cops if she came." Aphrodite sucked in her breath. "You think she's a suspect?"

"For Cliff's murder? Could be. I heard that she and Chantelle both worked at the same club--Cheetah's in Vegas?"

"Nah. Chantelle and Bianca together?" She gave a nervous little laugh. "Who told you about that?"

"Sarvonsky. You think it was her?"

"Causing the ruckus? Maybe. There's something real sneaky about her. I only tolerated her cause--" She broke off

as though she'd changed her mind about what she had intended
to say.

"Thanks for Rocky's things." Frankie opened the box
and riffled through its contents, noting several credit card
receipts, an envelope from the Wachovia Bank, recent
photographs of Gordie and Autumn, and several opened letters
and bills. She stuck it into her handbag.

"No problem. I gotta get in there." The actress
smiled at Autumn. "Bye, sweetie!" She leaned in close to
Frankie and kissed her cheek. "I'll be thinking of you." She
hurried back toward the theater, wobbling a little in her high
heels.

"Is she a princess?" Autumn asked in a tiny voice.

Frankie smiled. "Yes, she is."

She closed the window and, before she put the van in
drive, dialed Sarvonsky's number. She stuck the phone into its
holder and, adjusting her Bluetooth, turned her attention to
driving, easing the van out of the parking lot. A long dark limo
was sitting at the far end with its lights off and she vaguely
wondered who was getting the VIP treatment. Sarvonsky
picked up; she launched into a report.

"I'm at the Playhouse," she said. "I just talked to
Aphrodite. She says Thornton's widow was at the hotel today,
having a screaming match with some other woman. And the
cops want to talk to her. Bianca." Glancing in the rear view
mirror, she became aware of car lights following too closely
behind her.

"They interviewed her before the funeral." Sarvonsky's
voice was faint.

"I guess they weren't satisfied." She was recounting
what Aphrodite had told her as she turned onto the dark
curving Buttermilk Falls Road that led back to Route 209. The
lights behind her were too close. She peered into her mirror: It
was the limo she had noticed in the lot. There was traffic
coming from the other direction, heading for the Playhouse in a
steady stream, but as she turned onto 209, it became much
more sparse.

"I've got a limo riding on my rear bumper," she told
Sarvonsky. "I'm going to pull over to let it pass." She edged
the van to the side of the road and the limo squeezed past but

then pulled over directly in front of her. Someone got out and came toward the van.

She only had time to scream. What happened next was a blur. A hulking figure appeared at her window wielding a tire iron; the glass of her window shattered. A gloved hand yanked the door open and she was being pulled out, screaming and fighting, and dragged towards the limo. She was barely aware of the cold night air or the opening of the limo door before she had been thrust inside. A wad of cloth was stuffed into her mouth. A woman was helping him now, pulling something over Frankie's head and she was being shoved face down on the floor. The man wrenched her arms behind her, knee in her back, tying her hands. She was choking, blinded, totally panicked.

"Get the kids!" The command was a low growl. Something, a blanket or coat, was thrown over her. Doors slammed, and the engine came to life. They were soon jouncing over rutted roads, she could tell that much, but she became disoriented in the utter dark. Her face rubbed against the rough material that covered her face.

The limo had started up immediately after she'd heard the order to get the kids. The woman must be driving the van. She tried to choke down her panic, to think. Who were they, and where were they taking them? One quick glimpse of the figure at the window had not given her much to go on, the head had been well covered--but from his bulk and voice, it could have been the bodyguard.

Hadn't Sarvonsky said the club bouncer also worked for a limo company? Who was the woman? Chantelle? Bianca? Had Aphrodite set her up? She'd caught a whiff of scent, something musky and cloying, like Opium, as the woman yanked the hood over her face.

Frankie fought back another surge of panic. She couldn't let fear overwhelm her. The kids! Her baby! Autumn must be terrified. Had the boys been awakened by the sudden onslaught? She would kill anyone who touched her babies, she thought; rage swept through her like a firestorm.

She twisted her hands behind her back. The cell phone had been on--Sarvonsky must have heard her scream! He had to have heard something before the driver realized that it was still connected. Or was it connected? The Bluetooth had been ripped off as she was pulled from the van. What had she actually said to Sarvonsky? Had she mentioned the limo?

The car raced on through the night while she strained to loosen her hands. The radio came on, and rap blasting from the speakers caused her as much pain as the ropes cutting into her wrists.

She felt she should pray, but it had been too long since she had even tried. Who could help her now? Rocky, she thought, Rocky, please, help me.

The limo finally came to a halt, and the music stopped, though the hum of the engine continued. She heard a rapping, an electric window sliding open, and a woman's voice. "What the fuck are you sitting there for?"

"Fucking Christ," he said, "She looks like the other--"

"You plan to screw this up, too? Lou says you fuck up again, he kills you. I swear to Christ he should have--"

"Shut the fuck up," the man said.

"If you weren't so stupid--"

"Maybe I'm not as stupid as you think. And maybe you're not as smart. Maybe I'm not Loucasto's dummy--"

"And maybe you are--"

"Shut up and get the asshole on the phone. The stupid fuck doesn't realize--"

The car door opened and closed. Moments dragged, and the only sound Frankie could make out was the purring of the engine. She squirmed, trying to adjust her position to relieve the pain in her back and neck. Her mouth was dry, and a heavy, lemony scent, air freshener mingled with gas fumes, overwhelmed her. She coughed and choked on the gag. The door opened. Strong hands pulled her roughly from the floor and onto the seat. She felt thick fingers reach beneath the hood to remove the gag.

"What do you want?" Frankie gasped. "Where are the kids?"

"The kids're fine. So far. If the asshole cooperates, they'll be home in a few hours."

"Do you want money?"

"You got money?"

"I can get some." Her mind was working feverishly, thinking of the cash from Rocky's cache. If only she could reach Sarvonsky. . . .

"You got a hundred grand?"

A hundred grand? Was that ransom for the kids, or did Gordon owe him that much? "I could get a down payment," she stuttered.

"How much?"

"About a third of that." He didn't respond. After a few moments she asked, "Can I see the kids?"

"In a little while."

"Could you take off my mask? I can't breathe."

"Just chill, bitch." He leaned over her so that she could feel his breath, warm and rank. She rubbed her head against the back of the seat, trying to dislodge the hood. Her sweaty hands twisted against the bonds.

Suddenly, he seized her and hauled her from the car. She staggered a little, her legs numb, a supporting arm guiding her for several hundred yards. She sensed his bulk as the man shoved her against the side of a vehicle and pressed himself hard against her. A meaty hand groped at her breasts. The stench of his warm breath permeated the material of the hood as his face pressed against hers. "Too bad I don't have time for you now, slut," he muttered. "A little later, maybe--"

She heard a child crying. Another car door opened. She was deposited on the front seat of the van. Autumn emitted a high-pitched shriek; Frankie tried to reassure her through the hood. "Honey, it's Aunt Frankie! Don't be scared! It's just a game!"

"I want my mommy!" Autumn screamed, and Gordie's wails continued unabated.

"Mommy! Pick me up!" Jeffrey shouted. "Pick me up!"

"Jesus Christ," a woman's voice snarled. The man made a garbled response; the door slammed shut, and the voices receded. Autumn's shrieks subsided, and Gordie's wails became softer, diminishing to noisy sniffles.

"Could everybody play the quiet game for just a minute?" Frankie demanded. "Autumn, honey, can you see anybody? Where are we?"

"They went away," Autumn sniffled. "They went out that door. Aunt Frankie, take that thing off your head."

"Want to pull it off for me?" Frankie suggested in a light tone.

"I can't reach you."

"You know how to unbuckle your car seat, honey. Unbuckle it."

"I'm not allowed to," she said. "Daddy said I'm 'posed to wait for a grown up to get me out."

"This is a special time. I need you to help me. Okay?"

"Okay, Aunt Frankie." She heard a deep shaky breath and then the sound of a buckle clicking. Little hands tugged at the head cover. It came loose with a few yanks. Frankie's eyes adjusted to the dim light. The van was inside what seemed to be a huge warehouse; she could see several limos parked in the dusky light. The keys had been removed from the van's ignition, and her cell phone was gone. Autumn clambered onto the front passenger seat.

"Could you do me another big favor?"

"That mean lady smacked me," Autumn told her, "cause Clarence was growling at her."

"Look here at my hands." Frankie turned so the little girl could reach them. "See if you can help me get the knots untied." Autumn grunted with the effort. After a while they seemed to be loosening but not enough for her to free them.

"Look if my purse is still there on the floor by your feet." Autumn found the scuffed leather bag and lifted it with two hands toward Frankie.

"Dump everything out there on your seat," she told her, and Autumn complied. Frankie scanned the items and located a nail file among the debris. "Put that file right in my hands. See if you can find my little scissors, too." She found she could maneuver the file to saw at the ties. Autumn held up a pair of tiny manicure scissors.

"Help me cut it!" she told her, extending her hands. The little girl tried, jabbing at Frankie's wrists as she worked them with both hands. The boys began to whine again. Jeffrey kept pleading, "Pick me up!"

"Be quiet, boys! I mean it! Everybody has to be very quiet!" She worked frantically with the file; Autumn was utterly serious.

"I made you bleed!" Her voice was trembling.

"It doesn't matter; it's okay. Keep cutting!" Finally the ties had stretched enough to pull one hand loose. Frankie tore off the remnants and rubbed at her wrists; blood was trickling in several places.

"All right! Good girl!" She kissed her niece, taking the frightened little face in her hands and pulling her close. The boys squirmed. She looked around the dim garage. "Stay right here, and be real real quiet!" she ordered them. "I'll be right back."

"Don't go! Don't go!" Autumn reached for her.

"You have to be a big girl and take care of the boys just for one minute! Put every thing back in my purse for me." Frankie slipped out of the van and looked about her. Moving stealthily through the dim warehouse, searching for some way of escape, she found an overhead garage door but was unable to open it.

She peered into several of the limos, but none had keys in the ignition. She moved swiftly around the perimeter of the building, noting the presence of a security system, then found a high window that opened into an office, dark behind the glass. A faded yellow sign in the corner of the window read Loucasto's Limo Service--Makes Special Occasions More than Special! Her face barely reached the bottom of the window, but she could see a corkboard with numbered keys hanging on hooks. If she could get in without alerting anyone, she could reach the keys.

She felt as though she were outside her own body, watching from somewhere above, as she gripped the windowsill and pulled herself up. She could make out a desk with a chair behind it. The sliding glass window had a lock on the inside. Could she risk smashing it and drawing the attention of the two who must be somewhere nearby?

She had a vision of Rocky teaching her to escape from their second story window when, as children, their father locked them in. How fearless Rocky had been, leaping to the porch roof and clambering down the rickety trellis! Frankie herself had faltered, terrified, until Rocky goaded her on.

She dropped back to the ground and looked around for a tool. One of the limos had an extended antennae. She snapped it off. Blood was rushing loud in her ears. How many minutes had elapsed already? Back at the window, she slid the slender tip of the antennae between the panes of the sliding glass and pried with all her strength. There was a crunching sound and the right pane slid a little.

She held her breath and crouched against the wall. When no approaching sounds reached her, she slid the pane of glass all the way to the left, pulled herself up on the sill again, and managed to crawl into the office, ignoring the shards slicing into her hands and knees.

She crept toward the keyboard, passing a panel of buttons and a security hook-up with a sectored screen that showed a door, an outside view of the garage, and a lounge area in which she could make out two people sitting in chairs, feet on a table, watching TV, a Coke machine in the background.

She reached for a set of keys with the number 3 on a disc and a small remote attached, removed it silently, and slipped back to the window. When her feet touched the floor she was already running low toward the limos. She did a quick inspection and opened the door of the one with the number three on a small sticker.

She left the door open as she slipped back to the van. "Okay, kids, let's go! We have to be very, very quiet!"

"Where are we going, Mommy?" Jeffrey whined.

"We're having an adventure." She was undoing car seat belts and hefting Gordie onto her hip, grabbing Jeffrey by the hand.

"Autumn, honey, come on. Follow me. Be as quiet as little mousies." She shoved them into rear seat of the limo and then down onto the floor.

"Hide!" she instructed them in a hoarse whisper. "Stay down on the floor, and hold onto Gordie." Autumn clambered in, dragging her blue monster with her.

"Christ! Autumn! You brought that? You could have grabbed my purse!" She was in the driver's seat, inserting the key into the ignition. The engine purred. She pointed the remote as she drove straight at the door. It didn't open. Realizing she had been holding it backwards, she flipped it and pointed it again. The door rose with a noisy clatter and they sailed out into the night! Had she only imagined the noise and voices behind her?

The limo was unwieldy, the terrain unfamiliar. They seemed to be in a commercial district, but the streets were dark and narrow. She hurtled past garages, warehouses, a closed Mobil station. She floored the gas pedal, swerving on the still-slick road. She realized that her lights weren't on and searched for the control, nearly swerving off the road as she fumbled. Ahead there was a cross street and a blinking light, a highway sign ahead. They would make it if she could only find Route 80.

CHAPTER 24

Frankie glanced into her rearview mirror and saw the lights of a van hurtling toward her. Rocky's Lexus? She couldn't make it out, caught up in her own headlong rush. A sign for 80 West flashed by and she swerved to turn onto what she thought was the onramp but suddenly saw, looming before her, a huge neon-striped trestle blocking a dead end. She slammed on the brakes but couldn't stop. The limo crashed sideways into the wooden barrier with a horrible screeching, sending splintered wood and snow flying into the air, and, with a thud and a deafening crunch, half embedded itself in a huge snow bank. She felt, rather than saw, the children hurtled from one side of the car to the other. Autumn screeched, and one of the boys let out a terrified howl.

"Are you all right?" She turned toward the back, nearly crawling through the partition to see her babies. "Is anyone hurt?"

"Clarence is hurt! Clarence is scared 'cause you wrecked us!" Autumn sobbed. She saw that they were frightened and tumbled about, but unharmed. There was no way to tell how badly the limo was damaged. She put it into gear and stepped on the gas. It refused to budge, wheels spinning in the snow. She saw the lights of the vehicle that had been following her go past the dead end, then reverse and turn into the service road toward her. She tried again, throwing the shift into reverse. The car shuddered but remained trapped in the snow bank.

"Stay on the floor!" she screamed to the children and then checked that all of the doors were locked. The van came to a stop several feet away, the door opened, the interior lights revealed a man's bulky figure step out, and, as the dark shape rushed toward them, Frankie looked frantically about for something to use as a weapon. His face was a mask of rage as he came into the glare of her headlights. She turned on the flashers and leaned on the horn, desperate to attract attention. She pushed the alarm button on the key chain remote, and when he wrenched at the door handle, the alarm detonated with a series of yelps, sirens, and flashers. The traffic on Route 80, only yards below them, flowed on undisturbed.

He punched at the window, his face near the glass, screaming something that was drowned out by the alarm. He screamed again and kicked at the headlights. Frankie opened the glove compartment hoping to find something, anything, but all she came up with was a tablet and pen. She clutched the pen like a knife in her hand. He was turning away, going back toward the van. She tried the engine again, stomping frantically on the gas pedal; the only response was the sound of tires spinning vainly in the snow.

Then he was returning, his goon face vivid in the flashing lights, carrying a small, evil-looking handgun. He came up to the windshield and pounded on it, pointing its nose through the glass directly at her. He was shouting something that she couldn't hear.

Her only option was to comply and play for time. She hit the button and shut off the alarm. He motioned for her to lower her window. She retracted the window a few inches, conscious of the children huddled on the floor behind her, terrified into silence.

"What the fuck do you think you're doing, you stupid bitch?"

"Please put that away," Frankie said, her voice hoarse. "I'll do whatever you want."

"Get the kids out of there, and come with me! No more fucking games!"

"Okay. Please, don't scare them." She opened the driver's door slowly and got out, sinking into deep snow that prevented easy movement. She moved towards the rear door, as though to open it, while he watched, holding the gun with casual menace.

"Jesus Christ! Look what you did to my car!"

With a desperate effort she turned and lunged at him, jabbing with the pen. It caught him in the throat and although it failed to puncture, he was so startled that he staggered backwards. She attempted to kick him but her feet were buried in the snow and she fell to her knees. Before she could move he had recovered his balance and charged like a bull with a goad in its flesh. He grabbed her by her hair, bellowing. Then he had her in a chokehold, thick arm tight around her throat, and he was holding the gun to her head.

"I ought to blow your fucking head off right now! I don't need you anyway! You stupid bitch!" He took a deep breath, as though making an effort to control himself. "Get those fucking kids into the van."

She was reaching for the door when, over his shoulder, she caught sight of another set of headlights veering onto the service road. A vehicle was moving with startling rapidity towards them. The man turned toward the sound, and she used that moment to drive an elbow hard into his gut. As he reeled backwards, she yanked open the rear door of the limo and dove inside. It slammed behind her. She landed almost on top of the three little bodies huddled on the floor, pulled them as close to her as she could, shielding them with her body. She heard a series of pops that could have been gunshots, and the man swearing as the vehicle careened nearer, brakes screeching. The limo was jolted as something heavy slammed against it.

She peered up from behind the glass partition and saw the face of the man who had been in control now being bashed against the windshield of the limo. His features were grotesque, flattened against the glass like soft clay, blood smearing; then his head was lifted and smashed down again. She caught a glimpse of a tall man in a leather jacket leaning over the immobile figure and, daring to creep up from the floor, she recognized Sarvonsky. The bodyguard was prostrate across the hood of the limo, and Sarvonsky appeared to be twisting his arm at an impossible angle behind his back. The sound of sirens quickly shattered the night, and a line of police cars roared up the hill toward them. Frankie began to sob with relief.

"Aunt Frankie, don't cry! Clarence will bite that bad man!" Autumn's voice, thin and shaky, had come to her out of the darkness; she pulled her up onto the seat. The two little boys crawled over to her. Gordie started to scream, arching his back in a belated tantrum, and she took him into her arms. He was soaked and smelled as though he needed a serious diaper change. But they were safe!

Moments later, through the smeared windshield, she could see the man being cuffed and shoved into a police car. The rear door of the limo opened and Sarvonsky leaned in, his face pale in the dim light, but with the crinkle around his eyes that told her he was suppressing a grin.

"What the hell are you doing out here on a dead end road, woman?" he asked her. "I thought I told you to be careful." She reached toward him, stifling the sobs that were still shaking her whole body. He took her in and held her against his chest and she sagged against him, forgetting her need to be strong, in command, allowing herself to feel protected and safe.

CHAPTER 25

A police sergeant, a tall, heavy man with sparse, straw-like hair and darting gray eyes, drove Frankie and the children home. "You were lucky tonight," he told her. "The whole area is filling up with scum." He shook his head. "They used to stay in the cities--New York, Philly, all of them raping and killing each other. The Poconos was a different kind of place then, clean, lots of family resorts. Now we got all these cheap developments, massage parlors, stripper clubs, gambling."

Frankie was too shaken to even attempt a response. She held her little son and nephew each on a knee, and Autumn huddled close to her, ignoring the ongoing monologue.

"The Gardiners, now--you know they're one of the oldest families around here," he went on. "Mrs. Gardiner's people, too, the Irewoods, settled all of Paradise Valley. Ran the two finest resorts between here and Shawnee. 'Course, Mrs. Gardiner, was adopted by the Irewoods when she was about ten years old. She inherited the Irewood resorts, three of them, catering to New York society people.

All the other fine old places are run down. Except for Mount Airy. Used to be a ghost town, all boarded up before the gambling bug bit the Poconos." He turned to look over his shoulder at her. "Everything's being chopped up, trash moving in. You ever go into one of them Wal-Marts? Looks like a goddamn United Nations in there." He droned on like a fly buzzing around her head.

At the house, the sergeant helped her get the children inside, reassuring her that a black-and-white would patrol the area, and that Lake Nakomis security had been alerted as well.

"The regional station's sending Bobby Clarke over. He grew up here, not like some of these other new guys."

Frankie, still trembling with fatigue and shock, faced the formidable task of calming and putting the children to bed. The boys were asleep in a matter of moments, but Autumn hung close. Frankie coaxed the little girl into bed, rubbed her back, and sang her favorite lullaby. Finally she drifted off, clutching the stuffed monster that had replaced Wilby and murmuring, "Mommy?"

Sarvonsky called to say that, after his debriefing, he'd be over. Frankie brewed a pot of strong coffee. When he buzzed at the gates, she opened the front door and, as soon as he was inside, punched in the security code.

No one had been able to reach Gordon; Frankie had left messages on his cell phone with only the broadest outlines of their ordeal. He had not called or returned by the time Sarvonsky entered through the breezeway.

"Nice place," he said glancing around the kitchen. "I could fit my whole cabin into that corner." He carried her purse under his arm like a football, and tossed it onto the table. "Thought you might need this," he said. "I grabbed it from the van. I know how you women get when you can't find your favorite lipstick."

"Thank you." Frankie smiled wanly, not yet up for banter.

"You'll get the van back after they've dusted it for prints--" He saw her ashen face and stopped mid sentence to open his arms to her. She went to him and he held her. She hadn't had time to shower yet and felt sticky and dank, as if the smell of fear had penetrated the very fibers of her clothing. His leather coat was stiff with cold and scratchy against her cheek; she leant into him, breathing in the clean scent of the outdoors.

After a long moment she pulled away and looked up at him. Her expression was still grave. "What can I tell Gordon?" she asked.

"More to the point, what can that bastard tell you?"

"This changes everything, doesn't it?" she asked.

"He's in deep shit of some sort!" Sarvonsky took off his coat and hung it over a chair.

"That guy wanted a hundred grand. How could Gordon possibly--?"

"That guy is Dominick Maggoti, a bouncer from the Paradiso. A low level thug--they call him 'Maggot'--works for Loucasto."

"Maggot? He's the guy in the pictures?" She shuddered as she poured Sarvonsky a cup of coffee and set it down on the table. "The name suits him."

"You got anything stronger?" he asked. She went into the den and brought back the half empty bottle of Dewars. He found a glass and poured himself a generous slug. Frankie reached across the table, took the bottle, and sloshed some into her coffee. Sarvonsky found ice cubes, and dropped several into his glass.

"I mean," Frankie asked, "was it--?"

"Could be he owes them."

"Who? Maggot? Loucasto? For what?"

"Gambling debts?"

"Would they let him get in that deep?" She held onto the cup with both hands, still feeling vulnerable.

"His family's got money. That's well known. Maybe they counted on that."

"But he couldn't get it! He told me that his mother had control of everything, all the business accounts. And something else. He said everything was his mother's fault, something about her control of the money. Maybe--" She gulped her coffee, choked, started to say something but stopped.

"What?" Sarvonsky asked reaching across the table to take her hand. She noticed the thick dark hairs curling on his wrist from beneath the edge of his sleeve. His touch sent an electric shiver through her whole body, and she pulled back.

"Do you think that maybe he killed Rocky because Gordon owed them money?"

"Possibly." Sarvonsky's eyes were dark. "I didn't think you were ready to consider anything like that."

"But Rocky had all that cash hidden away. I don't get it." She put her head into her hands for a moment. "Everything looks so different after what happened tonight. I'm ready to consider anything."

"Even that Gordon wasn't the killer?"

"That he wasn't directly involved," she said.

"But still involved?"

"Yes. Somehow. When I was in the limo I heard one of them, say--'she looks like the other one,' something like that. So he must have been--"

"Personally, I think Maggot's the killer. But I doubt they planned it that way, the way it went down. Loucasto would have wanted his money. And none of the scrutiny that a couple of murders by one of his employees could bring. My gut feeling--Maggot's a pit bull off the leash." His eyes remained dark. "Could you deal with it? If Gordon turns out to be innocent?" He raised one quizzical brow. "You got a lot invested."

"I never thought he was a cold-blooded murderer." She blew out a long sigh. "But if he's involved with these criminals--"

"Lie down with the devil. . . ."

"What?"

". . .eventually you got to screw him." He drank his whiskey.

A shiver ran through her. "Only it was Rocky who paid." Another small shiver shook her. "God, I was terrified. That gun at my head. Those cold eyes." She rubbed at her eyes, trying to erase the vision. "And Gordon must have brought it all home. I know he's a liar, a cheat, probably on drugs again!"

"Yeah, okay, let's assume he got in over his head-- gambling debts, drugs, whatever, and couldn't pay up. They kill Rocky to show they're serious? That's a drastic step. There are more effective ways of getting their money out of him." He twirled his glass, sloshing a bit over the rim. "And there's still the matter of Cliff Thornton. There's a connection we aren't seeing."

Frankie took a gulp of her whisky-laced coffee. It felt good going down, hot and burning in her stomach. "It's got to be Chantelle! She was involved with Gordon, and she tracked Rocky down and stalked her. Somehow she convinced Rocky to meet them that night. Maggoti was looking for her because she set them up."

Sarvonsky scratched at the dark stubble on his chin. "If Rocky was her target, why hawk her?" The crease between his brows deepened. "Who would benefit from Thornton's death?"

"Thornton's career was fading. He was a big spender and he screwed around. Maybe his wife was sick of that and so Chantelle set him up as a favor for her old pal. Maybe Bianca paid Maggot to kill him before he spent all his money--or traded her in for a new flavor."

"So Chantelle's the catalyst?" He toyed with the vase that sat on the table, its poinsettia dried and shriveled. "Old friends—maybe more than friends--meet by coincidence, and mayhem ensues? If Chantelle is involved, why would she agree to meet me?"

Frankie reached for the wilted bouquet and threw it into the trash. "Maybe she thinks she can use you."

"What about the photos?" He got up and wandered over to the refrigerator. "Got anything to eat?"

Frankie joined him at the open door. "Not much." She took out a carton of eggs and checked the expiration date. "I could make an omelet."

"I'll do it," he offered. "I know my way around a frying pan."

Between them they located a wilted onion, some frozen red peppers, a half box of mushrooms, a head of garlic, and several small red potatoes. Frankie lifted a copper frying pan down from its hanger. "Okay. What if Chantelle thought she could turn Rocky against Gordon? Sent her the photos herself?"

Sarvonsky expertly broke six eggs into a white bowl and tossed the shells into the sink. He whisked the eggs with a swift professional motion. "The money, too?"

"Well, not the money. Aphrodite said--"

"What's with Aphrodite? She won't return my calls and she's out when I stop by the Inn." He gave her a significant look, and taking in his weathered face she realized that the scar hadn't detracted anything from his appeal, and that he knew it. "She's been in a few scrapes."

"Aphrodite? What?"

"Minor stuff. A disturbance at a club. Possession of prescription drugs." He poured the eggs into the pan. "She and Thornton were friends?"

"Yeah, sort of. Apparently they both liked to party." Frankie set plates on the table while he tossed the omelet and caught it mid-air. Rummaging through the breadbox, she found a stale loaf of bread. "I haven't thought much about Thornton. Poor old guy." She choked back a sob. "Shit! I was so scared!"

Sarvonsky put the frying pan down and took her by the shoulders. "You were fine! In fact you were fucking terrific! Kept your cool. Saved the kids." Embarrassed, she turned away.

He spooned the omelet onto the plates, sat down, and began to attack his portion with gusto, tearing into the bread. "Maybe Rocky didn't show at the Willowtree because Gordon knocked her around. But she could have met Thornton later." He looked at his watch, shook his wrist, and banged it on the table, then glanced around the room. "What time is it? This damn thing--" Frankie indicated the wall clock. It was almost eleven-thirty. Her face felt suddenly feverish. She pushed her omelet away. He glanced at her plate.

"You planning to eat that?"

"My stomach's too queasy," she admitted. He scraped her portion onto his own plate.

"You think she'll really be there?" Frankie asked. "After tonight?"

"The garage was deserted when the cops got there," he said. "If she thinks Maggot will give her up, she might run to Loucasto for help, an alibi."

He finished eating, put his plate in the sink, and took his jacket from the chair. Frankie shivered again, feeling hot and flushed at the same time. "You're going to be okay?" he asked.

"No," she said, her voice breaking a little. "Not for a while."

He dropped his coat back onto the chair and came toward her. There was no hint of humor in his dark eyes then. She moved toward him and he held her against his chest, her head reaching just to the top of his chin. He cradled her like a child who needed comforting after a nightmare and rocked her a little.

She rested her face against the fabric of his shirt and allowed herself a long shuddering sigh. She was startled when he tilted up her face and leaned down to kiss her full on the mouth and even more shocked by the surge of warmth that began in her stomach and spread sweetly outward. His kiss was warm, insistent, a little rough, the stubble of his chin scratchy against her face. She made no move to break away. He brushed her unruly red hair back from her face, trailed his finger along her neck, leaning in to kiss along the same line, nibbling.

Some part of her wanted this closeness, wanted to blot out the memory of the last two weeks, to rush toward oblivion. His hands moved, unbuttoning her sweater, warm on her breasts. She froze. It was the wrong reason, the wrong time. "No," she said, stopping his hands with hers.

He pulled back, disconcerted. "I'm sorry. I didn't mean to do that."

"I'm feeling so--"

"Shhh," His voice was rueful. "Please, just forget it. I was seriously out of line." He looked about for his jacket. "I should be going anyway, find out what I can. You sure you want to stay here?"

"We're getting special protection. And for what it's worth, Gordon will be back."

"It's Gordon who worries me," he told her. "Call my cell if you need anything. Otherwise, I'll call you tomorrow."

"Let me know what you find out tonight."

He leaned close and kissed her lightly. "I will," he told her. She let him out and punched in the security code. His truck rumbled off into the night.

She loaded the dishwasher and was about to turn off the lights when she heard the sound of the garage opening and closing. Gordon came through the door like a tornado.

CHAPTER 26

Gordon's eyes were wild, his face livid. "Where are the kids?" he demanded, looking around the kitchen.

"They're asleep."

"Nobody's hurt?"

"They're shaken up, bruised maybe, but by tomorrow they'll be fine!"

"What the fuck were you thinking?" He came close to her, trembling with rage, his pupils dark pinpoints. He was obviously high, and he was blaming her for what had happened.

"I just took the kids out for dinner. We stopped at the theater after because I--"

"I thought I told you to let me handle things!"

As he stormed past her and up the back stairs, she noticed a small gym bag under his left arm

A little later he stomped back down, unzipped his Thinsulate parka, and flung it away. He was wearing a dark turtleneck and black jeans, an unusually casual look for him. A bit calmer but still jumpy and with a feral look in his eyes, he found the nearly empty Dewar's bottle on the counter, tilted it to his lips, and drained it. He began rummaging through the cabinets, looking for another bottle without success, before he went into the den. She heard him open the liquor cabinet and the small refrigerator.

She followed him, turning on the table lamps. The Christmas tree hadn't been taken down or even watered, and it was becoming a fire hazard, she thought. She was aware of the sound of wind howling in the fireplace chimney.

Gordon had stopped by the window, drinking his scotch in thirsty gulps; the hand holding the glass shook so badly, the ice cubes were clattering. He stared out for several moments as though looking for someone in the dark. He turned back to her.

"Who was that guy in the truck?" he asked. "What the fuck was he doing in my house?"

He must have passed Sarvonsky at the gates, she thought. He was on the attack instead of on the defensive.

"That guy--that guy rescued your kids from a crazy thug!"

"A cop?" He took another swig.

"A private detective." Frankie said.

"You hired a private detective?" His face was only inches from hers, visibly damp with droplets of perspiration. Coke, she thought, or amphetamines.

"Not exactly." She could stand unflinching before him, but the flush that rose from her throat was beyond her control.

"I can't believe you--" Frankie felt tongues of fear licking along her spine. Still she wouldn't let him intimidate her. "Who the fuck told you to drag another asshole into my business? Ever since you got here you've been nosing in where you don't belong!" He drew even closer and though she flinched inwardly, she stood her ground. "What were you doing snooping around with my kids in the car? You could have got them killed!" Flecks of spittle dotted his lips. His right fist was clenched.

He's out of control, she thought. This was how Rocky had seen him just before he struck the blow that sent her staggering against the fireplace.

She choked down her own anger, though she wanted to claw his face--scream out, "Fuck you!"--as Rocky had probably done. The moment froze. He looked ready to snap, to attack her. She took slow, deep breaths. She had to stay in control, soothe him as she might a vicious dog.

She almost whispered, "Gordon, stop. Please, stop." They stood for another moment, eyes locked, her heart thudding in her chest. Suddenly he shuddered, blinked, and turning away, collapsed onto a chair.

She remained unmoving while he shook, head down. Finally, he wiped his face. "I'm sorry," he said, his voice low and hoarse. "Frankie, I'm sorry."

"What's going on?" she asked.

"Christ! Christ!" He snorted, got up, went into the kitchen, and came back with a wet paper towel. He wiped his face and blew his nose. "My life is a fucking nightmare! Everything's out of control!"

"Why did they grab the kids?" Her own voice was shaky.

"Frankie--" he gulped, his lips quivering, "I have to ask you something." A harsh sound ripped out from deep in his chest. "Something bad happened tonight--"

"I know, Gordon. But they're safe now. They caught the guy, Maggoti, and they've assigned us a special officer--"

"But it's more than just him," he stammered. "He's got friends. They're still--after me! If something happens--" he faltered. His stare had gone blank. "If something happens to me--I want you to take care of the kids."

"You know Rocky and I always promised that to each other. But who--"

"I'm in trouble." He took the last gulp of his drink. "I don't know what to do."

"Maybe you should talk to the police."

"I can't!" He choked out the words. "It's too late for that!" He closed his eyes. "Maybe before. Not now. I've really fucked up this time. I may have to just--disappear."

"Sarvonsky, the guy who was here--maybe if you just talked to him--"

He stood up, anger flaring again. "How could you think--?"

"Gordon, I still don't know--how--why?"

He looked away. "There are people--fucking bastards! I owe--a lot of money. They think I ripped them off. I had money for a deal."

"Did they kill Rocky because of the money?"

"Christ! I never thought--I would never have left her like that--"

She felt contempt rise like vomit. How had Rocky loved this man? "Like what? Lying out cold on the floor after you hit her? Did you accuse her of taking your money?"

"You don't know shit, Frankie. She didn't understand how serious it was. She started ragging on me about petty shit, accused me of cheating on her--"

"But you weren't?"

"Of course not. I loved Rocky. I knew she wasn't hurt bad. She was faking, trying to scare me. Look, I don't have time to go into it." In a sudden jerky motion, he pulled out his wallet. "I got to get out of here! Here's a little money for food and stuff, diapers, for the kids." He peeled off three one-hundred-dollar bills. "I'll send more when I get--" He looked toward the window, confused, his fear fueled, she thought, by drug-induced paranoia.

"Get what? Rocky's life insurance?" When he turned back she saw that his anger was ready to flare again.

"No! No, of course not. I never insured Rocky."

Liar, she thought, fucking liar! She forced her face to remain impassive. "What then?"

"I'm working on something. I could get things cleared up in a week or so. I'll let you know as soon as--"

"Where will you go?"

"I'm not sure yet. I'm meeting someone, a friend, with connections in Vegas. I may still be able to straighten things out."

Chantelle, she thought. How could he straighten things out when Rocky was dead? Chantelle might help him out of his mess if she had to flee, too. Maggot could connect her to Rocky, to Thornton, to the kidnapping, no doubt.

He was leaving the children with her. A sudden fear struck her. "What if your mother wants the kids again?"

He let out a harsh sound, somewhere between a bark and a bitter laugh. "That won't happen," he said. "Oh, Christ!"

He went upstairs. She heard him moving about overhead. A few moments later he came down without the gym bag but carrying a large duffle and headed toward the door. He put the parka on and zipped it.

"Gordon!" She caught him at the door. "You're sure you can trust this friend?"

"I can't trust anybody!" he groaned. "But I can't stay here either!"

"Wait Gordon," she held onto his arm. "I know how stupid this is, but Autumn won't stop looking for her Wilby. Do you know--"

"I had to burn it. Rocky got blood all over it and I didn't want Autumn to find it."

He grabbed his bag and slammed out through the garage, muttering as he went. She watched his car roar off into the dark night. In daylight the snow had begun to look dingy, but by night it still glowed as white as the surface of the moon, cut only by the dark line of the driveway and the moving Suburban.

Her head was throbbing to the beat of her racing pulse. She couldn't release her anger, perhaps because it helped to dull the knife-sharp edges of grief. She looked at the clock. It was nearly 1:00 AM. She had to reach Sarvonsky, find out if he'd talked to Chantelle, warn him that she and Gordon were planning to flee together.

She dialed his cell and got only the message that he was unavailable. She tried his home phone, but his machine picked up. She left a garbled message saying that she thought Gordon and Chantelle were heading to Vegas.

Should she call the police and inform them of Gordon's flight? But on what grounds could he be prevented? He apparently wasn't even a suspect in Rocky's murder. She should sleep but she knew she couldn't. She reached for the TV remote.

Media attention had surged and dwindled; no doubt the kidnapping would stir it up again. She channel surfed and paused when a local news report caught her attention. A perky reporter, the one who had been at the scene when Rocky's car was found, was reporting live from another scene.

"A prominent Monroe County couple was beaten and robbed tonight in a brutal home invasion. They were taken to a local hospital where the well-known developer, Garrison Gardiner remains unconscious and his wife in serious condition."

"Damn!" Frankie whispered, already reaching for the phone.

CHAPTER 27

When the dispatcher answered, Frankie hesitated. What could she say? That she believed Gordon had robbed and attacked his parents?

"Could I speak to Detective Ransome?"

"This is the emergency line."

"I have information about the robbery at the Gardiner home in Marshalls Creek. It was their son, and now he's escaping."

"State your name, please. Then clearly state any information you have to give." The beep indicated she was being taped. She identified herself and words spilled out, describing Gordon's appearance, his Suburban, and license plate, all the while fighting against an insidious sense of betrayal. She shook it off. She refused to feel remorse for trapping the bastard. She was signing off when her cell phone rang across the room. She slammed down the receiver and dug frantically through her handbag to locate the bleat. It had stopped by the time she found it, but the missed call feature indicated Sarvonsky's cell number. She jabbed at the return button.

"Sarvonsky here."

"I've been trying to get you."

"What's up?"

"Gordon is heading for Vegas. He says he's meeting a friend who has contacts there!"

"Chantelle?"

"It's got to be! His parents' home was robbed tonight! His mother--" Frankie remembered Gordon's distress. Perhaps he believed he had actually killed her. "He did it!"

"You're sure?"

"Well, he didn't confess, but--!"

"He took off? How long ago?"

"Thirty minutes, maybe. I think he's meeting Chantelle! I--I called the police!"

"I got it covered." His voice was calm.

"Where are you?"

"I'm waiting for her outside the Paradiso." His phone crackled.

"She's not working?"

"The bartender claims he hasn't seen her. But her Acura's parked out back."

"You don't think Gordon will meet her there?"

"Hang on," Sarvonsky said. "Looks like we got some action."

"What?" Frankie demanded. "What's happening?"

"Someone's coming out of the back door. . .looks like a woman. . .yeah, she's putting something into the Acura, luggage, maybe." There was static for a few moments before he came back on. "She's heading out. I'm tailing."

"Call the police."

"You telling me what to do, woman?" His voice was light. Her own nerves felt taut.

"No, no, of course not. But shouldn't you?"

"Maybe. I'll keep in touch."

"Wait, Roman--be careful." The phone went dead. There was nothing else she could do; she knew she couldn't sleep. She went upstairs to check on the children. The boys were sleeping soundly. Only Autumn seemed to show signs of trauma, clutching Clarence even in sleep, eyes moving spasmodically behind closed lids, and now and then emitting little whimpering sounds. Frankie tucked the comforter around her.

Downstairs, she sat on the floor in the den and did some deep breathing and yoga stretches, easing her mind and muscles.

She looked through the small box of her sister's odds and ends that Aphrodite had given her, read the notes and letters, looked over the bills. She found records of two incoming calls, which, like the call on the night of her death, were made to Rocky's cell from Paradise Valley. She phoned the number and found that they had come from an all-night diner. No one knew who had made them. She sat down at Rocky's desk and made a to do list for the next day.

She closed the notebook and tucked it into her handbag along with the jewelry box. Then she snuggled down on the sofa, wrapping herself in the soft brown and tan throw. How was it possible that her sister was gone? She could see her still, so vivid and vital, moving, laughing, talking. Where had that energy and animation disappeared? Evaporated into the air? Wrapped in Rocky's handiwork, she felt her presence around her. Was it only the intensity of her longing? Her eyes closed.

Rocky came into the room and sat on the sofa at her head. Frankie gradually became aware of her sister's long fingers gently stroking her hair, as she had often done when Frankie, young and fearful of nightmares, was unable to sleep. She reached out sleepily for her sister's hand and felt Rocky's familiar diamond wedding band.

"I thought you were dead," she murmured.

"I'll never leave you," Rocky whispered. "You know that, don't you?" Frankie felt her whole mind and body flood with joy. She looked up into her sister's smiling eyes but her joy suddenly retreated, tainted by confusion.

"But I went to your funeral."

"Don't dwell on that, Frankie."

"Can you tell me why it happened?"

"I made mistakes. I was chasing the wrong things. Love is what matters. Thank you for taking care of my babies."

"I'll always do that."

"I know." Rocky leaned close and kissed her sister's cheek. Frankie noticed the small gold locket that had been Rocky's after their mother's death. Her fingers reached up to touch it and Rocky suddenly took it off, put it into Frankie's hand, and closed her fingers around it.

"It's yours now," she whispered. Then Rocky tucked the blanket, kissed her, and tiptoed out, and, feeling her love, Frankie slept on.

When she woke hours later, it was nearly seven; the dream lingered along with a sense of her sister's presence. She even felt for the locket before she remembered that it had been only a dream. But had Rocky sent her a message? The locket had not been found. She became obsessed with the loss of the locket.

While the children remained asleep, she attacked her list. Sarvonsky didn't respond to her several calls. She punched in the numbers for the Swiftwater barracks and asked for Ransome.

"He's out on an assignment," the desk sergeant told her. "Can someone else help you?"

"Is there any information about the Gardiner case?"

"Who's requesting it?"

"I'm Rocky Gardiner's sister, Frankie Lupino."

"I can't give you anything new on the investigation."

"I was calling about the robbery at the home of the senior Gardiners in Marshalls Creek."

"Do you have information on that?"

"I spoke with someone last night. I gave a report." Frankie felt frustration churning deep in her solar plexus. "Could you have him call me?"

She tried Sarvonsky's home number again with no success. To distract herself, she dismantled the Christmas tree, packing away the decorations in egg cartons and bubble wrap. Dragging the carcass, she left a trail of needles on the Persian carpet, filling the room with the pungent scent of pine.

By nine-thirty, the children were awake and remarkably animated considering the ordeal of the previous night. They seemed to have suffered no physical effects but Frankie's muscles hurt and big purple bruises were developing along her shoulder and thigh.

She bathed the three children together in the Jacuzzi, bribing them with bubbles and yellow plastic ducks. After only a minor struggle, she managed to dress both boys in warm sweatsuits sporting cartoon figures.

Autumn had insisted she could dress herself, but reappeared wearing the same torn pink tutu and stained sweater that Frankie had peeled off her several days before. Frankie convinced her it was time for something clean, and she settled for a Winnie the Pooh sweatshirt and black tights, submitting as well, to the hairbrush with quiet resignation.

When Frankie asked if they would like to go to visit Lourdes and Kiki, the boys responded happily. Autumn's brow furrowed. "Can Clarence come with us?" She had refused to relinquish the ugly toy, dragging it with her, inventing conversations, and pretending to feed it whatever she ate; a smell of sour milk clung to its matted and grimy blue fur. Choose your battles, Frankie thought. "Why can't Mommy come back?" she asked.

"I'm sorry, honey. She just can't."

The day was sunny although still icy cold with a knifing wind. When they reached the gates, Frankie saw the media trucks still milling around. She reported to the officer on duty that they were going to Pinewood Trails and hurried past, ignoring the reporters' attempts to intercept them. One van followed for several miles, and she was considering ways to lose it when she looked in her rearview several miles later still, to see that it had abandoned pursuit.

Lourdes greeted them at the door. Little boots lined the entryway, and the children added their own. Frankie assured her that the officer would be keeping a discreet eye on them and promised to pick them up by six. She had matters to attend to.

CHAPTER 28

At the courthouse in Stroudsburg, Frankie learned that certain adoption records remained sealed despite current, more open policies. She could find no entry for a birth certificate under the name of Edwina Irewood but did locate the record of her marriage to Garrison Gardiner with her name listed as Edwina Mauro Irewood. She perused birth records for Mauro, hoping to find a clue. A Mauro family in Tobyhanna Township listed three children, among them Edwina, born in 1938. Death certificates indicated that both parents and two children had died in 1948. She copied names and dates.

At the Stroudsburg library she found in the newspaper archives the story of the tragic fire which claimed the lives of Edwina's birth parents and two siblings, including a front page photo of a pathetic looking ten-year old Edwina. She filed it for future consideration.

Next she went to the Wachovia bank where she asked for a conference with the manager. The nameplate on the walnut desk read Olivia Dalton. A large, pale woman with flat eyes, she had squeezed her massive frame into a navy blue suit. A pair of red-framed glasses sat low on her narrow nose. Frankie explained that she needed to know if Rocky had any certificates of deposit or other funds for the care of the children.

"I can't divulge that information. I'm sorry." The woman removed her glasses. "I'm sure any money you spend will be reimbursed when the estate is settled."

"That would be just fine," Frankie replied, her voice tart, "if I didn't happen to be already overextended." The other replaced her glasses, a tight smile indicating dismissal.

Frankie continued to call Sarvonsky's cell at ten-minute intervals, without success. Shouldn't he have checked in by now? The bank was near the Stroudsburg Medical Center, where she could check on Edwina's condition. When she reached the hospital parking lot, before getting out of the car, she made a call to Ransome. His voice was crisp with anger.

"Where the hell did you get the idea that Gordon broke into his parents' home?"

"It had to be him!"

"You have any evidence, Miss Detective?"

"If you'd seen him last night! He packed a bag--"

"Well, first of all, Mr. Gardiner is free to go anywhere he wants, and second, according to his parents, who were home during the robbery, the perpetrator was a stranger."

". . .Are you sure?"

"Am I sure? Have you talked to his parents?"

"No, of course not. Can Mr. Gardiner even talk?"

"He's unresponsive--another stroke--but Mrs. Gardiner is talking."

"She's out of the hospital?"

"No. But she's out of intensive care as of this morning. I talked to her myself."

"What about all their security? The dogs? And the people who work for them? How could anyone break in?"

"Somebody did."

Edwina had to be covering for him. "So nobody's looking for Gordon?"

"I'd like to talk to him, but I can't put out an APB when his parents say he's not involved."

She was terrified that this was the wrong choice, but she'd had no word from Sarvonsky. "I have something to report about him--Sarvonsky."

"Tell me when you come in."

"That might be too late. He could be in trouble." She spilled out the information she had been hoarding, the money, the photos, the legal papers, and the fact that she hadn't heard from Sarvonsky since he said he was tailing Chantelle. During the following silence, she felt the cell phone growing hot in her hand and imagined it was Ransome's fury leaping over the airwaves.

"You're a very stupid woman!" he finally snarled. "Do you know the penalty for withholding evidence? I want you down here to make a statement about last night's incident."

"You took a statement from Sarvonsky, didn't you?"

"Yeah. I need yours, too. Be here in an hour or I'm putting out an APB on you. Eleven o'clock."

She checked her watch. "Yes, sir. I'll be there."

She tried Sarvonsky's number again. No luck. The hospital was only minutes away from the Swiftwater barracks. She could run in before going on to the meeting with Ransome. The wind cut against her face as she got out and crossed to the hospital. Once inside she was assailed by the peculiar smells of disinfectants and illness. The clerk at the information desk gave her Edwina's room number without looking up from her novel.

Frankie took the elevator to the third floor and strode down a quiet hall and into Edwina's room, trying to look legitimate. At first glance she thought she had been misdirected. The old woman in the bed looked nothing like the chic and stylish Edwina Gardiner. Her face was swollen nearly beyond recognition and as discolored as a rotting apple. Her head was swathed in white gauze bandages, and her right arm hung in a cast from her stringy neck. She was propped into a sitting position by several pillows, eyes closed, open mouth emitting a gargling sound. Several exotic flower arrangements had already been placed on the side table; their abundance and sweetish stench made Frankie almost gag.

She gingerly touched the hand that lay on the white knitted blanket. The woman opened her eyes and stared out through slits of purplish flesh. She seemed to flinch at the sight of her.

"Mrs. Gardiner, I just want to talk to you."

"Do I know you?" The eyes were filmy. "You aren't Rochelle, are you?"

"I'm Rocky's sister. Frankie."

"Why do you use that ridiculous name?" Her voice was weak and querulous. "A woman should use her proper name. All of these young nurses call me Edwina. Or 'dearie'." The eyes flickered shut, and when they opened again they looked vague. "Are you a nurse?"

"I'm Rocky's sister. Don't you remember me?"

"I heard that Rochelle was murdered. Is that true?"

"Yes, it is."

"That woman ruined my son," she muttered. "She associated with sordid people. Never satisfied. She wasn't even a faithful wife."

"That's not true, Mrs. Gardiner. Rocky loved your son."

"She came from nothing! Nothing! He could have married anyone!"

"Is that why you hated her so much?" Frankie asked. "Because she reminded you that you came from nothing too?"

The old woman started; a look of cold fury flickered over her face. Then her eyes filled with tears. She turned her head away. "Get out! Leave me alone!"

Frankie thought she heard her choke back a sob and wanted to bite her tongue. In a softer tone she asked, "Can you remember what happened?"

"I tripped on the stairs," Edwina turned back a little too quickly, face flushed, eyes frightened. "I think my arm is broken."

"How did you fall? Did Gordon ask you for money? Did he hurt you?"

The woman peered at Frankie suspiciously. "Did I fall?" she asked vaguely. Perhaps the pain medication was causing her confusion. Had she told Ransome anything at all? Frankie wondered, scrutinizing the pathetic creature nodding against the pillow. It seemed hopeless.

She was about to leave when the woman's eyes opened again and she said quite clearly, "My son--my son--has very serious problems."

"Money problems?" Frankie prompted.

"Drugs. Gambling. Rochelle drove him to it. But now she's dead. If his father ever knew--" Frankie held her breath and moved closer to the bed.

"Did Gordon come to your house last night?"

"I had to cut him off--before he destroyed everything," the old woman said. "You understand that, don't you?"

"You have to tell the truth about him now."

"He's still my son. I can't send him to prison." Her voice had again become a quavery whisper, and her eyes closed. Frankie stood there for a few more minutes, frustration and anger roiling inside like tar in a hot pit.

At the police station she called Sarvonsky's number again, only to hear the same mechanical voice assure her that her party was unavailable at this time. She snapped the phone closed and entered the barracks.

When she entered Ransome's office, he glared menacingly at her and she realized she'd never seen him display emotion before. "Well, have you heard from your detective friend?"

"No. I don't suppose you have?" Frankie asked, unable to conceal her anxiety.

"He's too smart to jump into the middle of a homicide investigation!" the trooper fumed, eyes glinting. "What makes you think you're smarter than the police? What makes you think we should share information with you?" He glowered at her from beneath dark brows. "You're not playing with amateurs! Do you realize that?"

"I wasn't even--I was just picking up some of Rocky's things from a friend."

"Yeah. Your friend and I had a chat. Lucky for you she called 911 when that limo tailed you out of the lot."

"Aphrodite called?"

"Sarvonsky might have found himself--"

"Is anyone looking for him now?"

"That's our business." His face had resumed its bland expression and his eyes shifted towards the papers on his desk. "Could we first get down the details of what happened last night?" He pressed a button on the recorder and led her through the events of the previous evening, stopping her to refine impressions.   After he was satisfied he asked, "Now what's your story about Gordon attacking his parents and high tailing it to Vegas?"

"He obviously still needs money! He's running from someone. He hurt Edwina, probably thinks he killed--"

"Is it possible he's running from the criminals who killed his wife, kidnapped his kids, and attacked his parents?"

"He attacked his parents! Why didn't he come to the police?"

"You're making some pretty big assumptions." Ransome's face darkened again.   "A few days ago you were willing to swear that he murdered your sister. Now you say--"

"I still think he's to blame--"

"The evidence indicates otherwise.   In fact we're running prints on the same guy who grabbed you and the kids. We got an eyewitness says he was looking for your sister—"

"Yes, but--"

"There's strong evidence your sister was held in a limo at Loucasto's garage.   That's probably where the, uh, assault occurred."

"What evidence?"

"Enough to bring charges against Maggoti for rape and first degree murder."

Hearing it from Ransome suddenly made the reality palpable.   She swayed a little, feeling faint.   Images rose like poisonous gas--Maggot tearing at her sister's clothing, his huge hands at Rocky's throat.

"Are you okay?"   Ransome's voice, a bit softened, seemed to be coming from a distance.   "Take the advice I gave you the first time you came in with your theories--leave the police work to the police!"   When she continued to sit there pale and shaky, he asked, "You want some water?"

She nodded.   He brought her a paper cup and she drank. "But why? Why Rocky?" she faltered.

"We got some theories."

"Do any of your theories tie her husband in? Because he's obviously the reason behind what happened."   Her voice sounded weak even to her.

"You want me to call your friend to come down?"

"Who?"

"The actress."

"Aphrodite? I thought she was leaving." Frankie got to her feet. "I'll be okay." She should thank Aphrodite for making the call, she thought, later. But the blood rushed to her head and her knees wobbled; she sank back down on the seat.

CHAPTER 29

Aphrodite, looking like a young girl with a scrubbed face, braids cascading from beneath a fur-trimmed hat, arrived by cab twenty minutes later. She threw her arms around Frankie and hugged her tight. "Thank God you're okay!"

She drove Frankie's Honda to her favorite sushi spot, The Tokyo Teahouse, tucked into an out of the way shopping center and got them seated in a corner booth.

"Have some tea, girlfriend," she suggested when they were settled. "You're still looking pretty whipped."

"I'll be fine."

"Ransome told me about what happened!" Her huge liquid eyes fixed on Frankie's face with concern. "How are the kids?"

"They seem okay." The owner, Sue, a lovely woman with large almond eyes appeared to greet them. Aphrodite ordered sweet and sour soup and tea for Frankie and the special, chicken teriyaki, dumplings and hot Saki, for herself.

"Ransome told me you made the 911 call last night," Frankie said.

"Yeah. I just got this weird feeling when the limo took off right on your ass."

"You probably saved our lives. According to Ransome, Rocky was attacked at the garage, in one of their limos." She choked up. "They're charging the guy who kidnapped us. You know she was raped before--"

"Damn!" Aphrodite's lovely face was grave, dark brows knitted, full mouth turned down at the corners. "Damn! Why? Why Rocky?"

"If they know they're not saying. Sarvonsky thought possibly payback--for money Gordon owed. Ransome won't even connect him."

"He said my interview helped them out." She grimaced. "I just hope I didn't get myself into deep shit."

"You? How?"

"Well, I admitted that Chantelle was--" she faltered. "Our connection." She shrugged, cocking her head and grinning. "You know, some of the actors liked to party a little after the show."

"Who? Not Rocky? Rocky hated drugs!"

"Well, even Rocky smoked a little weed now and then. But, well, some of us, Cliff and me liked a little blow. Chantelle could always get us anything we wanted."

"I thought you hated Chantelle?"

"I said she was a sneaky bitch. She is. But she was handy to have around now and again. She was no friend, believe me."

Frankie felt that there was still some secret concealed behind Aphrodite's veiled eyes.

"But what about Chantelle and Thornton's wife? You sure they never let on that they knew each other?"

Aphrodite considered. "I never heard anything about that till you brought it up." The actress frowned. "But I don't go digging into people's business. You can't help noticing the two of them are similar, though. Together, they'd really be an eyeful."

Frankie felt she was holding a handful of puzzle pieces, but several edges were refusing to mesh. "You think Chantelle knew Thornton from before, from Vegas? That's where he met

Bianca, right? Could he have been playing around with
Chantelle, too? Maybe a triangle?"

Sue appeared to place drinks and steaming bowls of
soup before them. She saw that they were engaged in a deep
conversation and moved away. Aphrodite inhaled the fragrance
of her soup before replying. Her long braids swung around her
beautiful dark face.

"You mean were they hooking up? Nah! She was just
playing that man! She was trying to stay close to Rocky. I don't
think Chantelle likes men all that much if you know what I
mean."

"You know she works at the Paradiso?"

"What's that?"

"One of those gentlemen's' clubs."

"I only know she works the resorts--cocktail waitress,
bartender sometimes."

"She's also an exotic dancer--a lap dancer. A hooker,
according to Sarvonsky."

"Really? You think Cliff knew that?"

"You're asking me?"

"Right! You never met Cliff." Aphrodite smirked a
little. "He was always running after some female with his
tongue hanging out. And always the same type." She seemed
amused despite herself. "I guess it made him feel young."

Frankie glanced at her watch. It was almost one.
Where was Sarvonsky?

A waitress appeared to set down the rest of their order
and ask if there would be anything else. She placed the bill on
the table.

Frankie checked her cell phone. The battery was live,
but there were no messages. Was Sarvonsky following them all
the way to Vegas? She sipped half-heartedly at her soup,
stomach in knots, and forced her attention back to Aphrodite.
"But you were friendly with Bianca?" She thought she detected
a nervous flash in Aphrodite's eyes.

"I only met her when she came up for the show. Cliff
had the suite right across from mine. We got a little friendly.
But I told you, Bianca hardly left the hotel the whole time she
was here."

"But she came to the theater to see her husband's show?"

"The evening performance, a few times. Never to matinees. I guess she was too busy working out or getting a massage."

"You went with her to Cliff's funeral."

Aphrodite's voice rose with exasperation. "Her husband had been murdered, and she was here all alone! My Lord, wouldn't you?"

"Yes, but--she seemed really. . . ?"

"Devastated! The woman seemed devastated!" Aphrodite shook her head and her braids bounced.

"Ransome asked you about her?"

"I told you, he grilled me." Her half smile implied that she'd enjoyed the experience. "You know if he's married?"

"No idea. You're sure--"

"Now, girl, I know you're broken up about Rocky--I am too. But you're making me feel like I'm on trial here!"

"No, no. I just. . . ."

"I could be putting myself in danger." Aphrodite lowered her thick lashes and smiled her broad smile.. "Ransome says he might have to put me under his protection--as long as I stay around."

"His personal protection?"

"I hope so." Aphrodite smiled. "He is fine!"

"He may be fine, but he's sitting around twiddling his thumbs while Gordon's escaping."

"Escaping? I thought--"

"He attacked his own parents!"

"You know that?"

"And he's to blame for Rocky's murder. God damn it, I know he is! Even if it was that thug who did it!" Frankie found herself choking up. "He's got to pay for it."

The actress put a hand over hers and patted it. "I'm so sorry, baby." Her nails were long and red. Five silver bracelets jingled on her narrow wrist.

Frankie's cell phone rang and she grabbed it. Sarvonsky had resurfaced.

CHAPTER 30

Her relief revealed just how scared she had been, and how much his safety mattered to her. "Thank god!" Frankie breathed. "Where are you?"

"Listen. I need you to do something. You remember how to get to my place?"

"Why? Are you there?"

"No, I'm at a motel on 611, the Silver Lake Cottages, about forty miles from Lake Nakomis. I want you to go to my place and get the money. It's on a shelf above my bed in the loft. Bring it to me here."

"What are you doing? What's happening?"

"I'm in Unit 17. Take the driveway behind Gator Gill's Tattoos, about a half-mile up. How long will it take?"

"I don't know. Are you in trouble?"

"No. But I need the money." He started to give her directions to his place. She signaled to Aphrodite for a paper and pen and scribbled.

"Should I bring it all?"

"Yes. It's wrapped, inside a cardboard box. Come alone. Don't tell anybody. Understand?"

"I don't know what we're doing!"

"You want to prove Gordon's connected to Rocky's murder?"

"Yes, he--

"You want to nail him, don't you?"

"How?"

"We may be able to tie him in. Get the money."

Frankie looked at her watch; it was almost one-thirty. "Give me an hour and a half." She would have to drive to Whitehaven, and then locate the cottages.

"You got to do it in an hour at the outside. Time is crucial."

"Christ, I'll lose my license if I get another ticket!" she wailed.

"Can you do it?"

"Yes. I'll do it!" she said. "Wait, how do I get into your cabin?"

"There's a key in the little bird feeder."

"What about the dogs?"

"They won't bother you. They know you."

"What's going on?" Aphrodite's voice was a stage whisper. Frankie ignored her until after she'd signed off. "Who? Not Gordon?" she asked.

"No, not Gordon. Look, I got to go. You have any cash?" She found a five-dollar bill and counted out seven ones. Aphrodite dropped a twenty and followed her out. Frankie felt a surge of adrenaline flooding through her as she headed to the Honda. Her hands, inside the gloves, were hot and moist.

"Frankie, I'm going with you."

"No. He said to come alone."

"And I said I'm going with you. It is not safe for you going off by yourself."

Aphrodite opened the passenger's side and hopped in.

"Get out of this car. I can't take you."

"I'm not letting you go alone!" She sat with her hand on the lock, unmoving. "It's not Ransome, is it?"

"No. A private detective."

"Oh, Sarvonsky? That man is relentless. He's been calling me."

"He's got a plan to stop Gordon."

"Listen, Frankie, if I'd called the police the night I saw Rocky's car at the Inn, maybe I could have--"

Frankie started the Honda. She still didn't quite trust her but she didn't have time to argue.. Aphrodite was still buttoning her long shearling coat as they sped off.

On the drive she told Aphrodite about the money, and they speculated about Sarvonsky's plan. "Maybe he has Gordon holed up at the motel," Aphrodite suggested. "But why does he need the money?"

"Maybe Gordon found out that Chantelle set Rocky up and he's holding her for ransom."

Aphrodite's brow wrinkled. "You think she did? Set Rocky up?"

"Someone gave Rocky pictures of Gordon with sleazy half-naked dancers, including Chantelle, at one of those clubs."

"Gordon?" Aphrodite wrinkled her nose. "Men are dogs!" She laughed. "Sometimes I think lesbians are the only ones who got the right idea."

"I think Chantelle tried to cause trouble between them-- maybe even set her up."

"But I don't get it. The way she zeroed in on Rocky, I swear she was hot for her. Why would she want to hurt her?"

"Maybe she wanted to cause a riff between them."

Frankie maneuvered over the bumpy ruts to Sarvonsky's cabin; as they lurched to a stop, the dogs inside set up a chorus. Frankie found the key and entered. The dogs bounded up to them, sniffing and whining, and followed her up the stairs while Aphrodite stood nervously waiting at the door. She found the package on a shelf above his bed wrapped in newspapers as he had described.

When Frankie turned the key in the Honda, it sputtered as usual, but this time, despite several frantic attempts, it failed to catch.

"Now what?" Aphrodite asked.

"It must be the battery," Frankie groaned. "I should have had it checked." She tried again without success.

"Shit!" Aphrodite shook her head. "We're fucked!"

"Wait. If we could turn the car around to face downhill," Frankie said, "I might be able to pop the clutch and jump start it."

"What are you talking about? Clutches? Jump starts? Don't you need some kind of cables for that?"

"Just help me push!" Frankie said.

The two of the worked together, rocking the car backwards and forwards until it was finally positioned facing down the hill. Aphrodite got in. Another slight push got it moving. Frankie managed to leap into the driver's seat before it picked up speed, hurtling downward, and, as Angelo had taught her, she depressed the clutch, put the car into gear, and released it. The Honda shuddered and the engine roared.

She drove at top speed, an eye out for patrol cars.

Less than an hour later, she turned the Honda onto a small road that veered off Route 611 behind the tattoo place and they spotted a row of sagging yellow-and-white cottages along the ridge of the hill. There was an arrow with the legend Office pointing further uphill.

"He said cottage number 17," Frankie whispered.

"Why are you whispering?" Aphrodite asked.

"I don't know." Frankie took a deep breath.

"Do you have a gun?" Aphrodite's eyes glittered with excitement.

"No, I don't have a gun! Where would I get a gun?"

"Maybe he had one hidden with the money." Aphrodite leaned forward eagerly. "There--number 17!"

Frankie pulled the Honda into the parking spot beside the cottage. Sarvonsky's red truck was parked behind it, and near it a dark Acura. When she tapped on the door, Sarvonsky opened it. Her eyes searched his face. He looked a little weary, the scar showing darker and more ridged than she remembered. His dark curls were uncombed, the gray evident, but his eyes on hers were relieved and warm. "You got it?"

"Right here." She handed him the box. His fingers touched hers as he took it, and she was aware, even then, of the frisson it set off. When he saw Aphrodite his expression changed.

"What the hell? I told you to come alone!"

"I wouldn't let her!" Aphrodite moved into the doorway. "I wasn't about to let her get into trouble alone."

"Get inside, then, both of you," he growled.

"I'm Aphrodite." She extended a gloved hand. "You've been calling me?"

Frankie watched him appraise the actress, taking in her lovely dark face and lithe dancer's figure.

"Roman Sarvonsky." He took the hand she offered. "You're not an easy woman to track down."

She smiled up at him in a flirtatious manner, eyes bright. "I'm here now. I want to help."

Frankie shivered as she entered the musty room. The cottage, obviously chosen for its seclusion, was small and cramped, with drab green carpeting, a few dull prints on the walls, and a double bed covered with a worn green spread. Its sour smell reminded her of the series of progressively shabbier apartments, and finally the dingy trailer that had served as home during her father's downward drift.

A tiny kitchenette with an avocado sink and half-sized refrigerator occupied one wall. Sarvonsky laid the box on a small table near two Dunkin' Donut cups and an empty bag. Frankie noticed the lounge chair near the bed and a large overnight bag beside it.

The door at the end of a short hall clicked open, and a young woman with a tousled mane of blonde hair emerged, wearing a low-necked chartreuse sweater that revealed generous cleavage, tight black pants, and leather boots that increased her height by an additional three inches.

"Chantelle!" Aphrodite exclaimed in surprise, her voice cool but not unfriendly. "What's happening, girl?" The blonde glared at the two women; her big hazel eyes were heavily made up, eyelashes thick with mascara, lips outlined in a shade darker than the moist pink that tinted them. She was the woman Frankie had noticed talking to Gordon at Rocky's wake, perhaps the woman of the photos.

Chantelle glowered at Aphrodite but addressed Sarvonsky. "What's this Black bitch doing here? You sent out invitations?" She picked up a pack of Virginia Slims and shook one out.

"Could I have one?" Aphrodite, ignoring the insult, extended a hand. The blonde hesitated for a moment but shook one out. Aphrodite held it out for a light and after a moment the woman flicked a small gold lighter, and lit it for her. Frankie noticed a black-and-red viper, fangs at the ready, tattooed on the inside of Chantelle's left wrist. She closed the lighter, plopped down on the lounge chair beside her suitcase, and took a hungry drag. Aphrodite puffed delicately. They eyed each other as they blew out simultaneous plumes of smoke.

"You got the cash?" Chantelle's voice was husky, redolent of smoke, whiskey, and a Brooklyn girlhood.

Sarvonsky patted the bundle on the table, pulled out a wooden chair, and sat. "Sit down," he told the new arrivals. "You both know Chantelle Rojas?" Aphrodite puffed, nodding slightly, appraising the woman with interest.

"Yes. A one minute telephone acquaintance," Frankie said. "And a brief encounter in a limo last night. But I understand you knew my sister." She stared into the woman's face; it was definitely the woman of the photos, she decided.

Chantelle sucked deeply on the cigarette, eyes flickering toward Frankie. "I'm sorry about--what happened to Rocky." There seemed to be genuine regret in her voice, perhaps even a glitter of tears in her kohl-rimmed eyes.

"You're sorry? You're sorry?" Frankie was furious. This woman had the nerve to say she was sorry, as though her sister's murder had been some minor accident.

Sarvonsky stepped forward, interrupting.

"Chantelle and I had a long talk last night," he said. "And she agreed to help us out."

A deal, Frankie thought. She needs to bargain because Maggot's locked up. "How? How exactly is she going to help us?" Frankie asked, eyes still focused on Chantelle's face.

His voice reached her ears over the thudding of her own heartbeat. "She's been in contact with Gordon. And she has contacts with--certain people who are eager to see him."

"What kind of deal?" Aphrodite asked.

"Gordon thinks he and Chantelle will be heading to Vegas along with some high quality cocaine. But they'll be intercepted."

"Who? The cops? Ransome?" Frankie asked, and Chantelle shot her an evil look.

"Yeah, Ransome's in on it. We've set up a little detour."

"You're working with Ransome?"

"We traded some information," Sarvonsky said. "He's been sniffing around Loucasto's operation for some time. It looks like we can help them out. Gordon expects this coke deal to buy him time till he can get the money he still owes Loucasto. He could be useful to Ransome."

"So," Aphrodite interrupted, her voice gleeful, "Chantelle will flip on Gordon to save her own ass!" They all turned to her. She shrugged. "Am I wrong?"

Chantelle flushed an angry, blotchy pink, a crease appearing between her dramatic eyebrows. "Shut the fuck up, you stupid bitch! I'm not flipping on anybody! I'm not a criminal!"

"No offense, girlfriend! Just calling it like I see it." Aphrodite shrugged and moved across the room, putting space between them.

"No one's accusing you, Chantelle." Sarvonsky gave Aphrodite a warning glance. "We got a chance to help each other out, that's all." His gravel voice was mild, soothing. He wore a rumpled blue work shirt, open at the throat, that looked slept in, and Frankie noticed another thick, raised scar that started near his collarbone. Chantelle appeared momentarily placated as she sank back into the lounge chair.

Frankie felt as she had once on a runaway filly, hurtling out of control at breakneck speed. What if Chantelle wasn't planning to flip? What if she and Gordon escaped to Vegas with the drugs that Rocky's cache would be helping them to buy? Of course Aphrodite was right--Chantelle's only motive was to save her own skin. Maggoti could tie her to both murders. She must know exactly what had happened to Rocky--and why.

Impelled by some force outside herself, Frankie moved toward the lounge chair and knelt on the ottoman beside it, snaking an arm around the back of the chair so that Chantelle couldn't avoid her. The woman's eyelids narrowed over dark contracted pupils.

"I know you were there with Maggot last night," Frankie said softly. "Were you there when he killed Rocky, too?"

"You're crazy!" Chantelle gasped. She looked over Frankie's head toward Sarvonsky, trying to rise, her eyes frightened. But Frankie reached out to pin her where she was.

"Tell me how it happened! Why?"

"I wasn't there! It wasn't supposed to--" Chantelle' voice came out choked, high pitched. She tried to rise again, but Frankie's grip prevented her.

"I need to know. How was Gordon involved?" One of the woman's ringed and manicured hands struck out at Frankie but she seized it. Smoke from the cigarette stung her eyes.

"Get off me!" Chantelle writhed in her grip, and the cigarette flipped onto the rug where it smoldered unobserved.

"Why did Magotti kill my sister?" As Chantelle twisted away, Frankie noted a gleam of gold at the low neckline of her sweater and in one swift movement seized the fragile chain. Chantelle caught and pried at her fingers but she held on, ripping it from her neck.

"It's Rocky's locket!" At this, Frankie lost control, grabbing at the woman's thick hair, and planting a knee on her chest. "How dare you? My mother's locket!" At that moment the cigarette smoldering on the carpet burst into flame. Aphrodite noticed and rushed to stamp it out. Sarvonsky intervened, pulling Frankie away from Chantelle. She turned to him sobbing, holding up the broken chain. "She was wearing Rocky's locket!"

"Calm down," Sarvonsky said. "Listen to her! You're going to blow the whole--" He half-led, half-dragged Frankie to the other side of the kitchen counter. Chantelle sat up gasping, and rubbing at her throat. Looking back, Frankie saw that the woman's face had crumpled. She was gasping and tears trickled down her cheeks.

"You set Rocky up!" Frankie's voice was knife edged. "Because you wanted Gordon! Because she took Gordon's gambling money!"

"It wasn't like that! I never--it wasn't supposed to happen," Chantelle gasped. "I never saw Rocky that night. I didn't know until--it was too late." She faced Frankie, her face anguished. "I showed her what a prick she was married to! We had a plan! She was supposed to meet me that night! I would never have let--that stupid bastard screwed everything up."

"Who? Maggot?" Frankie asked.

"Yeah. The stupid fuck."

"Why?"

"Because he's a fool. He decided to write his own program!" She spat the words out angrily. "*I told her where Gordon hid the money.* I knew how deep Maggot had his hooks in." She faltered, her voice almost a whisper. "I would have done anything for Rocky!"

She lit another cigarette trying to regain control. After an angry drag she stalked over to the counter and stubbed it out in a butt-filled saucer. She spoke to Sarvonsky, who was still holding Frankie. "I'm getting the fuck out!" she said. "You're not pinning a murder rap on me!"

"Of course not." Sarvonsky's voice was paternal, soothing. "We've got a deal. We've already got plenty on Maggot." He let go of Frankie and moved toward Chantelle. "He's going down, not you. He's being charged. Murder. Kidnapping."

"I'm not going to jail!"

"Not if you stick to our plan. You'll get immunity--if you help put Loucasto and his crew away." He put his arm around her shoulder. "But we've got to move on it, now or we'll lose the chance." He turned to Frankie and looked into her face, his eyes holding hers. "I need you to trust me on this."

Frankie, still trying to process what Chantelle had said, nodded slowly. "Okay. If it means that Gordon is--"

He turned back to Chantelle. "Your contact is meeting you and Gordon at five, right?"

"Right." She looked for her coat. "That's what we said."

"And Gordon's convinced that you got the cash?"

"Yeah, yeah." She glanced down at her watch, gave Frankie another half-angry, half-apologetic look. "I found the locket in Maggot's limo," she said in a husky voice. "I wasn't gonna let him get away with what he did. And--I wanted to keep something that was hers." Frankie made no reply, merely looked down at the golden trinket in her hand.

Chantelle turned to Sarvonsky. "Let's go."

CHAPTER 31

Chantelle grabbed a long coat made of some furry, reddish material, a fuchsia scarf, and gloves. She and Sarvonsky briskly counted the bills and packed them into a plastic shopping bag. Suitcase, purse, and the money in hand, Chantelle went out. A car door slammed, and an engine started.

Grabbing his coat and gloves, Sarvonsky said, in measured tones but with an undercurrent of excitement, "Let's hope she doesn't blow it. Wait here for at least twenty minutes."

"How did she explain the money?" Frankie asked. "Wasn't Gordon suspicious?"

"We concocted a story. A loan from Bianca. Apparently she came to the club once with Chantelle. And he's desperate for a way out."

"So they really were in contact all along? Bianca and Chantelle?"

"Yeah. Looks that way. Sisters under the skin."

"Can't we come?" Aphrodite asked.

"Sorry. They're meeting a few miles away. We can't tip them off." The gleam in his dark eyes told Frankie he was glad to be back in action. He went out to the truck, and, as Frankie and Aphrodite watched through the little window above the sink, both vehicles disappeared down the snow-covered hill.

Aphrodite pouted like a child denied a treat. "I always wanted to be in on something exciting--a big drug bust!"

"Just so Gordon gets caught--"

"For attacking his parents?"

"For drug dealing, and conspiring with those criminals. For getting Rocky murdered." Frankie sat on the bed, hugging herself in the cold room. "Edwina is still denying that he attacked them. But I'm sure he went to beg her for more money. When she refused, he lost it——just like with Rocky!"

"Why do women cover up for trash like him?" Aphrodite sat down beside her and rolled her eyes. "It makes me sick!"

They waited nervously for a few more minutes, Frankie checking her watch while Aphrodite smoked one of the Virginia Slims Chantelle had forgotten. Frankie reached for her bag. "I can't just sit here. I have to see what's happening. I know this is crazy but I've got to help somehow. Sarvonsky could be in trouble if Ransome doesn't get there in time."

"I'm not due at Skytop until ten." Aphrodite was suddenly grinning like the Cheshire cat. "Let's roll, girlfriend."

They drove down the hill, alert for action involving the Acura or Sarvonsky's truck. Just as they were about to turn onto Route 611, they spotted the Acura parked at one of the small separate cottages behind Gill Gator's Tattoos. Gordon's Suburban was next to it, and a black BMW with Florida license plates had pulled up at an angle to the door. Frankie drove past the motel unit, parked in Gator Gill's lot a few hundred yards below, and opened the driver's door.

"What are you doing?" Aphrodite whispered.

"I want to make sure no one leaves before the police get here." She opened the trunk of her car and found a tool chest. Removing the longest screwdriver she could find, she crept toward the cars. Aphrodite started to follow, but she waved her back.

Not quite believing her own foolhardy actions, Frankie started with Gordon's Suburban, puncturing all four tires, listening to the whoosh of air before moving on to the other two cars. At the sound of sirens in the distance, she rushed back to Aphrodite, and they exchanged triumphant looks as she slid into the passenger seat.

Aphrodite stepped on the gas and they took off, passing two state police cruisers turning uphill toward the motel unit. Out of danger, Frankie found she was shaking and queasy while Aphrodite laughed as though it had all been a marvelous romp.

When Frankie picked up the children, Lourdes insisted she stay for dinner. She'd prepared arroz con pollo, and the aroma reminded Frankie that she needed to eat. The children were cheerful after a day of play, Autumn and Kiki cavorting in long gowns from the costume box and the boys no longer quarreling.

After dinner, Frankie packed then into the Honda and drove back to the Gardiner home. Clarke followed discreetly in a patrol car. The media circus had resumed. She counted three TV location vans as she drove through the throng of reporters, closing the gates behind the Honda as quickly as possible, ignoring the shouts pursuing her up the driveway. In her rear-view mirror, she saw Officer Clarke get out of the black-and-white and stride toward a location van.

The phone was ringing as they entered the house. Sarvonsky's voice greeted her.

"Where are you?" Frankie asked.

"I'm twenty miles away. Put on the coffee."

"It's already on," she told him, reaching for the pot. "Look out for the vultures at the gates."

A short while later they were sitting together in the den. She'd bathed the children and bundled them off to bed, taken a quick shower, dressed in a clean pair of jeans and a silk shirt, made sandwiches, and carried them on a tray, along with a jar of peanut butter, a box of crackers, and a tin of sardines, into the den. Sarvonsky sat down on the couch, and was already reaching for a sandwich as she set the tray on the cocktail table.

His eyes swept over her, sought out her eyes, and held them. "You're looking better."

"Better?"

"Calmer." He touched a strand of her loose, fiery hair and tucked it behind her ear. "Beautiful."

She flushed at his words and his touch, an electric current traveling through her nerves to a hot center in the pit of her stomach. "Gordon's been arrested?" she asked.

"Yep. And charged. Possession with intent to distribute."

"When did you start working with Ransome?"

"You wanted me to call him. I told him what we had, or thought we had. We worked out a deal."

"And they caught him with drugs?"

"Broke into the motel room. Money and drugs all laid out." Sarvonsky took a huge bite of his sandwich. "Eliminated the need for probable cause--to search his car--plus we grabbed his contact, one of Loucasto's couriers." His eyes were bright. "This guy Stefano looks like a real pimp--long greasy hair in a ponytail, a suit jacket over a tee shirt, like he's watched too many Tarentino flicks. He's counting his money, and Gordon's tasting the coke. Chantelle's locked herself in the bathroom, but nobody's suspicious yet."

"You were there?"

He nodded. "Ransome pulled me in a few hundred yards from the unit, says he and his partner are going to bust the door, I can follow up."

"Did Gordon recognize you?"

"Couldn't tell. He was too shocked to react. He stood with his jaw falling to his shoes, not even reaching for the gun right in front of him. They were both cuffed and on the floor before they knew what hit them. They started cursing each other out before either one remembered Chantelle."

"And they arrested all three of them?"

"Yeah, but the damnedest thing," Sarvonsky reported, his eyes glittering and that look of suppressed amusement tugging at the corners of his mouth. "Someone had punctured the tires on all three vehicles!"

Frankie evaded his eyes, but she felt the blush tinting her throat and cheeks. "Gordon's locked up?"

Sarvonsky nodded. "For the moment. Of course his laywer'll be there first thing tomorrow."

"Could he get out on bail?"

"Possibly. If he can get someone to post it." He was polishing off the first half of the turkey sandwich.

"Who? Edwina? Could she be such a fool?" Frankie remembered the pathetic figure huddled in the hospital bed.

"He could put up assets--horses, homes, his interest in the breeding farm. Anything that isn't already mortgaged to the hilt."

"I doubt he has anything else. Isn't that what those loan papers were about?" Frankie asked.

"Seems his father covered for him on a previous real estate scam, but this angle is mixed up with Loucasto's operation so he ain't gonna hush everything up so easy this time." "What about Chantelle?" she asked.

"She could get a break on the kidnapping charges if she testifies against Maggot."

"But won't she be incriminating herself?"

"She'll get immunity." He gave a dry mirthless chuckle. "Get this. She wants to claim the reward money the Gardiners put up--for fingering Maggoti as the killer." He reached for the second half of the sandwich. "But believe me, she won't be getting any reward money."

"So why did Maggot go after Rocky? What did Chantelle say?"

"She says he's psycho, a wild man. But I'm not sure that's all of it. Part of her story rings true, but she's still hiding something."

"What is her story?"

"That Maggot fronted Gordon money for a side deal, a big drug buy that would generate enough cash to pay off his gambling debts to Loucasto. But she found out where he'd hidden the money, went to Rocky, spilled the beans. She was in love with Rocky."

"In love? I doubt that. Obsessed, maybe."

"Yeah, well. She says she convinced Rocky to meet her that night to confront Gordon at the club. But they never met up."

"Because Maggot found her first?"

"He was supposedly planning to scare her a little--send a message--because Gordon botched the drug buy. But when he found her, Thornton was with her and he lost control of the situation, then had to clean up the mess." Sarvonsky was starting on the sardines.

"But you don't buy it?"

"Why did they need Thornton to go confront Gordon? Why murder Rocky when all Gordon needed was a threat? There's still a piece missing."

"What about Thornton's widow?"

"Chantelle admits that they've been close friends since Vegas, long before Bianca met Thornton."

"Friends?"

"Yeah, maybe more than friends. Maybe they were plotting together all along."

"Where is she now? Bianca?" Frankie asked.

"Chantelle claims she doesn't know. Vanished. Cleaned out the bank accounts and disappeared. But I tracked down some big life insurance policies on Thornton, so if she tries to collect they may be able to track her."

"And Chantelle?"

"Chantelle will testify that she helped push Rocky's car into the river. It makes her an accessory after the fact."

"But she knew it was Rocky's car! Doesn't that mean she lied about not being there--"

"Maggot told her Rocky was safe, waiting for her at the club where they were planning to confront Gordon."

"So Gordon was just a fool?"

"She used him. And she hates Maggot even more than she hates Gordon. But she's scared of Maggot. I still think he got something on her."

"Like what?"

"Maybe she set Maggot up with her girlfriend, to get rid of Thornton, and that was the deal that went sour."

"But she's willing to testify against both of them?"

"Yeah. The threat of a jail sentence can be very convincing.."

Frankie poured them fresh coffee. A lull in the conversation stretched, and she looked up to find him scrutinizing her. She thought of his promise the night she had halted his kisses.

The inevitable flush began at her throat and moved upward, making her cheeks burn. She had never cultivated the feminine arts of subtlety or indirection. She faced him squarely, meeting his gaze.

"I'll never be able to thank you." She offered him a wry little smile. The coffee mug trembled in her hand.

He took it from her and set it down on the low table. "Know why I got involved, against my better judgment?"

"Why?"

"You. Your face--the look in your eyes." He tilted her chin up with a forefinger and bent toward her. His kiss tasted of coffee, but it was sweet and tender and continued for a long time. His warmth, the woodsy scent of his skin, the pressure of his lips, sent frissons through all of her nerve endings. She felt as though she were spinning, dissolving. She could go on resisting, filling up the empty spaces in her heart with hate and the desire for vengeance or she could give in to what she could now acknowledge as her own need.

In an attempt to slow the sweet vortex that was pulling her under, she traced the scar on his face. "You said you'd tell me what happened."

"Later," he said. He kissed her eyes, her mouth again. He stopped and looked at her, his eyebrow raised in an unspoken question. She took his hand and led him upstairs. She chose a guest room far from where the children slept, with a door that locked. There was the momentary awkwardness of removing shoes, unbuttoning garments, pulling down the sheets and comforter, and his fumbling for a small foil packet. She wondered, then, if he had been planning for this, thinking of her, and was grateful for his concern.

The bed smelled of lavender and freshly laundered linen; the down pillows were deep and luxurious. Then he was warm against her, pulling her close. His large square hands moved surely, caressing her back, her throat, and her breasts. He kissed her deeply, and she returned his kisses with all of the passion that she stifled and denied for years. She noticed a scar on his left leg, like a piece of knotted rope, and the long raised scar on his muscled chest, and she pressed kisses on the lumpy, pinkish flesh.   She closed her eyes, squeezing back unaccountable tears, thinking, I'm alive, alive.   Behind closed eyelids, she saw flashes of blue and golden light.   This time there were no interruptions.

CHAPTER 32

Two days later, Sarvonsky told her that Gordon was going to be released on bail. They were at his cabin, lounging in the glow of the wood-burning stove, his head resting in Frankie's lap. Lourdes had kept the children, so they'd been able to spend their first full night together. Frankie felt like a mysterious continent as he discovered beauty in her green eyes, her Slavic face, and the splashes of freckles that dusted her cheeks.

Lying in his rumpled bed after they made love for the second time, they'd shared stories. She'd offered her memories of Rocky, as she'd been--alive, charismatic, her protector, her friend and inspiration.

He told her about growing up in Brighton Beach, his failed marriage, the daughter he loved. He spoke of his career with the NYPD and how it had ended, almost a year before the September 11 tragedy that had killed so many of his comrades, in what should have been a fairly routine undercover bust.

"My partner and I worked out of the forty-four in the Bronx. I was posing as a dealer trying to buy crack at a housing project," he told Frankie. "Mike my partner, Mike Marone--was tailing. I was counting on his backup." His eyes glazed over for a moment. Frankie nuzzled against him, breathing in the pungent scent of fresh masculine sweat. "To make a long story short, I fucked up, and Mike died. I got trapped--no gun, not even a wire. Three assholes decided to kill me so they could keep the money and the drugs. I found myself looking right into the barrel of a .38, knowing that I was going to die--at the hands of a scumbag in a rat hole that stank from garbage." He took a deep breath and exhaled. "But I got out alive, and Mike didn't." Frankie saw the glitter of tears in his dark, hooded eyes. His breath came short and ragged. "The irony was, they never even knew I was a cop."

"Mike saved you?"

"He came through the door, and the three of them started firing. I took a couple of bullets, but one hit him in the throat and he dropped to the floor like a sandbag. Blood all over the room. They thought they'd killed me, too." He shut his eyes, rubbed his temples, and was quiet for a long time. She knew he had opened a locked door in order to help her. The wounds had marked more than his flesh, Frankie thought, almost wishing she had physical scars to bear witness, too.

She'd fallen asleep in his arms, feeling the crisp texture of his curly chest hair and breathing in his scent.

In the morning, the whining of the dogs awakened them, and after Sarvonsky had tended to them, he returned, cold from the outdoor air, carrying hot coffee and day-old bagels. After breakfast, they made love again; she was learning about him from his obvious hunger, restrained as it was by tenderness and concern. Afterwards she felt all of her bones had melted, that her flesh was glowing like moonstone.

Temporarily sated, naked, and lazy, they lounged and talked. Frankie traced the lines of his forehead and ran her hands through his graying curls. That was when he dropped it into the conversation, casually: "Gordon's being released today. He's hired Wendell Hill Coburn, one of the best criminal attorneys in the state."

"He's the one that got that shady Philadelphia judge off last year?" she asked. "Can he afford him?"

"Edwina can."

"But she's still in the hospital!"

"She's been moved to a private facility. In fact, she might even be home."

"She sounded pretty confused when I saw her," Frankie said.

"I understand Gardiner senior's V.P.'s been the acting manager of the business since his last stroke. But it must be her decision. I guess that's what they call unconditional love."

"I guess that's what I call unconditional stupidity!" Frankie said. "Maybe if he'd actually killed her. . . ." Sarvonsky reached up to cup one of her small round breasts in his large hand, but she ignored the gesture. "So Gordon's out?"

"Until the trial. According to Ransome, he may be more valuable as a witness."

"You mean he won't be prosecuted? But they caught him--"

"They could drop the drug charges if he testifies about criminal activity at the clubs."

"Goddamn it! Won't he ever have to pay--"

"They need an in, a contact, to bust a private club. Even the state cops and the liquor control board can't get in without some employee to rat them out, some club member willing to file a complaint."

"Even if they know--?"

"There's a different set of rules for private clubs. Gordon can help them prove their case."

"So if your name happens to be Gardiner, you can get away with murder! Dealing drugs! Robbing your parents!" A nervous shiver ran through her. "Do you think he'll blame me for getting him busted?"

"He's probably too busy thinking about how to avoid Loucasto's thugs. They aren't impressed by the Gardiner name." Sarvonsky sat up. Frankie rose, too, and wrapped the plaid blanket around her body.

"I can't believe Edwina's still willing to buy him a big-name lawyer! And if Loucasto's clubs are closed down?" She paced indignantly. "He'll go right back to his own spoiled, rotten life. And Rocky! Rocky is dead!" She sucked in her breath to keep from howling.

Sarvonsky came to her; she opened her arms and enfolded him in the blanket, pressing her cheek against his chest. "I'll never forget her face when they brought her up from the lake. Gordon was too goddamn drunk to even look at her!" She sobbed, shaking with fury. "I hate that bastard! I hate him! And that creep Maggot! I could shoot him myself--I swear I could!"

"Hating's like acid," he said. "It eats up your heart and guts and don't even touch the ones you're hating." He stroked her hair. "Anger's different. Anger's about justice."

She pulled away from him. "If Gordon brings home one of his sluts and lets her raise Rocky's babies?" she sniffed. "Is that justice? Or if Edwina takes them and hands them off to a nanny?" She shook her hair back and rubbed her eyes with her hands. "I can't bear it! They're mine as much as Jeffery is!" After a few minutes she gathered up her clothing and slipped into bra and panties.

Sarvonsky found the jeans he had discarded on the floor. "You could get custody, at least temporarily," he said. "Edwina's in no condition to fight you, and she's thinking about Gordon right now."

"But she is their grandmother, and she has connections."

"And you're their aunt," he said.

Her head popped through the turtleneck sweater and he handed her the jeans she'd worn the previous evening. "I can't find any money in Rocky's accounts, and I couldn't touch it anyway," Frankie told him. "If I don't get back to work, I'll lose the job I have."

"You could request a custody hearing. Appeal for funds from the state."

"But that could take months. What about what he did to Edwina? Will he get immunity from that?"

"A separate charge. If we could prove he did it."

"But Edwina won't talk."

"If we had the tape from the security camera. . . ."

"Of course! From his parents' place! Don't the police have it?"

"Actually someone took the tape. Someone locked the Dobermans outside, opened the wall safe, and took cash, jewelry, and two handguns. Whoever broke in, obviously."

"Gordon, obviously." A rank taste rose in the back of Frankie's throat. "But wouldn't he have destroyed it?"

"Maybe. But maybe he stuck it with the loot from the safe. When they arrested him, he didn't have anything to link him to the robbery."

"Not even the money?"

"Well, there wasn't much cash and it wasn't marked." Sarvonsky polished off another peanut butter cracker and finished his coffee.

"Maybe he hid it in his car?"

"Nope. The car was searched. Not there. He got rid of it before he met Chantelle."

"He could have hid it at the house," Frankie suggested. "He had some sort of bag, a gym bag, I think, when he came in."

"We could take a look around," Sarvonsky suggested casually, but with a sparkle in his eyes. "Unofficially, of course. Any idea where could he have stashed it?"

"His office?"

She went to the window and looked out. The dogs trailed after her. Winter had continued to rage. Snow had been falling most of the night, and the view outside the cabin was pristine, hills and forests dramatic, snow like white cotton clouds wrapping the world in silence, topping the tall pines, and every out-building with whipped cream. Suddenly Frankie turned back to Sarvonsky, excitement in her voice.

"I   think   I   know   where   he   hid   the   tape!"

CHAPTER 33

Sarvonsky drove as quickly as possible on the ice-bound roads, their progress blocked by a Penndot truck spraying sand.

"We've got to get to the house before Gordon does!"

"Where do you think he hid it?"

"The nanny's room! I was camped in the room, all my stuff, so I just assumed--"

"That he hadn't gone in."

"But I heard him moving around! He packed, he checked on the kids, and he could have gone in there too! There's a small storage closet high up on the wall!"

Sarvonsky looked at his watch. It was two-thirty. "He's probably already been released."

Frankie felt excitement like bubbles rising in her chest. "I've got the keys with me!" she told him. "Let's chance it!"

Gordon's release, covered by late news reports had intensified the frenzy of the media encampment. At the gates three news channels were represented, and one truck, parked directly in front of the gates, blocked their way. There was no patrol car in sight. A videocam was thrust against Sarvonsky's window, and an aggressive reporter pounded on the glass. Other reporters were emerging from location vans. Sarvonsky rolled down the window a few inches, his voice polite.

"Could you move your van, please?" He indicated the Channel 16 truck. The reporter, a man with intent eyes and sharp little teeth, shouted questions at him. "Has Mr. Gardiner been cleared in his wife's murder? What about drug charges?"

"I just clear the driveways," Sarvonsky said, expressionless. "I don't know nothing."

The reporter looked over the battered truck with the small front snowplow and turned the videocam away. "He's nobody!" he shouted to the others, who returned to their vans. The blocking vehicle lumbered out of the way.

"Christ!" Frankie whispered as she jabbed the remote. The garage overhead door glided smoothly up. The Suburban wasn't there! "Hurry!" she gasped, half out of the truck. She ran through the garage to the door that opened into the house. Once inside, she stabbed in the security code and had to repeat it in her haste. Sarvonsky followed her up the back stairs toward the bedrooms. In the nanny's room, where her open suitcase and clothing were still strewn about, she dragged a chair to the built-in cabinets high up near the ceiling. Standing on it, she yanked at the topmost cabinet, the only one with a key lock. It refused to open.

"Do you have anything we could use?"

Sarvonsky dug in his pockets and pulled out a penknife. "Let me," he said, and she hopped down. He took her place on the chair, and as he inserted a thin blade into the keyhole and jiggled, she ran to the window in Rocky's room to survey the snowy landscape below. No sign of Gordon.

"Son of a bitch!" She heard Sarvonsky's voice ring out from the next room. "You called it!" She found him pulling a small gym bag from the open cabinet.

Frankie crowded close as he unzipped it and dumped its contents onto the bed. First a small jewelry case fell out, then a snub-nosed handgun and videotape. Frankie grabbed the tape and, holding it, wrapped her arms around Sarvonsky's neck, chortling, "We've got it!"

"Yeah, well, let's get out of here. I don't exactly have a search warrant."

In the truck again, heading toward Pinewood Trails, Frankie asked, "Should we call Ransome?"

"Maybe we ought to take a look at the tape, see what we've got, before we talk to anybody."

"I know what we'll find," Frankie said. "But I'm sure Larry has a tape player we can use."

The truck was turning into the Happy Face Daycare driveway. He pulled in beside Rocky's Honda, now transformed into a snow sculpture, and parked.

After Lourdes greeted them, Sarvonsky, all business, asked where they could view the video. She led them to the small entertainment center in the den. He inserted the tape and fast-forwarded until he found the date of the robbery, time and date superimposed in neon over the black-and-white, four-sectored image. They sat on the lumpy couch to watch, the three of them leaning slightly forward.

In the top left sector, the driveway camera had caught Gordon's Suburban arriving; at the bottom left, a front door camera showed him entering and greeting his mother; in the top right sector, a shot from a rear view of the house revealed a dark form leading three lean dogs to the outside kennel run. The last shot, again on the front door sector, caught Gordon about to leave, disheveled, carrying a dark bag, then turning back into the house. Then the tape went fuzzy.

They were quiet for a moment, the only sound the whirr of the rewinding tape.

"What will you do now?" Lourdes asked.

"We'll have to turn it over," Frankie said, "but we plan to wait until after the court decides about the drug charges."

"Just a thought," Sarvonsky said. "If we turn it over now, it becomes part of the package--nothing to bargain with."

"Gordon will testify about gambling and prostitution at the club," Frankie explained to Lourdes. "But if he gets off--" She caught Lourdes' expression and faltered. "He has to pay!"

"I know you want what is best for the children." Lourdes said, her voice gentle.

"Of course I do. What do you mean?"

Lourdes shrugged. "He is their father. How will it be for them?"

"Better! Much better!"

"They have lost their mother, and they will lose their father, too?"

"But he's a rotten father! You think they've never seen him hit Rocky? I've seen him scream at them and shake Autumn like a rag. Look what he did to his parents, for Christ's sake!"

"Yes, this is true," Lourdes, agreed. "But punishing him will not bring Rocky back to us. Even if you send him to the jail, he will return and he will still be their father."

"He doesn't deserve to be!" Frankie cast a furtive glance at Sarvonsky. He ran a hand through his thick curls, unzipped his jacket, and removed it.

"Lourdes, you're a smart woman," he said.

"You must understand," Lourdes continued in a mild voice, "I have lived in his house and I have bad feelings for this man, too." She glanced apologetically at Frankie. "But I have also seen him caring for the children. He is a weak man, yes. I am just wondering if going in the jail will make him a better father?"

"Nothing will make him a better father!" Frankie responded, confused and angry. At that moment the children ran in and interrupted the conversation.

CHAPTER 34

No one heard from Gordon after his release. She'd asked Clarke, the patrolmen assigned to keep special surveillance on the children, to alert her when Gordon returned to Lake Nakomis, but he had not yet checked in with the regional police. It was assumed he was lying low. Frankie debated with herself and Sarvonsky, unable to decide what she wanted to do with the tape.

She called Gordon's parents and was told that the senior Gardiner was still in a coma but that Edwina was home under the care of a special nursing staff. She called Ransome at the Swiftwater Barracks.

"What's your theory this week?" he asked in greeting. "You looking to file new charges against your brother-in-law?"

"Well, he was arrested, wasn't he?" Frankie responded.

"Mr. Gardiner is currently under our protection," he said dryly. "Is that your question?"

"No, this is my question. Has Dominick Maggoti been officially charged in Rocky's murder?"

"Two charges of murder have been entered, for Rochelle Gardiner and Cliff Thornton."

"Is he talking? Was it because of the money Gordon owed?"

"I can't give out any specific information about an ongoing investigation. He's been transferred to Snydersville, pending arraignment. Why don't you consult with your boyfriend, the ex-son-in-law of the ex-state district attorney, if you want all of the facts?"

"Who? Sarvonsky?"

"Apparently he's on better terms with his ex-father-in-law than he is with his ex-wife."

She filed that away for later. "What about Chantelle Rojas? Was she charged?"

"She was released on bail."

Frankie thanked him and signed off. When she called Sarvonsky he chuckled, then admitted that his ex-wife's father, who had retired six years before, still had connections in police circles. "We keep in touch," he added dryly.

"So he's your 'sources'?" Frankie asked.

"One of them."

"Well, could you consult your sources about what happened to Gordon?"

He told her that Gordon had last been seen with his attorney and was keeping out of sight until after Loucasto's clubs had been raided and closed.

"What about the tape?" he asked her.

Frankie thought of the look on Autumn's face the previous evening when she was tucking her in. She'd asked in a small quavery voice, "Did my daddy go far away too, like Mommy?" Frankie, assailed by pangs of guilt, had assured the child her father would return.

"Let's offer it to Edwina," she said.

The following day they paid a visit to the Gardiner home in Marshalls Creek. Fiona greeted them and led them to a conservatory at the rear. The sun-drenched enclosure was alive with greenery, snaky vines, broad-leafed shrubs, and palms that, together with the warm, moist, air, mocked the snow banks visible through the windows.

Edwina, propped on brightly flowered pillows, was reclining on a white wicker chaise longue, a turquoise turban wrapped around her head. Pills, bottles, and books were arranged on a small side table. She wore huge dark sunglasses and a long turquoise robe. Except for the sling that held her right arm and the purplish bruises mottling her face and throat, she might have been lounging on a Mediterranean beach. A very tanned and blond young man, muscles rippling, in a white tee-shirt and pants, sat at a discrete distance, engrossed in a handheld video game. He nodded to them and started to rise, but Edwina waved him back. She scrutinized them, managing a small tight smile. With her left hand she indicated several scattered wicker chairs. Roman brought one over, and Frankie sat down while he retrieved a second for himself. Edwina's eyes were invisible behind the dark glasses.

Frankie spoke first. "How are you feeling, Mrs. Gardiner?"

Edwina wasted no time on small talk. "Who is this man, Frances, and what do you want?"

"I'm Roman Sarvonsky," he said, extended his hand, which she ignored. He sat. "Were you informed that your son was released from police custody yesterday?"

"Is this an official call?" Edwina's voice sounded hoarse, but she had regained her regal bearing. "Are you a policeman?"

"No, ma'am," he told her, sounding sincere. "I'm just a friend. I'm sure you know that Gordon is facing some pretty serious legal problems."

Edwina peered at him suspiciously from behind her glasses. "Gordon already has the best legal--"

"You know," said Frankie, "how frightening all of this has been for Autumn and Gordie, losing their mother, the confusion. What happened to them."

"Something happened to the children?" The older woman's voice took on a frightened edge. "They weren't hurt?"

"Someone who had a. . .disagreement with Gordon tried to kidnap them--the three of us. It seems Gordon owes a lot of money to some very rough characters."

The color drained from Edwina's bruised face. Her left hand went up to her mouth. "My God," she muttered under her breath. "What next?"

"We just want to be sure they're safe and cared for," Frankie said.

"They should be here!" Edwina bit off the words. "I've already made that offer. I even engaged a nanny, but, as you know, Gordon refused."

"Rocky would want me to care for them," Frankie said.

Edwina turned her gaze toward Sarvonsky, and Frankie felt that she was studying the scar that bisected his face. He might look like a rough character to Edwina, she thought.

"How exactly are you involved in my son's affairs?" she asked.

"I've been involved in the investigation of your daughter-in-law's murder." He stood up and paced behind Edwina's chair. Almost immediately the young man was on his feet as well, but Edwina waved him back impatiently. Sarvonsky continued, "Gordon's problems, his addictions, got him involved with criminals, maybe even caused Rocky's murder."

"No! No!" Edwina whispered.

"In any case, he's in a legal mess right now. Frankie could care for the children, at least until he gets his life straightened out."

Edwina protested. "He loved Rochelle, despite all her--he won't go to jail!"

"Not on murder charges. And probably not on the drug charges," Sarvonsky admitted. "But certain other information could be quite incriminating--especially if it surfaces while he's testifying for the state."

Color rose in her throat and suffused her ravaged face. "I don't know what you mean--"

"I know you want to protect Gordon." Frankie put her hand on Edwina's. "But we know who hurt you. We found the tape." Edwina stared at her blankly until she added, "From your security cameras."

The old woman flinched but maintained her regal pose, chin high, no emotion evident. She reached for a tissue and daubed gingerly beneath her glasses. "This is blackmail," she muttered.

"Not blackmail. You know Gordon needs help. We think you could make him get it," Frankie said. "We're willing to settle for that, for him and for the children."

Edwina continued to daub at the tears that were trickling down her cheeks. She drew in a sharp breath and, removing her glasses, looked directly at them. Her eyes were slits surrounded by swollen black and purple flesh. Her lips, thin and trembling, moved with effort.

"I don't know what to do anymore," she said with a quaver. "Gordon's father--he's always been so tough on him." One more excuse, Frankie thought but continued to pat the old woman's hand. Edwina went on, "It nearly killed him when he found out that Gordon had put the company we'd built into jeopardy, involved us in dishonest transactions--" She clamped her lips tightly together, having said too much. After a few moments she regained her composure. "What about my jewelry?" she asked. "My great grandmother's pearls are irreplaceable."

"There's a small jewelry chest along with the tape," Frankie said. "I doubt anything was removed. And a revolver."

"You haven't reported this to the police?"

"Not yet. Maybe we won't have to if you're willing to work with us." Sarvonsky's gravelly voice was oddly gentle.

"What do you want from me?" She sounded resigned.

"I want to have the kids with me until it's safe to trust them to Gordon again," Frankie said. "I don't want to have to fight for custody. I always promised Rocky. . . ."

"You don't understand what these children represent. They'll inherit everything our families built." Edwina sat pensively for a few moments before she went on. "They both have trust funds, naturally. I'll make whatever you need available." She took several gulps from the glass on the side table.

"Thank you." Frankie tried to suppress her elation.

"The papers will be drawn up. You may stay with them in their home, if that's what you want. I'll arrange for a nanny if you require help. I'm sure they don't need any more disruptions." She cleared her throat. "Someone will get in touch with you as soon as it's done." She gathered her strength for a final effort. "You'll give my messenger the tape and the other items--without publicity, I trust?"

"Guaranteed. No publicity," Sarvonsky said, from behind her chair; he gazed over the old woman's head, meeting

Frankie's gleaming eyes. Edwina seemed to shrivel visibly as she slumped back in her lounge chair.

"Mrs. Gardiner" Frankie said, generous in her triumph, "I promise I'll bring the children here, give them a chance to get to know you. Rocky would want that."

"Rochelle hated me," Edwina replied matter of factly. "She turned my son against me."

"You've heard from Gordon?" Sarvonsky made the question sound innocuous, but she looked at him suspiciously.

"I've spoken with his attorney. He'll contact me when he's allowed to." She waved a hand in dismissal; they rose. The muscular young nurse followed them to the door.

In the truck, jouncing down the long driveway, Sarvonsky pulled her close to him and planted a kiss on her mouth. She smiled. He flipped on the radio and they drove for a few moments before the music was interrupted by a news report.

A woman found strangled this morning at the Silver Lake Cottages in Stroudsburg has been identified as Chantelle Rojas. She had been employed as an exotic dancer at the Paradiso Club, which was recently shut down due to a racketeering investigation. Although this murder appears similar to the recent double slaying that occurred near the Shawnee Playhouse, police claim they have no immediate suspects. Anyone with information is asked to call the Swiftwater State Police.

CHAPTER 35

"Christ!" Frankie murmured. "Who?"

"Sounds like Maggot's style." Sarvonsky's brow was dark. "I'd say it had to be, if he wasn't locked up."

"Wasn't she under protection? She was helping the police!"

Sarvonsky turned off Route 209 onto 80 West. "We could stop at the Swiftwater Barracks. See if Ransome's around."

"You two have an understanding, don't you?" Frankie asked.

"We respect each other."

"So why was he so outraged that I wanted you--"

"Implying he wasn't doing his job?" Sarvonsky gave her a sideways glance. "Accusing him of incompetence?"

"Not incompetence. Favoritism, maybe. The Gardiners are like the local Kennedy clan. Not held accountable."

"Ransome's a good man," Sarvonsky said. "But he's human." He grinned a mischievous little boy grin. "I understand he's become a jazz connoisseur."

"Aphrodite?"

"I hear they're spending time together."

"He's not married?"

"Not my business."

"She didn't show up for her last two performances," Frankie said. "I need to talk to her.   And she hasn't returned my calls. I don't like it."

They turned onto Route 611, driving slowly, fighting traffic that clotted and backed up at the stoplights, finally turning up the hill into the barracks driveway.

The young woman behind the window told them Ransome was not available. Sarvonsky mentioned a few other names unfamiliar to Frankie and he met with the same response.   As they were getting back into the truck, a cruiser pulled into the lot, and Ransome, along with a female officer, emerged from it.   Sarvonsky intercepted him, and the two conferred.

When he returned, Sarvonsky's face was grim. "Maggot escaped from custody yesterday."

"How?" Frankie whispered.

"On the way to his arraignment.   Jim Franklin, a Monroe County Deputy, up for retirement--was driving. Maggot starts screaming he's going to throw up. Franklin pulls over and hauls him out so he won't have to clean vomit out of the back seat. The fucker head butts him, knocks him over, and takes off."

"He wasn't handcuffed?"

"Sure he was cuffed. Franklin nearly had a heart attack trying to chase him down, but he disappeared into the woods."

"You think he'll go after Gordon?"

"Maybe. But Gordon's got protection. Unless he does something stupid, he'll be okay."

"Well, Maggot's not going to strangle him, anyway," Frankie said. "He's probably stronger than Maggot."

"Yeah, wouldn't that be a hell of a contest?" Frankie noted the look in his eyes, the subtle signs of an adrenaline rush. "He'd need a more lethal weapon."

"What about the kids?" she asked, suddenly concerned.

"We'll pick them up right now.   I got a shortcut to Pinewood Trails," he told her. As he stomped on the gas the truck jolted forward and he reached over to squeeze her hand. "There's plenty of surveillance." His grin was reassuring. "When all this is over, I'm taking you away for a week, to some sunny island."

She returned the squeeze but not the smile. When they reached the daycare there was a regional police car parked next to the Honda, and Larry's SUV was wedged next to that. Frankie burst into the house without knocking. Inside, at the kitchen table, Larry, Clarke, and Lourdes were sitting, the remains of a late lunch evident on the table, the children playing loudly below in the daycare. Frankie laughed aloud in relief.

Sarvonsky and Clarke offered to accompany her and the children back to Lake Nakomis and to check the premises. Clarke assured them that he'd be patrolling. "Security's tight. Nobody's getting in. The media's been all over the place. Maggot's not stupid," he assured them.

"But the police believe Maggot brought Rocky's body through the country club grounds," Sarvonsky said.

Clarke looked embarrassed. "That's the only way he could have got past. A snowmobile could travel around the edge of the lake. But we're patrolling the country club grounds, too," he assured them, replacing his cap and uniform coat.

"How long will it take them to catch him?" Frankie asked.

Sarvonsky shrugged. "I'm betting two or three days at most. Everybody looks incompetent as long as he's loose. His face will be on every channel, every front page. I could stay with you at the house for a few days," he offered.

The black-and-white accompanied them to the gates, where an eerie calm had descended. The media had decamped, and the sudden quiet seemed strangely ominous. Frankie unlocked the door to the house, leaving the children in the Honda.

Sarvonsky and Clarke went inside and made a sweep through the house, although she assured them it wasn't necessary--the security system was engaged, and everything was quiet. The two men spoke for a few moments before Clarke got into his cruiser and set out to patrol. Inside, the boys played quietly while Sarvonsky and Frankie talked in the kitchen.

Autumn dragged over her favorite toy. "This is Clarence."

"Hello, Clarence." He stooped down to her level and grinned at the little girl. "You can call me Roman."

"Did a bad man hurt your face?" she asked.

"You could say that."

"I did say that." Autumn look mystified. "You want to hold Clarence?"

"Honey, go play with the boys," Frankie suggested. "I have to talk to Mr. Sarvonsky for a few minutes. . . . You don't think we'll hear from Gordon?" she asked.

"He could call from his cell phone or figure a way to send a message. I doubt he'd show himself before Maggot's back in custody, though."

"His judgment's been pretty whacked lately," Frankie said. "He's drinking and drugging."

"Let's hope his instinct for self preservation improves his thinking. You got the tape and Edwina's jewelry"?" he asked her, "I'll have them delivered."

Sarvonsky was standing near the doorway, wearing his worn leather jacket. He wrapped his arms around her and nuzzled her ear. "I have to run up to the cabin to take care of the dogs," he told her. "Clarke's alerted, and there's a security guard at the Lake Nakomis clubhouse. I told them I'd be back in half an hour."

"You're going to fly?"

"Three-quarters of an hour, then."

"Bring the dogs back with you. Then you won't have to leave me alone to go feed them in the morning."

"You want me to be your full-time personal bodyguard, woman?" She noticed that he ducked his chin a little when he was teasing.

"Only till they catch up with Maggot. After that you can be my part-time bodyguard." He kissed her and slipped out.

She fed the children a snack of peanut butter and jelly crackers with milk. In the largest bathroom, after their baths, Gordie tried to push Jeffrey off the potty, screaming, "Me! Me!" Maybe he would soon be ready to give up diapers. After she had them in pajamas, their teeth brushed, prayers said, she allowed each to pick out a favorite video before bed. Even Autumn fell asleep quickly. Darkness descended, closing in around the house like a thick black cloak.

CHAPTER 36

Frankie tried not to watch the clock but noticed when Sarvonsky had been gone for more than the half-hour he had first promised. She wandered through the house, turning on lights.   In the dining room she noted that the long, lovely teakwood table was gathering a layer of dust. She fingered the crystal of the chandelier above it, and her fingers came away dusty.

She heard a noise downstairs and jumped. Her mind returned to the night Rocky's body had been found and she felt her heart begin to thump. Where was Sarvonsky? She knew Clarke would be patrolling, but where was he?

She went to the security monitor in the alcove near the door to the garage and looked at the flickering camera views. Everything looked quiet. The green light on the panel indicated that the system was engaged.   She went into the den and watched part of an HBO film, a Julia Roberts comedy, on the giant screen. If she allowed her thoughts to drift, she would suddenly find herself threatened by darkness, like deep, black water lying in wait to engulf her.

There was the sound of an engine, and she hurried from the den through the kitchen toward the garage. She hadn't given Sarvonsky a remote, so she'd have to open the gates when he buzzed. But it was Gordon's Suburban, not Sarvonsky's truck, clearing the gates and approaching.

He must have decided to take the chance, she thought in growing alarm. Had he talked to his mother? Did he know that they'd found the tape?

Lights came on. She stood in the breezeway door that opened into the garage and watched as the door slid smoothly up and then down again. Gordon opened the door of the Suburban and stepped down. He looked haggard but no worse than he had for the past few weeks. His expression, when he saw her at the door, was noncommittal.

He approached, and she opened the door for him and was already punching in the security code when her attention was caught by a blur of movement inside the Suburban. The passenger door swung open and, in a move that was so fast it seemed like darkness moving, a figure now catapulted itself toward them. Frankie jumped backwards, but the figure slammed into Gordon from behind, a little below knee level, knocking him through the door and into the breezeway.

Looking up at her over Gordon's prostrate body was the black clad figure of Dominick Magotti, now holding a gun to Gordon's head. He was dressed in dark clothing from head to toe, including tight black gloves, like some Ninja fighter. "Well, well," he said, in a low unpleasant voice, "a welcoming committee."

Frankie backed into the kitchen, too startled to make sense of what had happened. Maggot ordered Gordon to his feet, a hand in his hair yanking his head backwards, the gun at his temple, and walked him into the kitchen. He was a few inches shorter than Gordon, but his bulk was more than equal, more compact and better toned. When he pulled off his black skullcap, his face, beneath the bald skull, had the look of a demented Mr. Clean, with mean little eyes set too close together, a nose that had been broken more than once, and teeth that looked squared off inside a mouth slit like an unhealed wound.

"Sit down," he invited Frankie, shoving Gordon into one of the kitchen chairs. He caressed his wispy goatee with a glove-clad finger. When she didn't respond immediately, he shouted, "I said sit down!" She did, quickly, stealing a look at Gordon's face. He looked dazed and white with fear, a jaw muscle twitching.

"Listen, Maggoti," Gordon pleaded in a low, urgent tone, "I know what you think, but it wasn't me who ripped you off. I--"

"Shut up," Maggoti said quietly. "I'll tell you when to open your mouth."

"But you don't get it--"

"I get that you spilled your guts to the cops! I get that you ratted me out!" Maggoti lifted the gun away from Gordon's temple and smashed it hard into his face. There was a crunching sound and blood spurted from his broken nose. Gordon staggered to his feet roaring like the wounded King Kong and lunged toward Maggoti who took deliberate aim with the .32. There was a cracking noise and a spurt of smoke. Gordon fell backwards half on to the chair, clutching his shoulder. Frankie winced and started to rise but Maggot turned the gun in her direction. "Sit down," he said in a gentle voice. "The show doesn't start until the fucking asshole is on his knees." He looked at Gordon. "You dumb prick. You know what you cost me?"

Gordon, holding his right shoulder where the blood was seeping through the blue parka, looked at him dully. He's going into shock, Frankie thought, and then, Sarvonsky should be here by now. But he would come to the locked gates and have to buzz for admission. Perhaps his arrival would distract Maggot enough for her to reach the phone. Her eyes slid toward the phone base on the counter where the wireless receiver was parked. She noted the array of sharpened knives nearby, suspended at hand's reach on a magnetic strip.

"I said, do you know what you cost me?" Maggot repeated, leaning in close to Gordon's bleeding face. Gordon, enraged, half staggered to his feet again and hurled himself at Maggot, but Maggot, for all his bulk, neatly side stepped him, aimed, and shot him again, this time in the rear of his left thigh. Gordon fell onto the white tiled floor, blood spreading outward in a bright red pool. He raised himself to his hands and knees. "Almost, but not quite," Maggot said, his voice low and pleasant again. "I said on your knees, not on your hands and knees."

Gordon's eyes darted to Frankie and back to Maggot. The whites seemed enlarged, bulging in contrast to the blue iris. "Run, Frankie," he said in a hoarse voice. "Call for help!"

"Oh, no. Frankie's going to be part of the show, too," Maggot told him. He gestured to her with the gun. "Come over here, baby," he said. When she didn't move immediately he screamed the command and she came to where he stood. "I don't think he understood me," Maggot told her. "He's still not on his knees."

He moved Frankie so that she was standing in front of him, facing Gordon and he put his left arm around her. He aimed the gun at Frankie's temple now. "On your knees," he said. Gordon managed to pull himself up into a kneeling position. He was bleeding profusely, reeling, hardly able to remain upright.

"You're the stupid fuck," he said, "not me. You let that conniving bitch screw you over one more time. For the last time."

"Chantelle?" Gordon looked up at him dully.

"You should be thanking me. She played you like a yoyo. First time she set you up was when she pointed your wife to the dough I fronted you. She thought she was playing everybody else, telling me how stupid I was, but she wasn't so smart when I was croaking her."

"You didn't have to kill Rocky," he whispered. "I would have gotten the money."

"Not as much as I got from the bitch's girlfriend," he snarled. "She wanted both of them out of the frame--your pretty red-headed wife, along with her old man. And since you ripped me off, I needed to get paid." He leaned in close to Frankie, his nose in her hair, breathing heavily. "Course I didn't get paid to fuck her. That was just for me. Umm," he murmured, "she was sweet. It was romantic, in the back of a limo, just like after the prom."

Gordon made a last attempt to rise and Maggot took another shot, this time striking somewhere low in the chest

area. Gordon slumped back to the floor, where he lay. "The
perfect ending would have been you taking the fall--but at least
I got paid."

Magotti gave a snorting chuckle as he ripped at
Frankie's blouse, tore her bra open, and grabbed at her breasts.
He shoved her against the table and bent her over it, face
against the wood. He continued in a calmly menacing voice,
"Now you can watch while I fuck your wife's little sister." He
laid the gun on the table just out of Frankie's reach and began
tearing at her jeans. She was wearing a leather belt and it didn't
immediately give. He yanked her up and turned her toward
him. "Take the belt off," he ordered. She looked toward
Gordon lying on the floor, seemingly unconscious. Her hands,
shaking badly, fumbled at the belt buckle. If only she could get
enough space between them to bring a knee up hard.

Her mind raced to the children asleep upstairs. What
would they find when they woke? She knew Maggot had no
intention of letting her or Gordon live after he was through
with them. Her fingers felt as thick as sausages as she fumbled
with her belt.

"Let me help you," Maggot suggested. He pulled her
over to the kitchen counter and reached for one of the knives,
slicing through the leather and dropping it back onto the
counter. With both hands he ripped at her jeans. She eyed the
knife, just out of her reach.

The buzzer sounded. "Fuck! Who's that?" he
muttered. He grabbed a handful of Frankie's thick hair and
dragged her toward the monitor, giving Gordon a vicious kick
as they stumbled past him to peer at the black-and-white
images. She could see Sarvonsky's truck at the gates. "Who's
that?" he demanded

"I don't know," she gasped.

"I think you do," he growled. The buzzer sounded
again. She moved suddenly reaching out to slam every button
within reach, including the gate control and panic button. Red
lights flashed on.

"You fucking bitch," he screamed, slamming her head
against the panel. "Reset it now! Reset it!" She stalled,
fumbling before she hit the reset button, praying that
Sarvonsky's truck had cleared the gates.

Maggoti turned back to retrieve his gun from the table, a hand still in her hair, but as he went for it so did she, sweeping it off the table so that it fell to where Gordon lay on the floor. Gordon, perhaps not quite as stupefied as he seemed, grabbed it and rolled onto his side, aiming it at Magotti.

"Let her go, motherfucker!" Gordon gasped.

Maggoti yanked Frankie back hard against his body, using her as a shield. She felt his breath rasping in her ear. His left arm was around her throat, his right around her waist as he lifted her off her feet and backed them both toward the doorway. Gordon slowly pulled himself to his knees, elbows on the table propping himself up against it, Magotti's .32 caliber pistol held in his two shaky hands, aimed directly at him.

She heard the sound of Sarvonsky's truck slamming to a stop in the driveway. Magotti looked around and at that moment Gordon fired wildly. Maggoti froze, then shoved Frankie as he dove to the floor. She crawled toward Gordon who was still propped against the table holding the gun. She heard the sounds of breaking glass and the barking and growling of dogs. Sarvonsky came through the back kitchen door as Magotti scrabbled at the door leading to the garage.

The dogs flew at him and he fought them off, flailing and howling. Sarvonsky had his own gun trained on Maggoti now.

"Down, boys," he commanded and the dogs slunk away. "Don't move," he told Magotti who stood glowering and impotent, backed against the door. Frankie reached Gordon and was prying the gun from his shaky hands when he fired. A shriek came from Maggoti, who crashed to the floor. There was a red splatter of blood left behind him on the door. Gordon dropped the gun and slipped to the floor at almost the same moment. Sarvonsky approached the prostrate form of Maggoti, gun leveled.

"Fuck!" he said softly. He rolled the body over. He had been shot in the face, the bullet going through the right eye. "Son of a bitch!"

The telephone began to ring at the same moment they heard sirens and Autumn appeared in the kitchen doorway in her little white nightdress. They heard the sound of sirens approaching

Frankie clutched her torn blouse and ran to Autumn. She scooped her up, carrying her back upstairs, as she screamed, "Daddy! Daddy!"

CHAPTER 37

Spring came late after weeks of rain, but by mid June the mountain laurel had burst into flower, covering the mountains with frothy pink and white lace, and the sun had at last made an appearance.

On a late Sunday afternoon, Frankie was setting the long wicker table in the gazebo that Rocky had loved, while Lourdes unpacked a hamper of her special delicacies. The children were playing with Sarvonsky's dogs on the long sloping lawn near the garden, where outcroppings of rocks and clusters of azalea, mountain laurel, and lilac edged the lake, spread out below, like a sheet of blue glass. Wild geese moved across the smooth expanse, leading smaller, fuzzy goslings.

Sarvonsky had fired up the grill in the small outdoor kitchen area and was marinating chicken breasts while Larry chopped onions and skewered chunks of beef and vegetables for shish kabob. He stopped to reach into the refrigerator for a beer for himself and tossed one to Sarvonsky, who caught it with one hand.

"Where the hell is Gordon?" Larry asked. Lourdes gave him a look and he shrugged, gesturing with a skewer. "He said they'd be here by one, and it's three. I'm getting hungry."

"Edwina's driver called from the car. Traffic's bad on 209, especially on a Sunday." Sarvonsky popped open his beer and took a slug.

Frankie kept a wary eye on the children as they played near the edge of the lake.

"Kiki! Autumn! Don't let the boys go so close to the water!" she warned. The children circled the lawn, running up to the gazebo like a small herd, followed by the excited dogs, Gordie trailing behind.

"The boys were throwing stones in the water," Kiki informed her mother, "at the ducks." Autumn stood behind her, nodding in agreement.

"No, boys. We do not throw things at the birds," Lourdes told them.

"But Autumn and me just threw flowers," Kiki explained. "Autumn says there's a mermaid in the lake, and that's why we were throwing flowers."

"Flowers are fine," Lourdes told them, glancing at Frankie. Autumn approached her aunt and tugged at the butcher's apron she had on over shorts and tee shirt. Frankie's hair was pulled into a ponytail, and her cheeks were flushed with color.

"When is my daddy coming?" Autumn's voice was nervous with anticipation and, Frankie thought, a hint of anxiety. "Is he all better now, Aunt Frankie?"

"He's almost all better," Frankie assured her. "He still needs a cane to help him walk. He and your Nana will be here any minute."

"And Poppy isn't coming?"

"That's right, honey," Frankie said. "Your daddy and Nana are coming to stay with you for a few days."

"Why can't Kiki and Jeffrey stay, too?" she asked.

"Because it's a special time for you and Gordie to spend with your daddy and your Nana."

"Nana doesn't like Clarence."

"I told her that Clarence is going to be very good. Fiona will come too, and she'll take special care of Clarence."

"Okay." Autumn turned and ran down the hill again, followed by the other children and the dogs. Frankie turned to look at Sarvonsky, and he kissed her on the mouth.

"Don't start worrying," he told her. "Our flight leaves at nine, and you're going to be on it with me." She started to say something; he stopped her. "They'll be fine. Gordon hasn't missed a meeting since he got out of rehab."

"I still say he got off easy. Anger management. A joke!"

"Anger management, rehab, probation, and six hundred hours of community service," Sarvonsky pointed out. He looked casual in a frayed blue work shirt and faded jeans, freshly shaved and faintly redolent of a spicy aftershave. Younger, Frankie thought, enjoying the pleasurable sparks his touch sent through her. But she was unable to concede the point.

"It's still a slap on the wrist. At least his time with the kids has to be supervised."

"They'll have Fiona and Lourdes for back up. And Jeffrey will be fine with Lourdes and Kiki. I plan to have you all to myself for a whole week, even if I have to drag you kicking and screaming onto the plane."

"I know they'll be safe. It's just, after everything--"

"That's over."

"I know." Frankie walked to the other end of the deck to where Lourdes was setting out fruit in a large blue bowl and they talked quietly together.

Larry glanced to be sure the women were out of earshot. "You think Gordon got off too light?"

"Probably."

"But he never meant for Rocky to--get involved."

"No. He's just a weak fuck who can't resist any lure-- drugs, hookers, money."

"It wasn't the first time he beat up on her," Larry said. "You think that's why she took the money?"

"She took it because Chantelle told her how he planned to use it."

"To pay off Loucasto's thugs?"

"She convinced Rocky that Gordon was all set to make a big drug buy-- *and run off with her.*"

"You got this from Chantelle?"

"Some of it. Some of it we pieced together, me and Ransome," Sarvonsky said. "This is the deal. Rocky was supposed to meet Chantelle after the show that night but Gordon knocked her out cold, then left. Maybe she was still a little out of it when she drove off. Even though she missed the show, she was hoping to catch up with Chantelle."

"Why would she trust that hooker?" Larry was skewering chunks of lamb, tomato, and pepper for the grill.

"She had evidence. The pictures, the money. But Rocky didn't know the half of the wheeling and dealing going on."

"Which half did she know?"

"That Chantelle was willing to set Gordon up because she was in love with *her*." Sarvonsky took a slug of beer from the can.

"And the other half?" Larry asked, "That she didn't know?"

"That she'd arranged for Maggot to help her ex-girlfriend, Bianca, to get rid of Thornton. He'd been trailing the guy and grabbed him when he got back to the Inn. But that's where Chantelle got screwed over. Bianca thought once Thornton was dead they were going to pick things up where they left off."

"Bianca and Chantelle?"

"Yeah. Only now Chantelle was chasing Rocky and that pissed her off. She offered Maggot a better contract--for both Thornton and Rocky."

"And Maggot grabbed them together?"

"Almost. He was about to load Thornton's body into the limo when he spotted Rocky, waiting for Chantelle. He grabbed her just before Chantelle showed up."

"So Chantelle never saw her?"

"He convinced her he'd already dropped Rocky off at the club, got Chantelle to help him load Thornton into Rocky's car and dump it."

"But where was Rocky's body?"

"At this point, she was still alive--tied up and gagged under a blanket on the floor of the limo. That's the irony. After Chantelle helps him, she goes to the club, and he takes the limo back to the garage where he rapes and kills Rocky. He leaves her body in a storage locker until Christmas Eve when he drops it in the lake near her house. Chantelle doesn't figure it out till she finds Rocky's locket in the limo."

"So Bianca, the beautiful widow who betrays everybody just escapes?"

"She had other friends to help her get out of the states. She tried to collect on the insurance policies from somewhere in Mexico, before the trail went cold." Sarvonsky shrugged. "She had a South American passport." He glanced over toward where Frankie and Lourdes were engaged in conversation before he continued. "But then we got a break. A Mrs. Clifford Thornton bought two one-way tickets from San Francisco in early May."

"Two?"

"Her traveling companion was a tall, gorgeous African American actress."

"Not Rocky's friend? Aphrodite?"

"Her real name is Aphra Janelle Benis. We tracked her to where she grew up in Detroit. The trail went cold for a while. Then I got the word she was off for Acapulco along with Mrs. Thornton."

"Acapulco? Isn't that where you're heading on vacation?" Larry asked. Sarvonsky merely smiled.

A dark limo came to a stop in the driveway. A driver opened the door, and Edwina stepped out and waved in the direction of those gathered at the gazebo. The driver helped Gordon emerge from the back seat and handed him his cane. He and his mother slowly made their way across the lawn.

The End

I would like to thank my dear friend Margaret Carson and my loving sister Rose Shiner for their advice and moral support during the process of writing this book.

I would also like to thank the Pocono Mountain Regional Police and the state Police at the Swiftwater (PA) barracks for their help in answering many of my technical questions.

CPSIA information can be obtained at www.ICGtesting.com
Printed in the USA
LVOW08s1620051115

461246LV00003B/479/P